BLACKOUT

JOEY JAMESON

CHANCES PRESS

www.chancespress.com

Blackout

Chapter One

This was always the worst part. Those last few moments sitting back-stage, looking at myself in the mirror, and trying desperately to psych myself up. The same four words always on a constant loop in my head. You can do this. As each song would finish, and the crowd would start up, my stomach would lurch just that little bit more bringing me closer to vomiting all over my back-lit vanity.

Every night before I went on it was always the same. I would stare at my reflection for so long that I almost didn't recognise the person looking back at me. I would study each part of my face, every line, every pour so intently that my eyes would blur until each smooth contour got lost in the next. You know that feeling when your eyes just glaze over and lose focus?

What was I looking for?

The other guys would always take the piss; seeing me sitting there in front of the mirror, entranced by my own reflection. Barely even moving. In love with what he saw...

Tonight was no different.

Maybe it was nerves. The other guys say they all get them, too; we must just all deal with them in different ways. Maybe my zoning out was how I dealt with doing what I was about to do, kind of like my brain's way of coping.

Yeah, must be nerves.

Every night around this time I would also be hit with the sudden urge to run out of here, to just pick up my things, leave and never look back and to get as far away from this shit hole as I could.

What would I do? Would I be able to get another job? This place doesn't own me. Maybe I should get out....

But then I would shake myself out of my own head, straighten up, look myself in the eye and remember the real reason I was here, night after night, doing what I do.

Because I love it.

But the urge to suddenly stand up and run out of here was strong tonight. Usually I could get around it, talk myself down from it like a jumper on a ledge. It was like jumping, after all. I was about to jump and plunge myself into the shark tank, metaphorically speaking. Only these men didn't want to eat me. Well, most of them didn't.

My thoughts were interrupted by the sound of the outside beginning to seep in through the cracks in the walls, bringing me back into the room. I blinked hard, aware now of where I was. The throbbing base of the speakers was like a sudden assault to my ear drums.

A head appeared from around the corner delivering a message, "You're up next, Dice," came Vince's deep, husky voice from behind me. I turned just enough to catch a glimpse of Vince in his slutty, patriotic, Union Jack thong. And just like that, the sound of my cue forced the sick feeling in my stomach to melt away. I pried my eyes away from the familiar blonde in the mirror and looked down at the fat, white line in front of me. I stared down at it as if I expected it to suddenly talk to me. I drew in a sharp breath and reached for the rolled up note on the table. Adjusting myself in the plush velvet chair, and tucking my hair behind my ear I put the note to my left nostril and snorted deeply, inhaling it all in one clean sweep. I lifted my head and inhaled a second time, forcing the white powder further up my nasal cavity. Closing my eyes, I could instantly feel the sweet intensity as the coke traveled down my throat and hit my blood stream, waking up every nerve ending in my body. The skin on my limbs danced as I opened my eyes and once again focused in on the man who appeared before me. This man seemed different than before. Stronger. Confident. Sexy. I ruffled my chin-length surfer hair with my hand, and leaned in to look at my eyes; their aqua colour suddenly invaded by a widening pool of black. I took one final look at my face, admiring my high cheek bones, my sculptured jaw.

You look good.

I gave myself a cheeky wink as I pushed the chair back to stand for the first time in what felt like hours; ready, pumped, turned on. I adjusted my cock in my white tennis shorts and smoothed down my vest.

Showtime.

***

I stood behind the red velvet curtains, waiting for them to spread their legs and welcome me onto their stage. I could feel the electricity in the room, the air thick with pheromones.

This is my favourite part.

The song was finishing, and the crowd erupted in a fury of hooting and cat-calls. It was my turn. I shook with sheer anticipation. Fists pounded the stage, voices cried out, salivating for more. Mouths would be open and tongues practically hanging out of their mouths like dogs on a hot summer's day. When on stage, each shouting voice always seemed to melt into the next, morphing into one loud, obscene drone. Each face always seemed remarkably like the next. Didn't matter anyway; they were all the same. Nameless faces; husbands…boyfriends…fathers, didn't matter to me. None of them ever mattered. Except for one. The One. That special One.

*Would **he** be here tonight?*

The mere thought of him made my skin tingle. Picturing his hands made me hard. Remembering the last time could almost make me cum. Either that or it was the coke making me randy. Regardless, I could feel a smile begin to tug at the corner of my lip. I forced myself to think of something else entirely, so as not to get a boner too early in the show.

Fuck, I hope he's here tonight.

I told myself not to go there. If I thought about him, I would lose my game. So I focused on the pigs shouting out obscenities instead; sharing their dirty fantasies with anybody who would listen. So brave, as they sat there in the darkness. I knew the feeling they felt; they felt immortal as they sat in the audience, safe behind their façade. Faces masked by dark shadows. Pockets full of dirty notes, ready to throw at the next guy who got them hard. Here, they could be anybody. It was an escape from their boring, shitty lives. I gave them release, I gave them a portal from which to fantasise about being somebody else, or being with somebody else. I let them think they could have me. Let them think that for those few minutes I was actually impressed by their fancy suits and shiny shoes; let them think that I wasn't put off by their bulging bellies and double chins. When they sat in *my* audience, they felt like they were the hottest things alive, and that they could bag somebody like me. But none of them could, of course…except for one.

Who was I fucking kidding? I love my job. I love the power.

The curtains pulling back caught me off guard momentarily, as Ben strutted through them, cock hanging out of the red satin robe he had on. "They're all yours, mate," he hummed, giving me a high-five as he passed.

"Cheers, mate" I shot back. He paused to get a better look at me.

"Hot, Dice…Going for the pervy tennis coach this time, eh?" His eyes took me in from head to toe; my skin-tight polo and tiny white shorts hugging all the right places.

"You know it," I joused coolly.

He met my eyes and gave me a flirty wink, "Enjoy…" And with that he was gone; his bubble butt shaking from side to side as he walked. Cute, I thought as he disappeared out of sight. Ben was one of the hotter guys who worked here; flirted with anything that had a cock and two legs, but hot nonetheless. But I would never go there. I never fucked at work.

"Gentlemen…" boomed the DJ's voice over the speaker, startling me slightly, "the man coming up next needs no introduction," he paused for effect, letting the dip shits in the crowd realize who was up. "This Adonis looks like he just got off on the beach, and is here for your personal, viewing pleasure…" This sent the crowd wild. "Please…please take your hands out of your pants and put them together… FOR MISTER DICE VALENTINE."

At the mention of my name I straightened up again. I looked down at the floor, and raised my eyes seductively. This was it. The heavy velvet curtains opened on command and I was at once hit with the blinding spotlight as the music roared to life all around me, filling every inch of the room. And just like that, I came alive.

I looked up and out into the faceless crowd and stepped out onto the stage. My head had already shut down, and I became a slave to my own body, the music my only guide. It had always been this way, ever since my first time. No matter what nerves shook me before hand, once I stepped foot on this stage…I was home. I was born to do this, a natural, you might say…if one could ever be destined to grow up and be a stripper that is. I was built to do this. And I was good at it.

The crowd settled down into their seats, and the only sound left in the air was the sultry beat of my song. I peered around the room, the blinding spotlight giving the illusion that I was there alone. The bright-ness showcased my deep mahogany tan perfectly, and it made my hair appear almost white in the glare. With one foot in front of the other, I edged my way towards the shiny metal pole in the center greeting it with wide eyes like a long lost friend. Taking ahold of it in one hand I wrapped my right leg around it and swung around until I landed softly on the ground. Without letting go with my arm, my hips took over and began instantly grinding away at the pole intensely, not missing a beat. I dry-humped it as my hand slid all the way up taking my body with it, and then quickly back down until I was in a crouching position again with my ass hanging out exaggeratingly over my heels. I could feel myself getting fully turned on now, the pole becoming my phallic prop. I stroked it lovingly then harder with every bump and grind, even giving it a lick while naughtily surveying the area. I loved the tease; I got off knowing that behind the lights, there was a crowd of men getting off just looking at me on stage. And I loved making them beg.

I swung my arm back and caught myself with one hand landing behind me on the ground as support. Lifting my pelvis into the air in time to the beat, I began thrusting at thin air, my other hand moving down my body and caressing the contour of my dick. I thrusted slowly at first; then progressively more intense. I could see shifting movements in the crowd, shadows dancing on the stage, the sounds of trouser zippers being unzipped masked by the music.

Time to give them what they came for.

I propelled myself forwards, completely bent over. I peered over my shoulder; mimicking a look like someone was about to mount me from behind. With spread legs and a flat back, I lifted my chest with my hands safely on my hips until I was again in a standing position. Taking a corner of my skin-tight polo in each hand, I lifted it achingly slowly up and over my head, making sure to flex each defined muscle in my chest as the lifting shirt revealed my sculpted torso beneath. Letting it fall to the floor, I shook my hair back into place. I stood there for a second, and let them marvel at my chest: tanned, shaved, lean and muscular, sculpted to within an inch of its life, the result of hours spent surfing and a strict gym regime. Drawing my hands to my abs, I ran my fingers over them, the light casting shadows on the deep grooves of my six pack. I couldn't stop touching myself. The coke that was coursing through my veins had me in its grip. Rubbing my hands over my exposed skin, goose bumps appeared all over me as my massaging touch made me tingle all over. I was rock hard at this point. My cock fought against the restraints of my tight shorts, begging to be released. As I ground my hips forward, waves of pleasure began rippling through my body as my dick pressed up against my zipper. My hands found my pecs and couldn't resist giving my nipples a squeeze and my lips a lick for good measure. I flexed my biceps as I let one hand reach over my head and find the pole behind me for support, the other trailed downwards, past my treasure-trail that disappeared into my tight white shorts, and gently rested on the bulging treat inside. I was so turned on I wanted nothing more than to bust open my shorts and jack off right there on the stage. I drew in a deep breath, my eyes once again sweeping the room, my head tilting back in ecstasy as my back bent and my hand massaged my dick from on top of my shorts. I slid almost all the way down the pole, my crotch swelling even further with each movement and pointing skyward.

The music picked up momentum and the crowd shifted accordingly. The smell of sweat and alcohol mixed with the sweet scent of cum hit my nostrils as I bent even further backwards creating a bridge with my body. You could almost feel the testosterone in the room.

I crouched down again before sliding my ass back up the pole this time and faced the crowd. The front part of the stage was already littered with notes. Fives, tens, twenties. Even a fifty I noticed. Fuck… and I hadn't even got my dick out yet.

I let my hands drop by my sides, giving the allusion I was finished. Then with a devilish grin on my face, I reached for the button of my shorts and undid it. I waited. My smile got deeper as I pulled the zip south, exposing my white Calvin Klein's. I let the shorts drop to the ground and stood there for a moment, like an underwear model waiting for his close-up. I rested my hands on my hips as if they belonged to someone standing behind me, and imagined how I'd react if I was dirty dancing with someone in a club. My hips rocked in a wide circle, moving to the sounds of the deep base. My head fell back, and my lips parted. I looked down at my own body now and while still grinding the pole from behind, ran my hands all over my naked skin. I ran my fingertips over the smoothness of my pecs, then my rock hard abs, before tucking my thumbs into opposite corners of my briefs. Then with my gaze focused intently at the spotlight in front of me, as if staring into the eyes of a lover, I dragged them down ever so slowly , inch by inch revealing more and more flesh with each tug. My hands slid them down over the curve of my hips, then my ass cheeks and finally revealing the dark trail of pubic hair that led down to my cock, my stiffie pitching an obscene tent in my underwear. Most male dancers had to either wear a prosthetic or pop a hit of V before going on stage to get a boner during a performance. Not me. I always stood at attention, so to speak.

Then just as I was about to reveal the prize, I paused, the cheeky grin reappearing on my face as the crowd moaned in protest.

You've got them exactly where you want them. Keep them here for another moment, hold onto them as long as you can.

But it was then that I saw him... He was here. There was no mistaking him, even from behind the lights, his stance gave him away. Powerful, broad, manly. Always in the same place of the club, to my left, two tables from the bar. A martini glass in hand. His short spiky hair shaping his shadow in the dark. I couldn't believe he was here. At once all the memories of our last encounter came flooding back into my head; his hands, his grip on my hips, the taste of his mouth...

I got distracted only for a second, my smile fading and momentarily replaced by a look of surprise, before I regained my composure and remembered what I was here to do. No matter what was going to happen later, right now, I had a job to do.

Strip.

Taking a deep breath I let my head fall back against the pole as I pulled my white Calvin's down the rest of the way. They fought for a second against my stiff, swollen cock until finally it was free and my underwear slid down my legs and landed at my ankles. My cock sprang up and bounced against my chest before standing at attention, practically saluting the crowd. Once again the men in the audience drew themselves forward on their chairs, trying desperately to close the space between their mouths and my dick just that little bit more. I could have just stood there and let them stare for ages. Let them just imagine their mouths around my 8 inch penis; the taste of my cum, the smell of my pubes, the look in my eyes as they bob up and down on it. God knows what they dreamt of doing to me as I got naked for them. I don't usually think about that too much. Some things are better left to the imagination, I always say.

I tore my eyes away from the crowd and looked down at the thick meat between my legs.

Time to bring it on home, Dice.

Slowly I lifted one hand to my dick and gently touched it as if it were the most fragile flower in the world. Softly, I let my fingers explore the thick, pink shaft, until they grazed the engorged purple mushroom head at the tip. It trembled and twitched from underneath my touch, as if begging to be grabbed and jerked off. The thick purple veins running along the shaft pumped more and more blood through it, causing it to vibrate like it had its own heartbeat. I looked out into the crowd once more and saw jerking shadows of men about to get off. My tease was working.

Not so fast, fuckers.

Tonight I wasn't going all the way. Not with *him* sitting only a few yards away. If *he* weren't here, I probably would have reacted differently. I probably would give them what they came here to see. On special nights my touch wouldn't be so gentle; other nights I would have a firmer grip and not leave this stage until I had properly had a little fun and sprayed my cum all over it. That kind of behaviour was usually frowned upon in a club like this one. But I was no *usual* dancer. I had a bit of a gift, some might say; my orgasms were practically explosive. They were so loud and vocal that I swear I could make windows rattle. When I came, my whole body got overtaken by a tremor so fierce that I couldn't help but cry out. And not only that, but I once measured how far I could shoot when aimed in the right direction…10 feet was my record. This was why the front row was always packed when I danced. The pervs loved getting wet, if you know what I mean. Sometimes I even caught them sitting there with their mouths open, as if trying to catch rain drops from a cloud with their tongues.

Filthy.

No…this wasn't going to happen tonight. Tonight I was going to take complete control of this stage and perform the ultimate tease…I was going to stop.

As if planned to perfection, the sultry tones of the music were beginning to fade. I took one final look out into the crowd, my hand still resting on my cock that was screaming to be sucked off. My eyes squinted in the brightness as I scanned *his* table looking for a sign of him, wanting to know that he was watching and that he was wishing it was his hands on my skin.

But he was gone. The sudden disappointment that seeped into my body was overwhelming.

Where the hell did he go? Did he fucking leave?

It was almost poetic in a sense; I guess this is what it feels like to get a taste of my own medicine.

Fucking tease.

It took all I had left to remember where I was, and to shoot the crowd one final devilish grin before exiting, even though all I wanted to do was pout. My hand dropped from my still throbbing and totally unsatisfied dick, and the music finished, and the lights dimmed.

The crowd was speechless.

***

As the curtains closed in front of me, I dragged my heels all the way back to the dressing room. I felt spent, tired, slightly achy. The intense rush of the coke and my strip were fading quickly and leaving only irritating remnants in their wake.

I couldn't believe he had left.

I was immediately reminded of the last time he had come to see me dance, and I quickly felt a flutter in my crotch.

Did I do something wrong tonight? Was he not turned on? Is that why he left?

I had to shake my head to stop myself from becoming a victim to my own dance.

"Hot dance tonight, Dice," came Tim's deep voice from inside the dressing room.

I reached the doorway and let myself fall against it slightly. My hands down at my side, lifeless and defeated. I let out a sigh and met Tim's probing eyes reflected back at me in the mirror. He was sat forward and applying some guy-liner to his lids. He kept his back to me as he continued to talk.

"Was kinda hoping you'd do one of your *special* performances, if you know what I mean…always gets the kiddies primed," his voice trailed off.

I didn't respond. Instead I carried on standing there in all my naked glory, the blood having drained from my cock leaving it flaccid and pointing southward, but ever still the lust-worthy specimen that gay dreams are made of.

Tim sensed my withdrawal and turned his chair to face me, the guy-liner still in his hand. "What's wrong handsome, someone tip you a fiver again?" he mocked sarcastically. I shot him a look that was bathed in sarcasm, and was about to shoot him a 'fuck you' when my eyes were suddenly drawn to something on my dressing table. I squinted to see it better in the dim lighting as I inched cautiously towards it.

As I approached, a single long-stem red rose came into view, staring back at me from across my table. I picked it up and shutting my eyes, put it to my nose and inhaled deeply. The sweet nectar invaded my nostrils and filled me with a rush that made my stomach flinch and flutter. Next to it there was a small white card with black writing scribbled across it.

Meet me in our spot…15 minutes,
-D x

"Looks like someone made an impression," Tim giggled to himself more than to anyone else, before turning back to the mirror.

I grabbed my clothes I came in with and turned on my heels.

"Hey handsome," Tim called stopping me in my tracks. I turned to him without saying anything, the cheeky grin on my face giving away my excitement. "A little pick-me-up before your encounter?" he nodded towards the mirror in front of him, littered with a series of thick lines primed for the taking.

I didn't hesitate in the slightest.

"You always know just what I need," I said, grinning widely, as I took the rolled up note from his offering hand and railed the line farthest from me. I lifted my head in complete ecstasy, instantly back in the mood. I could feel myself begin to harden again then and there.

"Go get 'em, partner," he said in his best cowboy impression, eyes still on the reflection in the mirror. I turned on my heals once more, clothes in hand, a spring in my step, dick no longer swinging idly.

Let's role, Dice.

***

As I pulled open the back entrance to the club, I was still buttoning up my shirt. I kept it untucked from my ripped jeans; cool, casual. Flip-flops on my feet, and hair ruffled, I felt the epitome of understated sexiness. My heart was pounding in my chest, reverberating in my ears. Fuck, I was so horny. Sheer excitement mixed with anxiousness coursed through my veins.

As I stepped outside, I stopped for a second to let my eyes adjust to the surrounding darkness of the alleyway. I was breathing heavily as I squinted to make out any shapes. It was a cool evening for August, the light breeze making my nipples hard, pressing up against my tight white shirt.

It was then that I saw him. He was leaning up against the far wall of the alley, one leg bent at the knee, heel resting on the wall behind him, hands tucked in his jean pockets. He wore a dark shirt, the top of his tanned and sculpted chest visible above the deep V-neck plunge. The image of the moonlight illuminating his skin in the darkness made my mouth begin to water. He didn't move at first, and neither did I. We just stood there, taking in the appearance of the other, mentally undressing each other with our eyes. I opened my mouth to say something, then stopped myself, suddenly unsure of what words were about to come out of my mouth.

I wasn't sure how long we stood there. The expression on his face was hidden in the shadows. The anticipation was killing me, but I was rooted to the spot, almost as if his gaze was keeping me still. I couldn't move until I saw his eyes and they told me I could.

At last he did. Pulling his hands free from his jeans, he shifted his weight back on to both feet and took a few slow steps towards me. I stayed exactly where I was. As he moved, the shadows disappeared and the dim light of the sky finally hit his face. He was even more beautiful than I had remembered. Totally the opposite to me; dark hair, cropped short around the back and ears, almost black in this light. His face was stubbly, adorned with short neatly trimmed hairs the same colour as the ones on his head. As he moved, his muscles reacted simultaneously, flexing through the confines of his shirt to the point where the material screamed out as if it was about to split. I could see the contour of his perfect pecs. He was more muscular than I was, and the cool night air was obviously having the same effect on his round, hard nipples. My eyes trailed down to his snug-fitting jeans. They were slung so low I could just about see the top of his neatly-trimmed pubes poking out.

He's hard, too.

I licked my lips without even knowing it as my eyes focused in on the bulge that appeared before them in his trousers. I was sure that if it could speak it would cry out to be released and tended to. I wanted nothing more than to sink to my knees then and there and service that cock like I had before in this very same place. No shame, no words, just complete and utter pleasure. But I couldn't move. I was totally powerless as his dark eyes held me there, staring back at him, a battle of the wills almost as we saw who would be the one to break first. The tension between us and the anticipation of the sweet release that was inevitably about to occur was almost too much for me to bear. I was afraid that I was going to cum in my pants right then and there, just from looking at him in front of me.

But he broke first.

Before I could react his hands were on me, so sudden and intense that my breath got caught in my throat. Both of his hands were instantly on my wrists, lifting them above my head and holding them together as the weight of his pelvis against me sent me reeling back against the brick wall behind us. For a moment he just held me there. I didn't struggle against his grip; instead I gave into it, my body relaxing at his mercy. His face was inches from mine. I let my lips part without closing my eyes, begging for him to kiss me. Those lips…full, bee-stung and sensuously shaped. I immediately remembered what it was like to run my tongue over them, and what it felt like to have them all over my body. His breath was warm against my face, sweet and slightly cinnamon scented. As if of its own accord, my face moved towards his, only to be rejected teasingly by his own. A grin played with the corners of his mouth; he was enjoying torturing me. He began to move his hips slightly, pressing his crotch up against my own as if greeting it. We stayed like that for what felt like hours, staring each other down and dry-humping each other through our jeans. Each thrust of my cock against material made me harder. Our erections were the only language necessary. We never spoke more than a few words to each other when we met. This meeting was like my dance personified; I lived for the tease, I performed it on stage almost every night. And now, this; this silent seduction must be what it feels like to just watch someone else on stage. A feast for the eyes, but without physical release.

I couldn't take any more. The effect of his body against mine was too much, and suddenly our clothes were a barrier between us that we couldn't get rid of quickly enough. Without letting go of my eyes, he freed my hands and backed away from me just enough to reach above his head, grab the back of his shirt and tug it off. The dark smooth material fought against his muscular physique. My eyes drank in his appearance as he let the shirt fall to the ground at our feet. In the moonlight, his smooth hard chest appeared almost like granite. He had the most perfect pecs I had ever seen; full, pert, and with perfectly formed nipples that were fully erect now in the cool night air. His narrow waist encased a deep sculpted six-pack of abs whose grooves were even more defined in the shadows of the alley. His only chest-hair was a light treasure trail of dark thin hairs that disappeared down into his tight fitting jeans. He let his arms rest at his sides, almost mimicking my stance from when I was on stage a few minutes earlier. He rested his weight on one foot; the classic underwear model pose.

Cheeky git.

He was mocking me. I tore my eyes away from his chest to see his eyes grinning back at me. Before I could protest, he reached at my shirt, helping it over my head, and wrapped his strong arms around me in a tight embrace. It was then that our lips finally touched. The pillowy feel of his soft lips against mine made my cock even wetter. His hot wet tongue was in my mouth, lapping and battling against my own. I closed my eyes and let my mouth do the talking. The passion I had bottled up for him suddenly exploded, and I literally lost myself in the moment. I didn't think, all I wanted was to touch and caress and lick every inch of his body.

I pulled away from his mouth and my tongue found his neck. I traced a line with it down from his ear lobe, before resting it in the crook of his collar bone. He tilted his head back, obviously enjoying the sensation. My hands found his perfect pecs, and caressed his smooth flesh as my tongue followed their lead. I gripped each nipple gently with my thumb and index finger, giving them a pinch, before opening my mouth and devouring first the left and then the right. His skin was freshly washed and smelled like soap and musky after-shave. My tongue couldn't get enough of his hard nipples, licking and sucking gently, each in turn as my opposite hand tweaked the other. I looked up to see his expression; a look of pure lust plastered across his face. His lips parted in an o-shape, his hands rested lightly on my broad naked shoulders. Returning my gaze to his chest I slowly slid down, tracing the contours of his tight stomach with my tongue. I took my time on his abs; licking them up and down. They were so tight and profound that I swear I was afraid I might cut myself on them. My hands stroked the skin on his sides as I continued to slide further down his body until I was safely on my knees. I looked up at him and again met his eyes that were now slightly closed, anticipation showing on his face. This was such a vulnerable moment. Right before the revealing of the cock. Each at the utter mercy of the other. With expert ease, I unbuckled his belt and then unfastened his button, all the while keeping his eyes on mine. He let his hands fall loosely to his sides, as I carefully slid his jeans and pants down inch by inch, until finally the prize was fully revealed.

I paused then for a moment, not even looking at the thick piece of meat between his legs. He was still staring down at me intently, his brow now furrowed in anticipation of what I was about to do. I let my eyes linger a moment longer before they sunk to his cock. It truly was a piece of beauty; long and pink, a thick veiny shaft leading to the most perfect mushroom head I had ever seen. The tip was wet and glistening in the dim light from the alley. It trembled as I brought my hand up to it and began my slow caress, up and down, developing a rhythm with each stroke, slowly at first, then with two hands; each twisting slightly in opposite directions. The action on his cock seemed to be having catalytic effects as I peered up at him and saw his head tilt back slightly, his mouth opening further and eyes closing. A deep moan escaped from his lips like a naughty whisper and his hands found my head, taking hold of my hair and urging me down onto his shaft. I resisted at first, making him twitch in longing as I teased him with a devilish grin on my lips. Then I couldn't take it any longer, I wanted him, every inch of him, inside me as much as possible. I parted my lips and opened wide, and without letting my tongue make contact I guided him into my mouth as far as my gag reflex would allow until he grazed the back of my throat. I kept him there for a moment, letting the muscles in my throat relax before I began sucking. After what felt like minutes, my tongue made contact…the reaction was priceless…

Immediately I felt his whole body shudder beneath the power of my sucking. I moved my head all the way up and down his long, hard dick, keeping a hand on the base for support. I had full control at this point. He was like putty in my hands as I modified my sucking; all tongue, then more lip contact than anything else. Hard, deep, fast, slow, then intensely fast. I could feel his body reacting as his grip on my head got progressively stronger. He spread his legs further and I took the hint and slipped both hands around his thick thighs and cradled an ass cheek in each palm. With a firmer grip on his body I was able to truly press him further into my mouth. I literally couldn't get enough. I didn't know how much longer I could go before I needed him to fuck me.

The moans coming from his mouth told me I was hitting his spot. Feeling a little daring, I cheekily let one hand slip down in between his ass cheeks and gently massaged his asshole. He twitched and stiffened suddenly, but I didn't shy away, instead kept on massaging and then quickened my sucking, harder and harder, swallowing each drip of his pre-cum that trickled down the back of my throat. My finger then found its way into his hole, just superficially at first, letting him adjust to the sensation of me inside *him*.

"Oh, fuck…" were his only words as my finger slid deeper inside; curving, once past the threshold, searching for that special spot that would make him cry out. He twisted his fingers around my blonde locks and continued massaging my head into him as if to tell me to keep going.

He's going to come in a second if I keep this up.

I opened my eyes suddenly and withdrew my finger from his ass, and slowly let his cock fall from my lips. With strong knees, I stood, letting his hands find my shoulders. Before I could fully stand up properly, he was spinning me around to face the wall behind me. His hands once again found my wrists and pinned me against it. The stone was cool and rough against my hands. He pushed his cock up against my fully clothed ass so hard I could feel the exact outline of it against my own asshole. The sensation was tantalising, and I started to speed things up by undoing my own jeans. He quickly caught on to my plan and roughly replaced my hands in the position that he had left them, pinned up against the bricks. He kicked my legs apart, and I sensed him pull his jeans off completely until he was stark naked behind me. Then he moved onto me and pressing his naked self up against me again, began removing the rest of my clothes. His erect nipples grazed my back, and his short raspy breaths felt warm against my neck.

He was so flustered and horny that he stumbled to get my belt undone. Grunting slightly in frustration he ripped the jeans apart and I heard the button fly off and roll away somewhere down the alley. With that he yanked them down over my rock hard dick and slid to his knees behind me.

Oh fuck…

I knew what he was about to do, and I braced myself for the sensation. As his tongue made contact with my asshole, I'm sure I let out a yelp of utter pleasure. He didn't waste any time going to work on my backside; each lick of his tongue sent waves of ecstasy soaring through my whole body. I closed my eyes and was in heaven as he expertly tongued my hole. One hand pulled my pert cheek away to make room for his lips. The other hand reached around and caught hold of my own penis and rubbed the head gently. I immediately saw bright vivid colours through my closed lids, exploding before my eyes and disintegrating into beautiful colourful ash. With his one hand massaging my cock and his tongue darting in and out of me, I began to shudder knowing that my orgasm was close. Sensing me on the brink, he pulled back quickly and stood up without warning. I opened my eyes at the sudden loss of contact from his lips on my ass, and was thrusted away from the wall and onto a tall pile of boxes that lay stacked in a corner of the alley. The positioning and level of the boxes were perfect. I was bent over the boxes, my exposed ass at a perfect level to his crotch. His hand pressed down upon my back, guiding me down until I was fully bent over comfortably. He put a hand on each of my hips and pulled me away from the boxes, positioning me and getting me ready to be invaded by his cock. There was a pause for a moment as I heard the familiar sound of a condom being unwrapped. A second later and I could feel the latex-covered head of his dick rubbing itself all over my ass. He slapped it with his cock a few times for good measure, and I closed my eyes and grabbed on tight to the sides of the box.

This was going to be good.

Then there was the sound of him spitting into his hand. Homemade lube. Then the warm sensation of his saliva inside me, as he prepared me for what was coming. And without another moment's hesitation, his hips pushed his mushroom head into my backside. My grip tightened even further on the box, and I gritted my teeth as my asshole began to spread and contract around his girth. The muscles in my sphincter screamed out against the invasion of him inside me. He paused just then, letting my insides adjust and relax. He was about half way in. Slowly he pushed further in, centimetre by centimetre until I felt like he was poking at the front of my stomach. I groaned through my clenched jaw as I felt the familiar pain that went hand in hand with being fucked. I breathed in deeply, forcing the air down and into my lungs, breathing into the space and praying the pain would pass and that pleasure would take over. My back arched and my nails dug into the wood that I was using for support. It was like this we stayed for a minute or two. One body. His hands caressing up and down my back, calming and relaxing me. Me, his property. Vulnerable as I lay there, bent over beneath his weight. He could have done anything to me at that moment. It donned on me just then, as thoughts swam around in my head, intermingling with the pleasure indicators my nerve synapses were firing; he was a part of me at that moment. Disappearing inside me, someone I barely knew. In the most intimate of positions imaginable…and I wanted more…

I turned my head around until I could see him from the corner of my eye. He was looking at me, his eyes searching, as if for permission.

"Yeah…Go ahead," I breathed. It was the reaction he was waiting for. He nodded in acknowledgement and immediately pulled his cock almost all the way out of my ass. Then, just when I thought he was going to withdraw, he began thrusting. His hips rammed me so hard I could feel his balls slap against my ass. Again. Pulling out almost completely and then thrusting into me all the way, his entire cock disappearing into my ass. I bit down so hard just then on my tongue that I'm sure I drew blood. A grunt from deep down in my belly made its way out and echoed loudly around the walls of the alley. Every thrust pushed me forward further onto the boxes, my elbows scraping against the wood. Again, and again. Harder, his thrusts deep, fast, and so strong that I thought he was going to split me in two. I could feel his thighs grow moist as they slapped up against my own. He had his hands on my hips now, gripping me tighter and tighter with each thrust of his pelvis, his fingernails digging into my skin. I wanted more. My cock was screaming out for attention, now frighteningly close to coming. With one elbow for support, I reached the other hand around and grabbed my own dick and immediately began jerking it off. The feeling was incredibly intense, his cock pumping furiously away at my ass, and my own hand mirroring his thrusts by working away at my own member, back and forth, pulling the skin backwards and forwards and paying extra close attention to the head. I closed my eyes and just concentrated on both sensations at once.

Before I could place the sound, I realised that we were both moaning and groaning loudly, the confines of the walls making us sound louder than we were. Somewhere, someone was getting a free show as our voices grew louder and louder with each thrust. The smack of his thighs against my ass only adding to the reverberations of the alley. Just then his hands slid from my hips up to my shoulders, and with one in each hand, he forced me to stand up straight. The movement only drove his cock further up inside me, until it grazed my g-spot and sent waves of electricity through me. I cried out without being able to hold it in. He wrapped one hand around my front and returned the other to my hip for leverage. He was close, I could feel it. The hand he had on my hip moved nonchalantly down towards my penis and took over. All I could do was stand there and experience it all. Seconds passed, and I drew closer and closer to exploding my juices all over the alley. Deeper and deeper, faster and faster until each movement disappeared into the last. I was cumming. My voice lifted an octave, signaling to him what was about to happen, and as if in response he sped up his hand motion on my cock, never slowing down the rhythm of his thrusts. After a few more hand jerks suddenly the blackness I saw behind my closed lids was replaced with shooting stars. I orgasmed then and there in pure technicolour. I felt my cum rise up from the depths of my shaft and explode out the tip of my dick in a hot steaming sticky mess over his hand. My body trembled and shook with each ejaculation, as more and more of my spunk rained down on our surroundings, my body shuddering with each wave of ecstasy. I swear I went blind for a whole minute, even with eyes open the only thing they could see were the bright vibrant colours that danced before them, a personification of my orgasm.

I didn't even realise that he had stopped pumping. He was waiting for me. Waiting for me to finish before he finished. As my body returned to normal, the only residue left were the goose pimples that rose out of my skin all over my naked body. He was still inside me. His whole shaft still rammed up inside me. I could feel the blood pumping through his dick like a second heartbeat that copied my own. When he felt my trembles subside, he moved his hips again and drew himself out, all the way this time, withdrawing completely making me believe he was finished. Then just as I was beginning to regain composure he caught me by surprise by slipping it back up into my asshole. Hard. All the way. My exhale caught in my throat as his thrust knocked all the remaining air out of me. Before I could protest, he carried on fucking me. The feeling of him fucking away at me was almost enough to make me hard again. His thrusts were short and quick. He was close. Again and again, fucking away at me like a fever that wouldn't subside. His grip tightened once again on me and I braced myself for his release.

With a loud groan that was almost a roar he finally came. His body vibrated violently as he came inside me, filling up the condom with his sticky mess. It felt like he came forever. His hips gyrating with each release. If he had let it go outside, I swear it would have created a small puddle at our feet. When the last drop of cum had been released, he stopped.

A few seconds passed. My cock was slowly starting to deflate, returning to its normal size for the first time in what felt like hours. I loosened my grip on the boxes and straightened my back. Pain shot up my spine from having been bent in one position for too long. I paused and let the blood return to my limbs. He slid out of me slowly, and without turning I could hear the smack of a condom being pulled off and then landing on the ground somewhere a few feet away.

I breathed in deeply, the air entering my mouth was cool and burned as it hit my lungs. It was then that I turned to face him again. We were spent. My body ached all over and felt sticky from the drying cum that covered it. I didn't reach for my clothes at first. I just took in the sight of him as he composed himself in front of me. His body was even more beautiful than I remembered. I drank in the sight of him, not knowing when I'd be able to lay eyes on him naked again. His memory already fading as he yanked his pants and trousers up over his perky ass. He raised his gaze to meet me and a smile spread out across his face, reaching his eyes and crinkling them in a way I'd never noticed before. His dark blue eyes held me there as he finished doing up his buttons. I didn't even try and get dressed. Why bother? It wasn't like I was modest in the slightest. I wanted him to see how comfortable I was, there, naked, at his mercy in the dark alley.

He broke his hypnotic stare and reached for his shirt that had been discarded on the pavement. He poked one of his huge arms through the hole, then the other. Even getting dressed he was sexy. Then he stopped and took me in once more, head to toe, lingering a little too long on my dick before climbing back up to my eyes. He snickered slightly and then stepped towards me and cupped one cheek in his right palm. His lips met my other cheek and he kissed me softly. The stubble from his jaw, scraping my face slightly. Then instead of pulling away he found my ear.

"Until next time…" he whispered. And with that he pulled back and turned away in the direction of the open alley, strutting down it like it was a runway. His ass swayed from side to side, an air of dominance in his stride.

I was rooted to the spot, not able to pull away from the sight of him walking away until he was completely swallowed up by the shadows. Gone. Just like that. The only remnants of his presence was his sweet scent that lingered on my skin. And as quickly as it began, my night came to a close. I breathed in a deep breath, my chest rising with the inhale. I let it out through my clenched mouth, and with it, a quiet laugh, more to myself than to anyone else. I turned to collect my own belongings that were spread out on the ground around me. I turned once more towards the open alley in hopes of seeing him there again, perhaps having forgotten something, or perhaps because he too wanted more than just a quick fuck. But he wasn't there. Nothing but dark shadows were to be seen. No movement in the slightest. I forced myself to look away, despite my insides aching for more.

Get over it, Dice.

Who was I kidding. This was all it was ever going to be. This was all I ever wanted it to be. Satisfaction. Quick, easy, no fuss.

Not a bad way to end my night.

Chapter Two

The sun was streaking through my venetian blinds, casting long narrow slivers of light across my otherwise dark bedroom. I could feel the heat from outside through the window. Somewhere out there children giggled as they passed by, and mothers scolded them, hurrying them along.

Shit, that means schools out. Have I been sleeping all day?

I rolled onto my back and stretched my long arms up above my head, as if reaching for something unattainable on the ceiling above. Shifting on the bed, I begrudgingly pulled myself up on my elbows, giving in to the late afternoon sunlight. As my weight shifted onto by backside, a quick flash of sharp pain shot up my tail bone.

"Fuck!" I exclaimed, suddenly reminded of last night's romp in the alley. Images of him and his hands all over my naked body appeared before my eyes like pictures in a dirty magazine. I moved a hand down to my ass to help me sit up properly in bed, the dark satin sheet shifting to reveal my naked bottom half beneath.

Jesus, guess I'm not going to be able to sit today.

I stood carefully, my late-afternoon stiffy piercing the air like a sword. I let my hand fall to give it a slight stroke adoringly, before finding my long dark robe hanging on the back of my door, and draping it across my shoulders. I yawned deeply as I walked over to the large bay windows to peer through the cracks in the blinds, my eyes squinting through the brightness outside. The world seemed eerily quiet despite the late afternoon time. I shifted my gaze from the window to the clock on the wall; half past four.

Such is the life of a night-shifter.

I wasn't due back in tonight until midnight.

What to do, what to do?

I wasn't much of a breakfast person. Probably because I was never up at what most would call the 'normal breakfast time'. To be honest, I only usually ate one meal a day. My life a never ending cycle of late-night dinners, mixed with booze and the occasional savoury snack, usually only whatever they had laying around at the club which was normally drugs and cheap wine.

Still staring out the window, my hands moved to my asshole and felt around the area tenderly. My hole felt stretched. Invaded. Fulfilled.

Oh my, he was good last night.

I couldn't remember the last time I was fucked like that. It's as if he knows my body better than I do. His expert hands all over me, caressing all the right places and bringing me to orgasm almost instantly. The thought alone of him and the effect he has on me was making my dick hard. I moved my left hand away from my ass and undid the tie from my robe. The fabric struggled around my stiffie that was now standing at attention. I let it fall open and to the sides, my eyes closing and head falling back as I took hold of my cock and squeezed gently. I opened my eyes and cast them down to my naked form; the light from the window illuminating the chest that was visible from beneath my half-open robe. My right hand was still at my crack and my index finger ventured to my asshole and circled it carefully. My breathing hitched as the feel of my own finger slipping inside me sent a wave of pleasure from my head to my toes. The grip on my dick tightened. My hand began to move up and down along my shaft in a slow and concise movement, as my finger moved in time inside me.

My mind wondered to last night's experience. *I could practically feel his hands on my hips, as he thrust himself deeply into me.* The memory of his nipples grazing my back as he fucked me made my hand quicken. Moving gradually faster and faster, I remembered the feeling of him driving his cock deeper and deeper into me, hitting my g-spot and sending electric shocks up my spine.

I slipped another finger into my ass and curled them as best I could , trying desperately to mimic the feel of his thick cock, my fingers causing the nerve endings around my rim to dance and sing.

Fuck, I'm close already.

I remembered the feeling of his breath against my neck as his hands tightened and tangled in my hair. Our bodies as one, moving together, matching each other's rhythm, faster and faster until both of us were on the brink.

Jesus, I was coming. I loosened the grip on my cock and slowed down as my orgasm tipped and I came all over my hand and the window sil. My two fingers still expertly probing my hole, sending me over the edge. My body bowed as I withdrew my fingers and grabbed the window edge for support, each wave of ejaculation shaking my frame. I opened my eyes and looked down out the window, my breathing slowly returning to normal. I stroked my sticky cock gently, as if congratulating it for a job well done. I smiled despite myself.

Alright, now I'm hungry.

***

Getting ready for work was always entertaining. For most people, getting ready for work meant coffee, shower, suit, tie, briefcase. For a stripper, getting ready for work meant showering, tanning, shaving entire body, press-ups and ab crunches. Instead of documents and files in my 'briefcase', I packed oils, lube, toys, condoms, an assortment of G-strings, briefs, hats, props, whips, cuffs...The list goes on.

Ask me who I think has it better?

I was lucky to land a flat in the neighbourhood I lived in. Close to the club, but not too close, Edgy, but with class. Safe, with just a touch of grime. I was hesitant to live so close to where I worked; I didn't want 'clients' seeing me outside of the club, walking down the road as I stopped into my local Starbucks. What's that expression, don't shit where you eat? But who was I kidding, I barely made it outside in the daytime, anyway! There weren't that many blocks of flats in the area either. Mostly businesses and law firms nearby. Translation- lots of horny closet cases looking to get off after their work day!

My best mate, Dale, from the club lived just around the corner from me. He was the one who got me the job in the first place. Dale was awesome, real stand-up guy. We met just after I moved into the neighbourhood; I was just out for a walk one day…ok, cruising…and we literally bumped into each other- spilled my coffee all over me. If it had been anyone else I would have been pissed. But one look into his emerald eyes and he was instantly forgiven. Dale is my exact opposite in almost every way. Green eyes to my blue, dark hair to my blonde. Our bodies are similarly built however, which is why we dance so well together. At the club we've earned the tag "Double D", and let me tell you, when Dale and Dice take the stage, you know you're in for a treat. As attractive as I find Dale, we've never actually hooked up. It's probably why we have such great chemistry when we dance together; if we started fucking, the magic on stage would surely sizzle. Don't get me wrong, we've made out a few times…purely for the show…and after a few drinks if he asked me to, I'm sure I wouldn't turn him down. But Dale is not boyfriend material. Aside from being able to give Christian Grey a run for his money in the *fifty shades of fucked up department*, Dale and I crossed over into the 'friend zone' long ago. He had a rough time growing up. Dad threw him out of the house just after he caught him sucking a guy off in his upstairs loft when he was 17. He spent the next few years of his life 'sofa-surfing' as he calls it, going from one dead end job to another; he was so down on himself for so long that I don't think he's ever really recovered. He still gets depressed sometimes and finds it incredibly hard to pick himself up from it.

I looked at a picture of Dale and I that was framed on my nightstand.

We do look hot together though.

I shook my head slightly, dismissing the thought. No, Dale's just a friend. A best mate, a surfing buddy, and someone to give me a lift to work!

I looked to the clock on my bedside table.

Shit, quarter past 11. Get a move on, Dice.

Dale would be here to pick me up in 15 minutes, and I was still naked. Opening up my top drawer, I riffled through my G's.

What to wear, what to wear?

I decided to play it safe and chose the black velvet briefs, my white lycra G-string and my cycling shorts with matching vest top. Tossing them into my gym bag along with my massage oil and a few condoms, just for good measure, I took one final look in the mirror. My blonde shaggy hair hung just right around my face, tousled with a touch of bed head. My skin practically glowed thanks to my quick dosing of St. Tropez. I looked out the window to check for rain. All clear. I reached into my underwear drawer and pulled out a pair of dark blue Aussie Bum boxer briefs and yanked them on, tucking my cock neatly into the built-in pouch. I pulled on a simple white ribbed vest top and cut-off denim shorts.

All set, baby.

And as if on cue, Dale honked his horn from downstairs on the road. Grabbing my gym bag and keys I set off.

"Hey there good looking," Dale crooned as I opened up the door to his jet black Mercedes, the leather seats pleading their discourse as I settled in. I couldn't believe Dale drove such an expensive ride. Sometimes I think he has more money than sense. If you ask him, he'd say he only ever got it for cruising guys, but secretly I know that Dale is more of a Man's Man than one might think. Although he can be somewhat camp after a few cocktails, underneath his glittery exterior is a man who likes to fix things and change car tires. What can I say? He's good with his hands…

"Hey there baby, what's shakin'?" I shot back, putting a little bit of extra gay-twang in my tone for good measure.

"Oh fuck, don't even get me started…Guess who rang me last night the second I got through the door?"

"Shut the fuck up, Dale? Don't even…"

"Yes, even…Dice I'm not even fucking joking, the second I walk through the door my phone goes off." Dale puts the car in reverse and backs out of my drive, not missing a beat of the conversation.

"Was he pissed again?"

"Oh, Dice, don't kid yourself, that shit only calls me when he's pissed," he says waving a perfectly manicured finger in the air for emphasis. Dale had been dating this 'seemingly perfect' guy a few months back; Lawyer, early thirties, and beautiful. They had met at our local gym when Dale initially told him off for not wiping down the elliptical after using it. But one look at Mr. Perfect's bulging biceps, and all hostile thoughts had evaporated. They had dated for a few weeks until it became frighteningly obvious that Mr. Perfect was still in the closet. Taking no pity upon him whatsover, Dale immediately broke it off. Part of me wanted to blame him, but at this stage in our lives if the only guys we can meet are bloody closet cases, we might as well give up now! Unfortunately, Mr. Perfect tends to go out and get trashed with his work mates on a regular basis and consequently rings poor Dale for a booty call. Dale usually stays strong. Usually.

"Dale, I'm seriously going to completely withdraw from any conversations about that fucker in the future, why the hell do you let him fuck you around like that?" As much as I love Dale, he had a soft spot for assholes.

"Dice, believe you me, if you saw what that man can do with his cock you wouldn't kick him out of bed either."

With these words we both erupted into a giggly fit.

"Now, enough about me…Spill, yourself you dirty slag," Dale shoots back at me, taking his green eyes off the road only momentarily to give me his 'all-knowing' gaze.

"What are you on about?" I fane innocently, in a very unconvincing manner.

"Don't you give me that shit Dice Valentine, Tim told me all about your little rendezvous."

I stare down at my knotted fingers, my cheeks reddening slightly in the car's shadowy interior.

"Dale Valentine, are you fucking blushing?"

"Don't be ridiculous you old queen," I spit back, not able to with-hold my widening grin.

"You fucked him again, didn't you?"

"Maybe…" I replied, sheepishly.

"I don't know why you're playing coy Mr. Valentine…I know you're just dying to gloat. Go on, then, I'm all ears…"

"What's there to gloat about?" I asked to no one in particular, "trust me when I say we're in the same boat."

"How's that, exactly?"

"Just that what I have with my mystery 'Alley Cat' will never amount to anything more than what you and your 'closet case' have. It's an open and shut case of 'never gonna happen.'"

I peered out the window and caught a glimpse of my reflection in the passenger side window. I let out a tiny sigh as my thoughts left a sour taste in my mouth. Saying the words out loud made me realise how disappointed I was about this whole situation.

Maybe I do want more.

Last night in the alley. Turning to steal one last look at him as he walked away. Willing him to turn around and see me staring back at him. Wishing he might say something that mirrored how I felt towards him. Disappointment stinging my belly, as he vanished into the shadows.

Shit. What's happening to me? I'm turning into a whiny chick.

"Oh, darling, you're really upset about this aren't you?" Dale cooed, his tone soaked in mock pity.

I turned to face him, my serious expression cracking instantly at the realisation that he was taking the piss.

"Oh fuck you!"

And with that the seriousness of our conversation ended. We spent the rest of the drive gossiping like school girls.

***

The club was packed tonight. More than normal. Some of the guys got more nervous the busier the place was. They probably get thrown by the crowds, find it hard to concentrate. Not me. I relished a full house. Whenever someone asked me how I stay cool when there's hundreds of faces studying my every move, I just tell them- I don't see faces when I dance. I see £ signs. The only one who's ever caught me off guard is…well, you can guess.

Dale led the way through the side entrance to the club, the muffled base reaching our ears already through the thick walls.

"Hiya Tony," we shouted in unison over the music as we approached Tony the doorman.

"Gents," he replied politely as we breezed past him.

Tony was our token straight staff member. Most strip clubs have one; usually to help keep the boys in check and step-in in case one of us gets out of line. Tony was a laugh, and if on his good side, would always have your back. He was a typical muscle-jock; shaved head, thick neck, and enormous arms. We all loved to flirt and tease with him, and he always takes it like a man…so to speak. You'd think that to work with a bunch of fags day-in and day-out he must have to be a little gay. But no, 100% hetero. Dale and I partied with him a little bit too much. We were his favourites.

"You alright, T?" I hollered with a smile, "Got anything good for your favourite boys tonight?" The glimmer in my eye giving away my true intentions. Tony was the best 'charlie hook-up' this side of the city. If he didn't have any on him tonight, sure as hell he would be able to nail some off some unsuspecting bloke railing it in the toilets later.

"Come see me later kiddo, I got your back," he shouted with a wink.

Grinning from ear to ear, Dale tugged me along impatiently further and further into the crowd in the direction of the back room.

"We gotta hurry D, we're on in like 20."

"Coming, Dad…" I teased.

"Are we good?"

"You betcha, handsome," I joked, my spirits instantly lifted, "he says to come hit him up later."

Dale shot me a ridiculously huge grin like a child on Christmas morning and squeezed my arm in pure excitement. And with that we were lost…

***

Well here we are again, big guy.

I stared straight ahead at the face in the mirror. Not blinking. Barely even breathing. I wasn't even sure how long I'd been sitting here like this.

Maybe he'll be here again tonight.

My heart did a little flutter at the thought of seeing him again tonight. I chastized myself inwardly for letting my feelings get the better of me.

Stop it. If he's here, he's here. Don't give him any more power than he already has over you.

My eyes glazed over, the background noise becoming increasingly muffled despite the proximity of the crowd beyond the curtain.

This isn't you anymore.

This last thought made me flinch slightly, breaking the trance and forcing me to sit up straight. My back suddenly aching, as if I'd been slumped over in the same position for hours.

How much more of this can you take?

I shook my head again, harder this time, in a desperate attempt to snap out of this sudden funk that was throwing me off my game. This wasn't like me. Normally at this stage of the night I was pumped, feeding off the energy of the other dancers. Tonight felt…different, somehow. A heavy feeling was weighing me down, making me feel a bit off.

However, it was almost showtime, and regardless of what thoughts were stirring in my skull, I had a job to do. A job that I was fucking great at. A job that under normal circumstances, on normal nights, I loved.

You want more than these drooling low-life douchebags can give you. You want **him.**

If it weren't for the change of song from onstage, I might have actually begun listening to whomever or whatever was putting these thoughts in my head.

A dark, grungy version of 'Smells like Teen Spirit' was unraveling from the speakers.

You're up next, fella.

As if on cue, Dale materialised in the mirror's reflection before me, stirring me and forcing me back into the room and out of my head. He caught the look in my eye and tilted his head in confusion.

"What you thinking about, fella?" he asked in a caring tone.

"Huh?" I asked, shaking my head, "Oh, nothing…just, ya know…daydreaming again…" I said dismissively.

"Well are you just gonna bloody stare at those lines all night, or are we gonna have some fuckin' fun?"

Dale's words jarred me further from the 'land of doubt' where I just was. I immediately remembered the small hand mirror littered with two fat white powdery lines in front of me.

"You know it," I said sniffing hard to clear my sinuses.

"Wait for me, you hog. If I know you at all the second I turn away, you'll have both of 'em up your schnoz before I can say 'boo,'" Dale teased, reaching into his back pocket and pulling out a note. Mirroring his actions I rolled a £50 into a clean tube shape. Our eyes met and we held up the notes as if making a toast.

"Here's to a fucking *gooood* night," Dale drawled, coughing to clear the pathways.

"Emphasis on the *fucking*."

Dale laughed under his breath, "You should be so lucky."

We leaned our heads down to the table, note in nose, and raked up each line in one clean sweep. Staring up at the ceiling, I tilted my head back and let sensation take over. Pausing briefly, I let my eyes close again and pictured the cocaine filtering through my system; down my nasal passage and straight into my bloodstream, igniting everything along its way until my insides were liquid fire, my nerve synapses firing in unison as the effects of my dopamine rush sent an immediate rush of intense pleasure to my limbs.

"Fuck me," I breathed, my eyes still firmly shut.

"You're not kidding."

When I opened my eyes I saw Dale rubbing the excess from the mirror over his gums.

"Bloody hell, Tony, you know your shit."

"Right, baby, you ready?" Dale asked, taking one last look in the mirror. I stood up beside him, my legs wobbling slightly.

"Easy, tiger…" he reached out to catch me, easing me back up. "You alright?"

"I think I'm getting too old for this," I mused bending over to look at the size of my pupils. As before their crystal clear hue was merely an eclipse behind the black disk of a pupil that was taking over.

"Oh spare me, D-you of all people aren't anywhere near retirement…"

I didn't respond. I didn't need to. He was right. Straightening up we both reached down our short shorts and adjusted our cocks inside our T-bars. Dale and I were the epitome of Heaven and Hell. He in black vinyl tear-away shorts, black mesh tank top, leather dog collar and huge black feathered angel wings. I, his complete opposite; soft white silk boxers, white ribbed tank top and plush, white angel wings strapped to my back.

We look hot.

I looked at Dale, who in turn was looking back at me, studying my face ever so carefully. I tilted my head, silently questioning his stare. It was then that I noticed a little glimmer in his eye that I hadn't noticed before. And the way that he was staring at me, almost adoringly, brought a smile to my face.

Dale is so cute. So wholesome. How have I never noticed this before?

We turned our eyes back to the mirror and studied the men who looked back at us. These men were different. Almost unrecognisable. We were merely their puppets. Dancing bodies tied to strings and doing as they were told. I was about to become a slave to my stage persona, and do what I did best. Dance for the crowd for money and thrills. Suck them dry for everything they were worth…And I couldn't fucking wait.

***

Dale and I stood behind the heavy velvet curtain. Hand in hand, our chests heaving beneath our costumes, patiently awaiting our announcement. The crowd was going insane, roaring so loudly I almost had to shield my ears. The glow from underneath the curtain suddenly faded, and was replaced with a dim blue glare; the crowd's cue to shut the fuck up.

Doing as they were told, the meatheads' cat-calls simmered until the entire place fell silent. Seconds passed and now the silence became almost deafening. The DJ was building anticipation. I could feel it in the air; heavy and seedy as if it would suddenly cause the floor to cave in. I was practically shaking, overcome by the sudden urge to jump out of my skin. Sensing my tenseness, Dale squeezed my hand in reassurance.

Good old Dale. Always knowing what I'm feeling without me having to mutter a fucking word.

I snuck a glance over at him and saw his eyes transfixed on a spot in front of him on the curtain. Willing it to open so we could take the stage. Then the familiar voice of Rick, the DJ, broke me from my bubble, filling the air with a sound that was soaking with filth and innuendo.

"Gentlemen…Gentlemen…Gentlemen…Please fasten your seat-belts, and keep your arms and legs inside the vehicle…" he shouted in his best 'fair-ground' voice, "…this is going to be a bumpy ride…"

The crowd went…Mental.

"Two for the price of one, is tonight's deal for you. Don't say we never do anything for you lot."

His voice oozed like silky smooth like vanilla as it seeped from the speakers and caressed everyone's skin in the room. Even I started to twitch down south. Rick knew what he was doing, and we owed the vibe in the club to him and his erotic ways. He was the absolute best at getting a crowd ready to open their wallets.

"I know I don't have to tell you… to put your FUCKING HANDS TOGETHER AND WELCOME BACK TO THE STAGE TWO OF YOUR FAVOURITE COCK-TEASERS…MR DALE LAVENDER AND MR DICE VALENTINE."

And with that the heavy velvet curtains parted slowly, letting blinding white light pierce us both, and causing the glitter that covered every inch of our exposed skin to shimmer beautifully in reaction. Rihanna's "Distrubia" started up, and without missing a beat I grabbed at the dog collar around Dale's neck and stepped out on stage, dragging him behind me.

The faceless crowd sprang to their feet in reaction to our costumes. Hands adjusted cocks in trousers. Some clapped, others sat in quiet anticipation.

You're all in for a treat.

Dale and I took center stage, a few yards spread out in between us. We faced the spotlights, hands on our hips. Our lips counting the beats, before our hips began to move in unison, drawing huge circles in the air. As we leaned back and our crotches faced the crowds we paused, giving them a glance of the outline of our cocks pressing up against the restraints of our shorts. When we were standing up straight, we both turned around and repeated the action with our asses facing out. This dance was one of my favourites. It was about the 'good' getting to be 'bad'. Dale and I had choreographed it ourselves and we had it pinned, right down to the very last second. We meant it to be dark, sultry and heart-stopping. It was the dark angel's turn to be punished...

As Rihanna sang about darkness and light, I stood up straight, skirted across the stage and took hold of the gleaming metal pole that stood erect in the center of the stage behind us, as Dale bent over slowly, hitching from his waist until he had an ankle in each hand. His tight vinyl shorts screamed as the material stretched sexily over his taught ass cheeks. He stole a cheeky side glance from over his shoulder as I took the pole in my right hand and swung myself around it, my right leg wrapping itself around as well until both my feet were off the ground, sending me spinning around the pole as if in flight. As I landed softly on the ground, I slid my right hand up the pole as far as I could and used the muscles in my core to propel myself back up to a standing position. As my cock made contact with the pole I let my head fall back and my eyes close. I stayed like this for a moment, enjoying the sensation of my increasingly hardening dick pressing up against cold, hard metal through the silk of my underwear. The crowd was obviously enjoying it as well as they fell eerily silent. Only the crooning of Rihanna's voice could be deciphered.

Don't lose yourself too much, Dice.

My subconscious was right. I wasn't out here alone tonight. Tonight there were two of us eager to do the pleasing, and I had to get back to my naughty little angel...

I sauntered over to a waiting plush velvet chair that stood off to the right of the stage. On it was a long, black riding crop. I picked it up and showed it to the crowd. Dale's ass twitched in anticipation from the other side of the stage. With feather light steps I made my way over to him and using the leather crop took a quick crack at his sweet spot.

The delicious sound of leather hitting vinyl reverberated through the air and the crowd winced at the sound. Dale, no stranger to whips and chains, faked a look of surprise crossed with orgasmic pleasure. Turning my gaze to the crowd, asking their permission to continue, they responded with an eruption of encouraging shouts. Dale bent his knees causing his ass to taunt my whip further as it bounced lightly in the air. Without warning I brought the crop down across his backside once more, showing no mercy. As it made contact with the taught vinyl fabric that coated his beautifully pert ass cheeks, he immediately straightened up to a standing position, his feet never leaving the floor. I turned to face the crowd, and Dale was immediately behind me, very close, his nose nuzzling the skin of my neck tracing an imaginary line from my shoulder to my ear. The sensation of him behind me and his growing erection pressing into my ass caused me to momentarily get lost in the moment and close my eyes.

It's all part of the show, baby.

Snatching the whip from my hand, Dale tossed it off stage. He was playing his part perfectly, all mock sexual frustration. I caught glimpse of his expression, which oozed fiery desire. He kicked my legs apart with his right foot, and still from behind pulled my wings off and peeled my white vest over my head, letting it slide off, discarded on the floor. His grasp was rough and sudden, and before I could react his hands were immediately on my skin; under my arms and gently grazing my nipples. He pinched them between his thumb and index finger, pulling at them gently until they stood perfectly erect. And as if we were one body making love, our hips began to move in unison, swaying from side to side and grinding into each other, until I could feel his rock hard cock poking me from behind. I let my eyes close slowly and let my arms fall to the side. My head rolled back until it rested on Dale's shoulder. I was completely lost in the moment. We were like lovers on the stage, each movement an exquisite part of the tease. Every second that passed was foreplay, and I was beyond turned on. My dick was aching to be released from my boxers. Heat pulsed through my veins causing my cheeks to flush and sweat begin to form a sheer layer over my skin. My breath hitched in my throat and my eyes darted open as Dale moved his hips just right so that the tip of his cock hit my sweet spot, a few thin layers of material the only thing separating us from barebacking.

His hands slid down my body, his fingers getting lost in the deep grooves of my abs, before finding their way down to the waist band of my silk boxers. Hooking his thumbs into the band he pulled quickly until the thin material slipped to the floor, leaving me in only my pearl white G-string which was barely containing my modesty.

The men in the crowd were all sitting now. Shadows dancing across the stage as they got increasingly more comfortable in their seats.

Let's give 'em what they want.

As if reading my thoughts, Dale slid his hand up my naked back causing me to instinctually bend over in front of him, my ass still perfectly in position for us to dry hump. And right on cue, Dale began to grind his hips into me further, taking me from behind even through the confines of our clothes. Both of us completely lost in the dance, our breathing getting quicker with every beat of the song that pulsated through us. I could tell Dale was completely turned on too as his grip on my hips got increasingly tighter, until his nails began to dig into my skin. This was roleplay. It was so easy to become lost in the scene. For a brief moment, I think I wanted him to take me right there on the stage. My thoughts suddenly shifted and the crowd melted away, leaving only Dale and I in the room, fucking mercilessly. Oh God, it would be hot, having him pumping away inside me.

I wonder what it would feel like to have him cum inside me? Would he be gentle or rough? I wonder how his mouth tastes. If I keep this up I'm totally gonna cum. I think he was sensing it too, because he tapped me gently on the thigh; our signal to change the tempo before it was too late. I stood up quickly and grabbing him roughly by the shoulder turned him to face me.

Your turn to get naked.

Dale looked incredibly sexy in his black mesh tank top. He had beautifully shaped pecs, and dark round nipples that were just barely visible through the sheer material of his top. His arms were intensely defined and muscular with deep tricep grooves and widely set shoulders. In short, he would give Adonis a run for his money. Thing is with Dale, he was incredibly modest and totally unaware of how beautiful he was.

Damn him for being so fine.

I took a moment to drink in Dale's beauty, letting my blood pressure return to normal after my naughty thoughts, and cheekily shot the crowd a wink and a nod which sent them into a fit. Looking back at Dale, I caught a glimpse of something in his eye that I had never seen or noticed before.

He looks almost…sad.

His expression was pained and lost somehow. He looked genuinely turned on. This was getting to him tonight. I needed to make this quick or I'd have him ejaculating all over the stage in a second flat. I snuck a glance at his tear-away shorts and the incredible bulge they were containing. His shoulders heaved with every breath he took in through gritted teeth. He let his hands fall by his sides now, his body language giving in and asking me to take him right then and there. I looked up into his eyes once more and instantly saw his expression darken. I winked at him so that only he could see, before taking his mesh top in both my hands and tearing roughly in opposite directions. The material didn't put up a fight, instead, disintegrated beneath my grasp, revealing Dale's gorgeous torso. No matter how many times I saw his naked chest, it still caught my breath every time.

Fuck me, you're gorgeous.

I let most of the mesh top fall to the ground and helped what was left of it as well as the angel wings, off his strong shoulders. He stepped towards me and with one hand around my waist, pulled me in close to him until we were nose to nose. We dipped our hips slightly in line with the thumping base, forwards and then backwards, dirty dancing on the stage, both completely bare except for my G-string and his tear-away shorts. Our mouths hovered inches apart. We parted our lips slightly, and I could feel his hot breath on my face. Our cocks were now firmly pinned up against each other, the friction sending electric volts of pleasure up and down my entire body making my knees quiver. It was like that we stayed for what seemed like hours, our erect nipples grazing together, sweat now glistening all over our bodies in the bright glare of the stage spotlights. I was practically panting now. I wanted desperately to move my head in that extra inch and taste his mouth, feel his lips on mine, his tongue gently lapping against my own…

This was the ultimate tease. The crowd was aching to see our lips touch. Wanted nothing more than to see us kiss, like actors in a love story. It was a moment of romance thrown into our filthy dance. As the music began to slow, the realisation that it was almost over swept over the men in the audience, forcing them to rise to their feet in protest. Catcalls and shouts reigned out so loudly that the last few bars of the song were lost under the voices.

Dale didn't let go or loosen his grip as the heavy velvet curtains began to race towards each other from either end of the stage. We held each other until the very last second, the light disappearing slowly and darkness swallowing us up as the curtain drew it's imaginary line separating us from the exposure of the audience. I couldn't move. He had me paralysed on the spot, not wanting it to end. Both of us waiting for someone or something to break the electricity that stood so heavy between us. But as the voices from the stage slowly faded, as did the mood, our breathing returning to normal. I think I broke contact first. Perhaps it was out of discomfort. Maybe I was nervous. But one thing was certain, the dance was over, as quickly as it began, leaving both the crowd and the dancers…wanting more.

Chapter Three

It was closing time. The club was emptying out slowly. Drunk guys heading home to wank over the men they'd just fantasised over for the past couple of hours. Some going home with others. Some still hoping for that last second hook-up in the parking lot.

Such was the anti-climax of spending the night in a boudoir of filth and decadence, such as this. The harsh realisation hitting that it was back to reality as the final curtain closed.

The dancers were starting to pack up and go too. Cabs waited out back, especially for us, away from prying eyes and hecklers. The club wasn't the classiest of its kind out there, but it did certainly treat it's guys right. Tony was always on hand to escort us to a waiting car in case any of the 'patrons' were hanging about trying it on. Good ol' T, always there to help out when needed.

I chuckled as the last of my coke buzz melted away. Part of me was considering having another bump and keeping the night going, but that unfamiliar heavy feeling was still plaguing my insides. After Dale and I danced, I had started to feel worse.

As soon as he let me go and turned away after our song finished, I immediately felt as if I was missing something. Even after only holding each other for a few minutes, and even if it was all for show, still, it was as if he had left an imprint on my skin.

After our song, Dale had backed away from me suddenly regarding me carefully as if I were a wild animal about to pounce. After he put a few yards between us he had turned and sauntered off in the opposite direction. That was the last time I saw him tonight. No words exchanged. He had left me standing there, hard-on raging, completely unsatisfied and filled with so many questions I was afraid my head would implode.

I stared at my expression in the mirror. So sullen and thoughtful. My body may have begun it's come down, but my mind was still whirring. Without focusing on the guys leaving behind me, I could feel the club continue to empty further. Before I knew it, silence had filled the dressing room. And there I still was, staring at myself, eerily still.

Get up. Go home and forget this whole night ever happened. You'll feel differently in the morning.

I forced myself to stir. Blinking broke the trance and my limbs began to move. A voice from behind me somewhere made me flinch. It was Tim.

"Hey babe, someone left this for you at the front door..." Tim said, handing me a small white envelope. "You alright, Dice?"

The look on my face was obviously giving away my solemn mood more than I was willing to let on. I reached for the envelope and regarded it carefully.

"Yeah, sorry..."

The envelope was sealed with my name emblazoned across the front in beautiful handwriting.

"Just tired, thanks Tim. Who sent this?"

Without even hearing his answer, I already had an inkling as to who must have left this.

Fuck, was he here tonight?

"Dunno, T said it was some guy...Didn't get a good look at him," Tim answered, shrugging his shoulders. I continued to study the envelope carefully. Running my fingers over the writing on the front. Tim caught sight of my tweaked expression and his look of concern suddenly melted into a wide mouthed grin.

"OOOH, I get it...It's from your mystery fella, *innit?*" he drawled in his cockney tone.

My eyes shot to meet his and the same shit-eating grin materialised across my own face.

"I'll leave you to it then, big guy."

And with that he turned on his heal to leave. Raising his hand to shoot me a wave as he walked away, "Wear a condom!"

I let out a stifled laugh as I turned the envelope over in my hand and tore it open. Inside there was a neatly folded piece of paper. Unfolding it, I let my eyes scan over the message.

You were so hot tonight...I can't wait to get my hands on you again. I'll be waiting when you get off...
-D

I immediately felt myself stiffen in my pants. Adrenaline began to fuse into my every limb and I suddenly felt revitalised again. All thoughts of Dale and our dance instantly melted away after reading the note.

Shit, he was here tonight. Tonight is looking up again.

I chuckled to myself as I stood and took another long look in the mirror. I ran a now-sweaty hand through my unruly hair and checked my nose and teeth. My bag was already packed. I had changed into white-stripped track bottoms and a matching white printed v-neck t. I liked to be comfortable after a hard day's work. Grabbing my things I headed straight for the blazing red exit sign. The place was deserted.

I'm the last to leave.

How was it that everyone else had left and I was still here, left to lock up on my own.

Where the fuck was Tony?

Tony was normally the one to kick us all out for the night. All the dancers had a set of keys to padlock the door in case of emergency. I had only had to use them a handful of times, mainly because some of the guys and I had stayed around partying well after last call. I must have completely fazed out and not noticed everyone else leaving.

The club had an eerie feel to it after everyone had left. It was so hollow and dark and had a stale musty smell in the air.

Jesus, I can't believe they've shut all the lights off.

I didn't care, I had a date to make now. As I made my way out onto the main floor, I had to squint and let my eyes adjust to the dark. Standing still for a few seconds, the glare from the exit came into view. I focused on the sign and began to make my way towards it. My flip-flops echoed against the four walls, making them seem louder than they should. When I was about half-way across the floor something caught the corner of my eye. Stopping dead in my tracks, I turned towards the shadow and grabbed at my chest in surprise.

What the fuck was that?

Against the far wall of the club.

Did something move?

I squinted into the distance and waited. My breath was caught in my throat as I watched. I waited. Part of me wanted to call out and see if something was there, but something stopped me.

Just go, Dice.

I started moving again, quicker this time and more determined. I inched my way closer and closer to the exit door with one thought running through my head;

Just get out.

I was practically jogging by the time I got to the door and pushed.

Fuck, the alarm.

Before opening the door I turned to the adjacent wall and the large alarm box perched at eye level. I stole another look into the club as I flipped the screen of the box back. Nothing stirred. I daringly looked further into the club. Still nothing. Nothing moving. No sounds. I turned back to the small alarm screen glowing before me and quickly punched in the code. It responded with a slow high-pitched beeping sound, which was my cue to get out. Not hesitating, I turned towards the door again and pushed hard. The large black door groaned in protest as I practically fell through the threshold. Turning I slammed it behind me, leaving one hand pressed firmly up against it as I fished in my gym bag for my keys.

Jesus, Dice, could you not have had them ready? Where the fuck are they?

Panic rised in my throat as I realised that I may have left them inside.

Oh please, God, no.

Relief flooded my body as my fingers made contact with the ring and immediately fished them out of my abyss of a bag. I locked the door in a swift turn of the key and let out a huge ragged sigh. With both hands on the door now, I let my head sag and stared at my feet.

Bloody hell, mate. Get a grip. Afraid of the dark now, are we?

Backing away slowly, I kept my eyes focused on the door as if I expected it to spring to life. When there was about two metres between me and the door, I paused, gritting my teeth in anticipation.

There was nothing.

I listened, barely breathing. But nothing happened. After god knows how long, I finally hauled in a deep breath of cool air. It stung my lungs as it went down, as if it were a foreign substance. I backed away slowly not removing my eyes from the closed door. When I was sure it was safe I swung around quickly and found myself practically nose to nose with Tony, who materialised as if from nowhere. I stifled a scream with my hand.

"Fucking hell!" I shouted, jumping almost out of my skin, "Where the hell did you come from?"

Tony didn't say anything. He just stared, wide-eyed straight ahead.

"Tony, you scared the shit out of me…What are you still doing here?" I looked him straight in the eye, but he appeared to almost be looking through me, as if he was finding it hard to focus. His arms were hanging listlessly at his sides, and his expression was completely void. I took a step back from him for a moment, trying to assess the situation.

My heart was still racing from my scare in the club, and I was clutching at my neck for protection.

"*TONY?*" I shouted, as if speaking louder would snap him from his trance. It appeared to work as he finally took notice of me standing there in front of him, as if I was the one who had appeared from nowhere.

"Are you alright?" I reached out to him just then, taking an arm in each hand and squeezing slightly. Even through his thick leather jacket, he felt cold to the touch, as if he had been out here for hours. There was a slight nip to the air tonight, but not nearly enough to cause him to be so cold. He still didn't respond even as I shook him slightly. I began looking him up and down, my eyes searching for some sign that he was hurt. I grabbed his hands and turned them over so his palms were face up. They were filthy, like he had been rolling around in the dirt or digging or something. Black mud was caked underneath his nails, and the skin on his fingers was red raw. My eyes travelled up his wide frame, trying desperately to figure out exactly what was wrong. I let his hands drop and they just fell to his sides like dead weights. Then Tony started to move. Slow steps, almost like how I pictured a zombie to walk in the movies. I moved back to get out of his way and watched in awe as he just staggered away into the empty parking lot.

"Tony?"

But either he chose not to respond or couldn't hear me. Part of me wanted to follow him. Something inside me was shouting for me to get to the bottom of whatever was wrong with him. But another part was itching to get to our spot.

I still had the note in my hand, and unfolded it again to reread the message from my Alley Cat.

I'll be waiting when you get off…

Even glancing at the words and considering the meaning behind them was enough to stir my legs into action once again. I heaved in a deep breath and turned away from Tony in the direction of the back alley behind the club.

This is so seedy. Meeting dark strangers in the alley after work. How the hell did I get here? I hope Tony is going to be alright.

I had to shake my head to get rid of the creepy feeling that was crawling up my spine.

This night is taking a turn for the worst.

As I made my way around the side of the building to the loading area of the club I was reminded of the sounds I heard from inside. My thoughts made me slow, and I considered turning around and heading home. I was at odds all of a sudden with the feeling in my trousers and the one in my gut. I stopped as I was about to pass through the part of the alley that was not lit-up. Letting my eyes adjust I searched the shadows for signs of my lover waiting for me. My imagination wondered, and I imagined him propped up against a wall, one leg bent at the knee and his foot resting sexily against the bricks. I remembered the smell of his skin and the warmth of his body pressed up against mine. I let my eyes close for a second as I lost myself in the anticipation of what was to come.

All fear and anxiety slowly drained from inside me and was immediately replaced by butterflies, fluttering madly against the walls of my stomach. My cock stirred in my pants as I thought of his hands on my skin. A grin played with the corners of my mouth as I stepped into the shadows and continued walking towards the alley.

It was completely black for a moment and I stumbled slightly, tripping over debris that was scattered over the ground. Turning the corner, I could see a sliver of light up ahead begin to grow from the lamp post above. Walking towards it I squinted as the fluorescent glow hit my eyes. Inching closer, the alley way with its piled up boxes came into view.

Shit, I'm nervous.

I clutched my gym bag tighter to my side and prepared myself for seeing *him*.

Then something stopped me dead in my tracks. Something on the ground caught my eye and drew it downwards. Something that shouldn't have been there.

"What the-"

I squinted in the assaulting light and craned my neck to see further around the corner. What I saw was like a sucker punch to my gut, instantly taking my breath away. My hand shot up to cover my mouth as sudden tears sprung from my eyes that were now as wide as saucers. My gym bag slid from my grasp and landed on the hard pavement with a thud.

There on the ground before me was the undeniable outline of a body lying splayed out on the ground.

Please, no…

I forced my feet to inch closer to the body, just close enough to see who it was. Bile rose in my throat as the face came into view.

Him…

I spun my head away from the sight and immediately vomited into the darkness. I coughed and spluttered as the contents of my stomach emptied themselves onto the pavement.

No, no, no. Please let it not be him. Please God, let it not be him.

But I knew it was. Suddenly I felt dizzy, as if I might pass out. I turned my head to once again take a look at the body that lay before me. My tunnel vision clouded, and I was sure that my thumping heart was about to burst from my chest. Wiping my mouth with a trembling hand I tried to suppress the rising panic that was slowly taking over me. I had to make sure it was him.

My head was saying *run*, but my insides were bleeding for this man who was here to see me. I closed my eyes momentarily to regroup myself before forcing them open again to take one more look. As I took another step closer to his lifeless figure, I suddenly wished I hadn't.

His face was completely splattered with blood, and black gleaming liquid oozed from a gaping wound just above his right eyebrow. His head was tilted away from me, but there was no mistaking his features. More blood than I had ever seen before was escaping from another wound, a puncture, from just about where I'd expect his heart to be. His arms rested extended at either side of his body, almost giving off an air of defeat.

Suddenly flashes of his beautiful, unharmed face snapped in my mind like photographs.

Last night. His devilish grin. His gorgeous eyes.

At that moment, something inside me broke. My chest heaved once more as I vomited again over the ground before me. The tears were flooding from my eyes now, as my body lurched a third time, dry heaving now, and completely empty. I had to get away. In an instant all emotion disappeared from my body and I was nothing but instinct. I staggered on my heel, one hand still clutching my mouth as if suppressing a scream. There was no logic in my movements, and the only thing driving me forwards was pure adrenaline. I'm sure my heart stopped working at that moment and my head took over in survival mode, calling the shots. I could barely see through the stinging tears that corroded my eyes.

He was here to see me…

I shook my head violently to rid myself of the thought. If I let myself think then I was sure I would die. All my body was telling me was to get away. Go home where you're safe. Nothing else mattered.

But before I could control it, the thought that whoever, or whomever had done this could still be close by, filtered through my thought stream.

Fuck me.

I felt like I was then being chased. Delirium surged through my veins at the thought that someone could be hot on my tail. I had the urge to turn back and check that I was alright, but I didn't. I wanted to scream, but I was sure I didn't have enough air in my lungs. I just had to keep moving, get home as fast as I could. Then I could call the police. My eyes darted around the car park, looking for someone, something to help, but were greeted with nothing but blackness.

Where the hell was everyone?

I couldn't believe the area was so deserted. It wasn't that late was it? There was bound to be someone around.

It took me a second through my hysteria to realise that I had left my gym bag behind.

FUCK.

My pace slowed for a moment before picking up again.

Forget about the bag; just get the fuck out of here.

Just then my flip-flop must have caught on something, and before I knew it, I was tripping. I stumbled at first before going completely ass over tit. The fall was practically in slow motion as I lost my footing and saw the ground gradually coming closer to my head. I was airborne for a split second before hitting the pavement hard with all the weight of my body. My hands connected first, skidding across the cold wet cement. Sheer white pain shot up my wrists and arms. My elbows and knees were next to hit before the right side of my head connected with the ground with a sickening thwack. I swear my temple bounced against the pavement, the feeling reverberating throughout my body and instantly numbing every inch of feeling I once had. Gravel scraped the exposed skin on my arms and tore through my jeans. The sound of bone being pulled along pavement rang in my ears until I almost lost consciousness from the sound.

Then everything stopped.

It was minutes before I started to feel anything at all, my body completely numb from head to toe. And then slowly, blinding pain appeared before my eyes like a white light clouding my vision until I was sure I had lost my sense of sight. I let out an agonised groan that didn't sound like me, but that bounced off the surrounding buildings. I gritted my teeth so hard I was sure I was going to crack my jaw in half. My hands felt like they were on fire; blistering heat spreading through my body. My body reacted by pulling itself into the fetal position as if to protect it from further attack, and I stayed there on the ground, rocking back and forth until the pain before my eyes subsided long enough for me to regain sight and realise where I was.

I didn't move for what seemed like ages. I was afraid something was broken. My legs felt wet, like I had landed in a puddle or something. When I finally was able to look down at myself, I saw the wetness was my own blood, soaking through the denim of my trousers. I winced at the sight. I could barely focus on anything. I wasn't even sure if I was still awake or if I had been knocked unconscious. Everything swayed and moved in and out of focus. Pain washed over me and then subsided briefly before returning again.

Am I dying? Is something broken?

In the darkness, beyond the alley, nothing seemed to stir or move. I strained my ears to hear footsteps, or the shuffling of feet. I listened as hard as I could. But there was nothing. A siren resonated from somewhere in the distance, filling the air with a distant wail. Or was that sound coming from my head? I strained my eyes to focus on something across the car park, but it was useless.

Get up, Dice.

My subconscious willed me onwards, but it was losing against the irrepressible urge to just let go. I was so tired. So listless. Drained and in pain. Without my permission my head eased itself back down to the ground until it connected with the cold pavement underneath. The cold stone actually felt comforting somewhat, and I could feel my body begin to relax and give in to the surrounding darkness. As I let go, the pain in my head began to let up; replaced with a warm comforting glow that began to fill me up from my toes to the very crown of my skull. I stared up at the inky black sky and the twinkling stars began to envelop me like a warm embrace. My heavy eyelids began to close slightly, drooping more and more as I began to slip into unconsciousness. My aching wounds and limbs eased as I imagined myself asleep in my bed. Comfortable, beneath the duvet. Warm and safe...

Chapter Four

I awoke as if from a dream, my head fuzzy and confused. I felt hung over. Tired. Exhausted, actually. I was in bed. Naked. Lying on top of my duvet. I felt heavy. It was only a matter of seconds before my brain registered the pain in my arms and legs. They throbbed as if they had their own enormous pulse. I gritted my teeth in response and bit down on my tongue so hard I tasted blood. It hurt to open my eyes. The sliver of light that crept in through the curtains pierced me like a sword. I squinted and managed to shift myself in bed until I was facing the ceiling. A cool breeze from outside made the curtains dance suddenly, letting in more light. It licked at my bare skin leaving goose bumps in its wake.

I stared up at the ceiling, disbelievingly, as my thoughts began to gather themselves and the memories of last night began to filter in and replay themselves in front of my eyes like scenes from a horror film. I frowned as I remembered what had happened.

What time was it? What happened when I got home? Did I call the police?

It suddenly dawned on me that I couldn't actually remember getting home. The thought made me shiver as I racked my brain trying in vain to remember what happened last night.

I fell…I remember falling…

I carefully inspected my naked body with both my hands, running them up and down my frame, checking for wounds. I winced as my palms made contact with my chest. Turning them over, I inspected their damaged state. Both my hands were badly scraped and caked with dried blood. Looking down at the duvet beneath me, I saw that it too was lightly splattered with blood. Presumably my own.

"Oh, shit."

I pulled myself up, first onto my elbows and then sitting. My right knee was also pretty badly banged up and stained with blood.

Fuck, all this from a little fall?

I had to get myself cleaned up. I swung my legs over the bed until my feet dangled over the side. Bracing myself, I stood carefully. The cold hardwood floor was cooling under my fiery skin.

Stop being such a pussy, Dice.

Doing my best to ignore my screaming cuts, I tore the duvet off the bed and swiftly tossed it in the washing machine. I smoothed down the rest of the bedding and inspected it closely for any dried sticky patches. The black satin sheets appeared to be fairly clean, having been protected beneath the duvet. Everything felt dirty, like my home had been infiltrated with grime and filth, and I was suddenly overcome with the need to clean and scrub everything.

I marched into the bathroom and caught a glimpse of the clock on the wall in the kitchen.

Jesus, ten past 11.

I carried on into the bathroom and flicked the switch. The dim lights sprang to life, catching me off guard slightly as my reflection appeared in the mirror in front of me.

I looked ghastly. Dark circles had formed under my eyes in the past few hours and my skin was blotchy. My blonde hair was limp and matted against my forehead. I ran a hand through it in a feeble attempt to make it look better.

"Fuck it."

Turning on the taps, I tested the water before beginning to rinse the blood from the scrapes on my palms. Slowly the clear water began to run red, instantly turning my stomach and making me feel queasy. I stiffled a sob as the cold brought tears to my eyes. Finishing quickly, I turned on the shower and prepared myself for the shock to my system.

***

After my shower, I was beginning to feel halfway normal again. I was just managing to keep the panic that was threatening to cripple me, at bay. I had wrapped my palms in some white medical gauze I had dug up in the first aid kit I kept in my medicine kit, and put a large plaster over the large graze on my knee. I looked like a burn victim as I emerged naked from the bathroom, but at least I could use my hands again. I quickly pulled on a pair of neon pink "Lick" underwear.

Why can't I remember coming home? Did I call the police? I must have...

The silence of the flat was abruptly interrupted by the sound of my mobile going off from somewhere in the bedroom. The sound made me jump as I stood frozen to the spot in front of my dresser.

I couldn't decide if I should run to it or ignore it.

What if it's the club? What if it's Tony? Maybe it's Dale, wondering where I went? What if it's the police? Oh fuck, what the hell happened when I got home? Everything's so fuzzy.

My heart started picking up momentum making my pulse drum even louder at my temples. The feeling mixed with my screeching mobile made my head throb. I put my hands over my ears in response, and willed the sound to stop.

Let them leave a message.

It rang for what felt like ages. When it stopped, silence filled the flat once again. I remained rooted to the spot, listening intently and wondering if it would ring again. After a few moments I realised that I was safe. I willed myself to dress quickly.

I swung open the doors of my enormous wardrobe and decided on a pair of faded blue jeans and a simple white V-neck tee. Easing the clothes over my aching body, I went in search of my mobile to check who had rung.

When I approached it on the bedside table, the screen was lit-up notifying me of a message. Part of me was dying to know who it was. The other part was happy being blissfully ignorant. Without a second thought I reached down and unlocked the screen.

Twelve missed calls.

A feeling of dread washed over me as I scrolled through my call history.

All from the club.

There was only one message. With a shaking hand I pressed the play button. I recognised the voice on the other end almost immediately; it was Joe, the manager of the club. The beginning of the message was muffled, but there was no denying the strain in his tone. I pressed the phone tighter to my ear to hear better.

"Mate, where you at? Dice this is serious, you gotta get down here mate. Cops are everywhere. Fuck, Dice…There's been a murder…I think you know him…"

I'm not sure how long he kept talking after that because all the strength in my arm suddenly left me, and the phone fell from my hand…

Chapter Five

The ride to the club was a bit of a blur. I must've rang Dale about fifteen times, but he didn't pick up. After about the tenth call, it started going straight to voicemail. Which meant either he was ignoring my calls or his inbox was full. Either way, it was just the cherry on top of this fucked up situation. If there was anybody I needed right now it was Dale.

Where the fuck are you?

After listening to the message from Joe, I went into auto-pilot. Suddenly the thought of being alone in my flat was almost too much to bear. I needed to get out and be around people, no matter who they were. I dressed quickly in whatever clothes were lying on my floor and rang a taxi to take me to the club. The late Summer sun was just beginning its quick descent over the horizon, casting a murderous pink glare on the earth below.

How suiting.

I shuddered at the thought. The taxi driver and I sped along in silence. Me, tapping my foot relentlessly, nervous energy pulsing through my veins. I chewed the skin around my thumb nail until it bled, a nervous twitch of mine since I was a kid, and looked out the window at the passing city. The people were a blur as they went about their daily business.

It felt like we were crawling by. As the world outside became merely moving images, like pictures on a film strip, I almost started to doubt how real they were. With my eyes transfixed on an invisible spot on the window I started to feel weightless in my seat, as if I was floating above my body looking down.

Fuck, I wish this was a dream.

"There's a road block up ahead mate," the driver bellowed from the front seat, "I'm gonna have to let you out here."

The roughness of his voice stirred me out of my trance. I blinked twice before I realised where I was. I reached into my jeans pocket and pulled out a tenner.

"Keep it," I said, chucking it over the seat and into his lap. Without another hesitation I opened the door and leapt from my seat without turning back.

I knew what the road block was going to be, even before I spied the yellow police tape and cones blocking off the road. I slowed only for a moment as I took in the scene up ahead.

There must have been three or four police cars, a police van and an ambulance. The ambulance's lights were still lit, flashing their neon glow around in circles, like a silent scream into the early evening sky. My mouth dried completely as the shock of what happened started to seep in. With each step I took my speed picked up until I was practically running over to the tape. As I got closer, an officer spotted me approaching and broke away from the group to meet me at the yellow and black crime scene tape. My breathing was becoming ragged even before I opened my mouth to speak. I didn't know what I was going to say or what would slip from my mouth without warning. All I knew was that I needed to know what happened.

"Woah, woah, stay right where you are," the officer said in a husky voice. He stepped in front of me and put his hands up, as if trying to block my view. I instinctually tried in vain to peer around him, desperate to get a glimpse of what had happened or to spot a familiar face beyond the tape.

"HEY, this is a crime scene. Sir, you're going to have to back up."

His tone was firm and oozing with authority. When I finally ventured a glance in his direction, I was caught off guard by his appearance.

He was taller than me, and much broader in the shoulders. His suit was clean and crisp but unbuttoned with tie slightly loosened, as if he had received the call while off duty and got dressed in a hurry. The hands he held up in front of him were large and smooth, and as my eyes quickly trailed up his seemingly muscular torso, they stilled on his face. His skin was tanned a deep golden brown and had the tiniest inkling of a five o'clock shadow across his jaw line. My eyes danced over his impeccably pronounced cheekbones that looked like they had been chiseled out of marble, before resting on his deep, dark eyes. His hair was a boyish mass of dark loose wavy curls which sat naturally on top of his head, sweeping slightly across his tanned forehead. I stood there in front of him, heart beating out of control and was momentarily stunned into silence.

His brow furrowed further as he took in my silence, possibly unsure as to what to say next. I broke his hypnotic stare by shaking my head slightly and desperately tried to avoid looking back in his direction.

"Sir? You're going to have to step away."

"I…I work here…"

I couldn't think of what else to say. My chest still heaving, I bent over half-way and rested my hands on my thighs.

"I'm sorry, you work here?" His tone sounded genuinely interested.

"Yes, yes, I work here, I need to speak to Joe."

My tone was beginning to give away the sense of impatience I was feeling wasting my time with stupid questions.

"Sir, can I just have your name please?"

The officer turned his head and snapped his fingers in another officer's general direction, beckoning him over to where we were standing. Another man in a police uniform carrying a clipboard joined us, eyeing me suspiciously.

"This gentleman says he works here," the husky voiced officer implied.

"Name, sir?" The second officer asked curtly, riffling through the papers attached to his clip board.

"Uh, Dice..." I stuttered, still not meeting any of their questioning glances.

"Dice?" asked the uniformed officer, his question dripping with sarcasm.

Finally I looked him square in the eye, straightening up, my annoyance shining like a beacon in the sky.

"Yes Officer...*Dice*...Dice Valentine."

Both officers exchanged looks. While the uniformed cop riffled through his papers again, the one in the crisp suit turned back to me, his expression even more stern than before.

"Mister Valentine," he paused, his mouth flattening into a thin line. "There's been a *homicide* here last night. Not much is known at this point beyond the identity of the victim. Police have locked down the area while they carry out their investigation."

His husky voice oozed with authority, and he almost stood a little taller after his police spiel. It was then that he took in my own ragged appearance. I was immediately self-conscious of the cuts and scrapes up and down my arms.

Shit.

He raised a perfectly shaped eyebrow at me, assessing my reaction to his words. But when my eyes didn't react to his news, he furrowed his brow once more as if contemplating what to say next.

"Mr. Valentine, may I ask how you got the cuts on your hands?" he asked.

I opened my mouth to speak but was interrupted by a voice calling out my name in the background.

"Dice!"

It was Joe.

"Dice, oh Jesus, thank God," Joe shouted, immediately coming over to where we were stood. "Where the fuck ya been, I've been ringing non-stop?"

Joe came at me with arms wide open, ready to embrace me right over the police tape. Joe looked a lot like Tony; shaved head, muscular build and olive skin. Usually the epitomy of calm and demure, Joe was obviously shaken by what had happened. Dark circles skirted his gray eyes and a few days' worth of stubble grew along his jaw. He was wearing a simple pair of faded blue jeans and denim jacket. As he hugged me, I could feel him shaking slightly and his sniffling was telling me that he'd been crying.

"Thank Christ you're here…"

I hugged him back, which felt weird. Joe wasn't normally so affectionate, especially with his dancers. We weren't friends by any means; he looked at us as staff, and nothing more. Pound signs with cocks.

"Jesus, Joe…I," I stuttered into his ear. He smelled like stale cigarettes and booze.

He pulled back suddenly to look me in the eye, his hands still grasping both my shoulders.

"Fucking hell, the police found a body…Someone found a body in the alley this morning…" Joe choked out, his voice breaking slightly. "Some fuck…Jesus…The cops got an anonymous call from someone early this morning…Fuck, I can't believe this happened in my club." Joe let go of my shoulders and buried his face in his hands.

Was I the one who phoned the cops?

"Joe…I need to talk to you."

The words just slipped from my mouth before I could stop them. Joe's eyes darted up to meet my own, a look of bewilderment slapped across his face. He opened his mouth to speak, but stopped himself. Before he could try again I grabbed his shoulder and ushered him away from the cops.

"Joe, last night…When I was leaving the club…" I began, pulling him further away from earshot. Joe was dragging his feet, his mind obviously reeling and thinking about what the hell I was going to say.

"Yeah?"

"Jesus...Joe," I whispered, stopping in our tracks, "Well, I don't...Fuck, last night when I was leaving the club..."

"Yeah?" he urged me on, eyes wide and expecting.

"I found him, last night."

I didn't know how else to word this, my voice coming out a whimper as sheer hysteria bubbled inside me.

"You, *WHAT?*" Joe shouted, a little too loudly.

"Shh, Jesus..." I whispered, my eyes slipping back to the pack of cops that waited a few yards away. "When I was locking up, I ran into Tony in the car park."

Suddenly I wasn't sure how to finish my sentence.

"What do you mean, you ran into him? When? What happened? Did you ring the police?" Joe started, his eyes searching my face. I looked behind me again at the officers gathered who were now eyeing us suspiciously.

"I mean, I ran into him...I was locking up and I heard a fucking noise."

"Was it him?"

"I-I don't know. It was dark..."

"Dice, what the fuck do you mean? Come on, man?" Joe urged through gritted teeth.

"Joe, shut the fuck mate, lemme think for a second."

"Dice, this isn't a fuckin' joke mate, what did you see?"

"I saw, I saw Tony. Joe, he was all messed up. I..."

I had to steal away from his gaze. I couldn't concentrate anymore. I looked over my shoulder to spot the Detective moving towards us, a look of intrigue on his face and something large and dark in his hand. As he inched closer to where we stood, the object in his hand came better into view.

No...Shit...It can't be...

"Gentlemen, if it's alright I have a few more questions for you…"

Joe crossed his arms over his chest and immediately broke away from me, both our eyes flitting down to the ruck sack in the officer's hand.

My ruck sack.

I looked straight into the eyes of the Detective, imagining the look of guilt that I must be wearing.

"Mister Valentine, I'm sorry, my name's Detective Smith with the Brighton and Hove Police Department. Were you working here at the club last night?" the Detective asked, getting right to the point.

"Uh, yes. Yes I was working," I answered, my bottom lip quivering slightly. A feeling of dread had completely washed over me, causing me to feel as if I was underwater. My chest felt tight and constricted. I balled my hands into fists at my side to try and stop them from shaking so noticeably.

"Mister Valentine, do you recognise this bag?" he asked, his question clearly rhetorical.

All of a sudden, it was as if I was mute. I opened my mouth to speak, but nothing but air came out.

"Can you confirm for me when you left the club last night?" he asked again, not waiting for me to answer the first question, his expression hardening.

Detective Smith had reached into his back pocket to retrieve his notepad and pen, which he immediately started to scribble onto as he spoke, not meeting my eyes again. When I didn't respond, he stopped and raised an eyebrow in my direction.

"Mister Valentine?" he implored, the tone of his voice losing patience.

"I'm sorry…This is all just…I, uh, I left the club…late…I guess…"

I looked down at my feet, my mind searching through the previous night's events.

When did I leave the club? Everyone had left…What time was it?

"Can you be more specific, Mister Valentine?"

The way he spoke my name made my stomach churn. Suddenly I felt like I was in a bad cop drama on TV. My mind was a total blank as I stood there, feeling like my feet were sinking into the ground and I was about to be swallowed up. My eyes flitted back up to Detective Smith, then to Joe who was staring back at me with the same wide-eyed stare, waiting for answers just like the Detective. His lips slightly parted in anticipation of the answers I might be able to give.

"I, I guess it was after three AM..."

"Were you alone when you left?"

"Yeah...Well, I think I was...I remember hearing a noise."

"A noise?"

"Yeah, a sound inside the club...Am I a...suspect?" I tripped over the word. "I didn't say that, Mister Valentine, but can you explain why your ruck sack was found near the scene of the crime?"

"I, I...well, I..."

My body was shaking so thoroughly that even my voice was coming out ragged. I looked down at my feet, searching through the memory of last night and frantically waiting for the light bulb to go off. All I could think about was how this must seem to Joe and the Detective.

Detective Smith must have taken a hint of my growing panic and quickly decided to take another approach.

"You said you heard a noise?"

"I...I thought it might be Dale..." I stammered.

Detective Smith looked from me to Joe expectantly.

"Dale...?"

"Dale Lavender. He...he's another dancer at the club..." my voice trailed off, praying he wouldn't ask me about him.

"And was it Mister Lavender you heard?"

"I don't think so...I mean, I don't know."

The Detective stopped writing and sighed a little too loudly in my direction. He turned his head to motion for the Officer in uniform to come over.

My heart was beating so loudly in my ear that I was sure the Detective could hear it. I looked to Joe for reassurance, but I was met with a look of uncertainty that only made my heart sink further.

The Detective once again looked into my eyes, his brow furrowed so deeply that a deep groove appeared between his eyes. .

"Mister Valentine, would you mind coming down to the station with us?"

"The station?"

"Yes, if you were in fact the last one to leave the club last night, and this is in fact your gym bag, I'm afraid we've got some more questions for you. Some more serious questions…"

"B-But, I…"

I looked over at Joe, my eyes silently pleading for him to interject. But the look on his face told me that he was as desperate as the Detective to know what I saw. He merely stood there staring, as I quickly dug my own grave right there in the parking lot.

"If you would feel more comfortable having a lawyer present, I would be more than happy to suggest a few names."

Detective Smith extended an arm, leading me to his unmarked police car which would take me to the station, the feeling of dread in the pit of my stomach growing increasingly larger with each passing minute.

Chapter Six

The Detective and I rode to the station in complete silence, but I'm sure he could hear my heart beating, even from the front seat. I couldn't have felt more like a criminal as I rode in the back seat, behind the steel gate partition. The feeling of panic and dread that I was trying so desperately to suppress was like a throbbing tumor in my belly. With each passing block I tried to ignore it. I tried to calm myself by breathing deeply. I tried to convince myself that they were just taking precautions and that this would all be over soon...

But what if it wasn't?

Every car that passed us sowed another seed of doubt in my mind and pushed me closer and closer to the breaking point. My thoughts were on a constant loop replaying what had happened last night. If I could just go over my story again and again in my head then I'd be able to tell it properly and then I'd be able to leave and let them get on with their investigation. After all, I didn't know much. I mean, yes, I was there last night, and yes I did find the body...but I was the one who rang the police.Surely, it was me.

Wasn't it?

That was all, right? I didn't know what the hell had happened after I fell...

What the fuck are they going to think when they find out I was there?

I didn't have time to consider this last thought as we pulled into the station without warning.

"We're here Mister Valentine," he said to me from the front seat, his eyes scanning my face from the rear-view mirror. "I'm sure this won't take long. Just cooperate with us, and I'm sure you'll be outta here in no time."

There was something completely unconvincing in his tone of voice that made me feel even more uneasy.

When we got out of the car, I half expected him to cuff me. Detective Smith came round to my side of the car and opened it gently. As I pulled myself out and stood so we were face to face, the Detective didn't step back to widen the distance between us. In fact, we were practically nose to nose. His sudden closeness caught me off guard and I found myself momentarily caught in the grip of his eyes on me.

Unconsciously I stood still for a moment, staring him down, almost daring him to move first. He kept his eyes firmly fixed on my own before letting them slide up and down my frame quickly.

Fuck, is he gay?

He must have sensed my thoughts for he backed down first, stepping back slightly to let me shut the door behind me. When he returned his gaze to my face I was sure I caught a glimmer of a smile sweep across his lips. My eyes were probably as wide as saucers as I followed him across the parking lot and into the station.

Damn it, he's a fag. Concentrate Dice.

Inside, it was exactly like they portray it on telly. The walls were painted a dull gray colour and the people who crawled around the many desks that littered the large open plan room, reflected the same dreariness as their surroundings. There was a faint smell of cigarette smoke lingering heavily in the air, mixed with cheap after shave and cleaning chemicals. I wrinkled my nose instantly as I breathed in the heady scent. My eyes surveyed the surroundings, taking in the panoramic view. The slight sexual excitement that tickled my stomach muscles in the parking lot was instantly deflated upon stepping into this apparent hell.

Without realising it, I had stopped in the entrance way of the building, like a deer caught in the headlights.

Jesus, I hope I get outta this place.

A passing officer knocked me accidentally and forced me from my trance.

"Shit, sorry!" I apologised despite the fact that he had knocked me. The offender didn't even look my way, but continued on his way with a purposeful stride.

"Mr. Valentine?"

I looked towards the voice, now behind me. Detective Smith once again had his arm extended, the flirtatious grin now replaced with something hard and official. I swallowed hard as I followed him into one of the side rooms.

The interrogation room.

***

I sat there in the cold linoleum chair, my arms resting on the equally frosty linoleum table. Detective Smith sitting opposite me, his eyes boring through me as if searching my face for the answers to his unasked questions. I couldn't help but stare at the mirrored window on the wall to the left, wondering who was behind it. The surrealism of this whole situation made me feel like I was having an out-of-body experience. Standing in the far corner of the room, staring at myself, taking in the horror of the moment.

Just breathe, Dice. You're not responsible for any of this. Just tell them the truth.

My mouth was painstakingly dry, like I had been chewing on sandpaper. I tried swallowing again in an attempt to appear casual, but it was like my throat was slowly closing up. I looked around the room and all of a sudden felt claustrophobic, like the walls were inching their way inward.

The Detective cleared his throat abruptly, making me flinch slightly. My eyes turned themselves to my knotted hands that were tightly pressed together. If I let them move apart, I'm sure their trembling would give away the utter terror I was feeling.

"Mister Valentine, let's get straight to the issue, shall we?"

He was a master at asking rhetorical questions.

"Can you tell me what happened to you once you left the club last night?"

I met his eyes briefly, before returning my gaze to my hands.

Fuck, he's got beautiful eyes.

I shook my head in an attempt to rid it of my lurid thoughts.

Neither the time or the place.

I realised then it was either sink or swim. I drew in a shallow breath and tried to put my stream of consciousness into words.

"Last night...I guess I was the last to leave..."

My brow furrowed as I tried to remember if my words were in fact true or imagined.

"Can you remember what time this was?"

Detective Smith's husky voice stirred something in me just then. His words washed over me in a way they probably shouldn't, considering the situation at hand. It was like everything that came out of his mouth was tinged with some sort of innuendo. I wanted to react to the urge growing inside of me, but had to mentally castrate myself. My eyes however, had less pure intentions and every time they looked up, drank in the sight of the beautiful detective in front of me. His chiseled jaw and cheek bones, broad shoulders and loose dark curls, every detail of his appearance made me harder in my jeans.

"Mister Valentine? What time was this exactly?" Detective Smith repeated, his tone beginning to sound annoyed and frustrated.

"Umm, I...I think it was about, three, maybe."

Detective Smith's mouth was pressed into a hard line and his dark eyes narrowed, obviously slightly unimpressed by the unspecificity of my response.

"Go on," he urged, shifting in his chair.

Mirroring his actions, I shifted uncomfortably in the hard chair. I rubbed at my thighs which were slowly falling asleep.

"I was surprised that there was no one else around…Normally people stayed after hours to have a few drinks, or whatever…But last night, there was nobody."

I still couldn't quite understand how I could have been the last one out last night and not known it.

"You said earlier that when you were leaving, you heard a noise?"

"Yeah…just as I was locking up. I remember feeling like I wasn't alone."

"Did you investigate the sound?"

"I…I called out…But…"

"Yes?"

His probing eyes were making me nervous. I was beginning to stutter. I never stuttered. I unknotted my hands and began chewing at the skin around my thumb.

"There wasn't anyone there. Anyways, I just remember wanting to get outta there as fast as possible. So I closed up, set the alarm, and that was when…" I paused then, trying to piece the story together before making an ass of myself in front of the police.

"That was when, what?"

"That was when, I ran into Tony."

Detective Smith riffled through his note pad at the mention of Tony's name.

"Tony…Is that Tony Matthews?" he asked, once again flashing his dark eyes my way.

"Yeah. He…he was outside."

"Did you speak to him?"

"Well, sort of."

"Sort of?"

I was slowly growing tired of him repeating every last thing I was saying. I glared at him, my eyes shooting proverbial daggers in his direction.

"I mean…he was acting strange…like he was, I dunno, on something I guess…"

"On something? Are you referring to drugs, Mister Valentine?"

"Well, maybe…I dunno, he, there was something definitely off about the way he was acting."

"Can you be more specific, Mister Valentine?" he asked, although his question sounded more like an order. "What did Tony say to you?"

"Well…he didn't actually say anything…That was the point; he just…stared."

I let my eyes stare vacantly ahead of me, focusing on everything and nothing all at once, remembering mine and Tony's exchange the night before. The tension between the detective and I made me shiver slightly as if a draught had just crept into the room.

Detective Smith sighed loudly and uncrossed his legs. Once again, I mirrored his actions unconsciously and shifted in my seat.

"Mister Valentine, we have been unable to track down the whereabouts of Mister Matthews," he paused for dramatic effect, "Do you have any idea of where we might find him?"

I shook my head, unsure of what else to say.

What the hell happened to Tony?

"Do you think that Mister Matthews could be responsible for the murder, Mister Valentine?" He asked, narrowing his eyes at me.

"Tony?" I threw back at him. I shook my head again, half answering his question and half trying to get the thought out of my head. "No, No, Tony was…No, Tony couldn't have done this…"

Could he?

The Detective sighed again, "So, after you ran into Mister Matthews, can you explain what happened next?"

I wasn't quite sure how best to approach the next part of the story. I must have sat there in silence for a few moments, the seconds on the clock ticking by.

Fuck, this is embarrassing.

"Mister Valentine? Can you tell me why you were in that alley way last night?"

"Well, you see…I…" I stammered, shaking from the inside out, "I was going…"

My voice hitched in my throat. A million thoughts racing through my head; if I said too much they'd think I had something to do with the murder, but if I changed my story it might all come out later anyway.

Did the club have cameras outside the building? Was there CCTV in the loading alley? Maybe the police already know something and they're just waiting for me to crack.

"Mister Valentine, if you'd feel more comfortable having a lawyer present…"

His voice trailed off, merely presenting me with options.

"I…I was in the alley…I was going to meet him…"

There was a pause from both of us just then. A heavy silence filled the room, weighing down on our shoulders like a wet blanket. Detective Smith's dark eyes burned into me. A look of shock crossed his face but disappeared almost immediately.

"Him?"

I didn't have to say anything. I just stared back at him, beads of sweat materialising on my forehead. The look in my eye said it all and the Detective sat back in his chair, his mouth opening to form an 'O'. He blinked his eyes a couple of times, as if in an effort to make sense of what I had just said. I could practically see the wheels in his head turning as he broke away from my stare and peered down at his notebook.

He pretended to scribble something down and then quickly recovered his composure and furrowed his brow once more.

"Mister Valentine, are you telling me you were having relations of a sexual nature with the victim?"

I swear I could see his mouth twitch up into a smile at the mention of the word sexual. My stomach muscles tightened hearing his question. I had to blink suddenly to remember where I was.

"I…well," I stuttered, again.

"Mister Valentine, were you or were you not having sex with the victim?" the detective shouted, slamming a fist down on the table's hard surface.

The unexpected sound his fist made as it connected with the harsh table made me jump.

"Yes, ok, fuck!" I shouted back, completely caught off guard.

This was it, enough fucking around. He wasn't letting me off without getting what he needed from me. The detective's eyes were wide and expecting. I took a deep breath and turned my eyes down to the floor.

"I slept with him a few times. He was just some guy from the club."

"Can you explain how you met the victim?"

"He was just some guy…a client…came to see me dance a coupla times…"

"Do you normally have sex with *all* your clientele?"

I shot him a look as his words slapped me across the face. "Hey, fuck you mate!" I shot back, before something inside me pulled away and told me to calm down. The detective put up both hands as his way of retracting his accusation.

"He came to watch me…quite often actually. I remember seeing him in the crowd…right up front…"

Shit, I hope I'm not making a mistake.

"Do you remember when you first noticed him?"

"I dunno…" I considered his question, "a few months back, I guess."

"How did he first approach you?"

"He always looked the same," I went on, half ignoring his question, "same hair, same dark expression on his face…he was different…"

"Different, how?"

"Different, like, he wasn't like the others…shouting and cat-calling. He was…respectful. That's what made him stick out."

The Detective raised an eyebrow at me and smirked. "Forgive me Mister Valentine, but I'm a homicide detective…Your little tale of puppy love isn't really why we're here."

I blinked harshly in reaction to his words, almost unsure that he'd actually spoken that way to me.

"Tell me how he first approached you in the club?" he continued, completely unaware of my being taken aback. I sighed again, long, intentional and slightly uncomfortable.

"Look, I had seen him around the club a few times and well, one night he, he left me a…note."

"A note?"

"Yah, a fuckin' note…you know…" I held my hands out making air quotations for emphasis. *"You're so hot…I want you…Meet me after work… You know…"*

I couldn't look at him anymore. I started to feel very self-conscious, which was bloody rare for me.

It's because he's so fuckin' hot.

I tried to ignore what my head was screaming.

"Let me get this straight…" He said, crossing his legs once more in his chair, "You get a note from a total stranger…in your line of work…and actually voluntarily meet up with them in a dark alley?"

"Jesus, it wasn't like that."

"Please Mister Valentine…enlighten me then!"

It was his turn to throw his hands up. He swiveled in his chair and turned to face whoever or whomever was sitting behind that mirrored glass. I could do nothing but stare at him, open-mouthed and slack jawed. My insides began to churn all of a sudden and my cheeks flushed.

I have never felt more cheap. He's bullying me and hoping that by making me feel like dog shit, he'll get something out of me.

As he swiveled back to face me, a slight smirk dancing across his otherwise beautiful face, I decided then and there to no longer participate in his 'guilt-games'. I could feel my face harden as something inside of me switched, my eyes narrowing on the Detective.

"Right… Detective *Smith*…" I said through gritted teeth practically seething, "I did meet him in the alley…a few times…joked around with the other guys that he was my 'alley cat'…and no, in case you're wondering that wasn't the first time I had fucked a complete stranger."

Betcha I've got your attention now.

"Didn't even know his name. I'd look for him every night I danced. If he was there, he'd usually find a way to get me to notice him…"

The Detective once again adjusted himself in his chair, his hands tugging at his trouser legs.

I'm turning him on.

"I'd meet him out back, we'd fuck like rabbits, and then he'd be off."

I paused, letting the image of me having sex with a stranger against a brick wall worm its way into the Detective's head.

Is he blushing?

"…Erm…" he said, clearing his throat, "Um, c-can you tell me the last time you saw him alive?"

"The night before last he had come to the club, left me a note and we had sex in the alley…"

Images of him pounding my ass as I lay bent over a pile of loading trays, flashed through my mind.

"Last night…after I danced, there was another note on my dressing table…"

"Are you sure it was from him?"

His question caught me off guard. I opened my mouth to answer right away, but stopped to consider. "I…I'm sure."

"Was it signed?"

"Erm…I…"

Fuck, was it signed?

"Mister Valentine?"

"He never signed his notes. Well, not his whole name. He used to sign them 'D'."

The Detective turned to write something in his notepad.

"And you've no idea what *D* stood for?"

"No."

Detective Smith riffled through his notes. "Mister Valentine, the victim's been identified as a Mister David Adams, born July 14th 1978."

He paused and looked up at me with his deathly dark eyes, taking in my reaction to this news.

I flinched at the mention of his full name. Part of me was shocked that he actually had an identity. Not knowing him had always made me feel more protected, almost like it was a dream and not really happening. I shivered despite the rising temperature in the room.

"Mister Valentine, tell me what happened after you found the body."

The tone in the room shifted and the tension from before returned, thicker this time, like a fog. My head was beginning to feel cloudy once more. I squeezed my eyes shut for a moment trying to return to last night and remember more of what had happened. Everything was so unclear. All I wanted was to go home and pretend all this hadn't happened.

"When I got…" I could feel my chest begin to tighten and the familiar sting of tears prick behind my eyes. All I could see were bloody pictures of him, lying on the ground, motionless, staring up vacantly at the night sky.

This is all my fault. If it weren't for me, he'd still be alive. What the fuck happened last night? Who could do this?

"Mister Valentine," his voice was harsh again, "What happened once you discovered the body?"

"When I got to the loading dock…in the alley…he was…"

I put a hand to my mouth, suddenly afraid I was about to be ill all over the table.

"He was…just lying there…"

Please don't make me go on.

"Mister Valentine, did you see anything suspicious when you found the body?"

"I…like what?" I asked, wiping my nose across the back of my hand.

"Anything out of the ordinary? A weapon, signs of a scuffle?"

"I-I don't think so…I mean, I don't know."

"Mister Valentine, if the victim was in fact *lying* there as you claim, did you check if he was breathing?"

"…If he was breathing? I-I guess I didn't think to…"

I furrowed my brow, suddenly unable to remember why I hadn't.

Maybe he was still alive…

"So you found the body lying there in the back alley of the club *you* work in, and it doesn't occur to you to check if he might actually still be alive?"

The Detective's tone made his question seem more like an accusation.

"No…No he was dead. He was lying there, covered in blood. He was dead goddammit," I pleaded, my voice beginning to crack.

"Are you a Doctor, Mister Valentine?" he asked mockingly.

I could do nothing but stare at him in disbelief. With every word that came out of his mouth I was beginning to feel more and more like a criminal.

"I…uh…" I could barely get the words out, my shoulders hunched as my throat filled with bile.

"Then why don't you leave declaring death up to the professionals next time. So after you allegedly found the body in the alley, what did you do next Mister Valentine?"

My breathing was ragged. If I looked up to meet his piercing stare I was sure I would crumble under its weight. Every question he asked caused me to near hysteria just that little bit more. I felt broken. Guilty. Confused. Unsure of what was real anymore. His interrogating was making my head spin, almost as if I was beginning to believe what he was saying and doubt my own thoughts and memories. The tears were flowing now, a slow and steady stream down my cheeks causing them to burn beneath their heat.

"WHAT did you do next, Mister Valentine?" came his question again.

"I, I think I called the police..."

Detective Smith almost let out a snort of laughter.

"You *think*?"

"I know..."

"You know?" he threw back.

I didn't respond. My eyes searched the floor as if the answers were written below my feet. The detective was sitting forward now, his elbows resting on his thighs, his eyes burning into me now.

"You know what I think, Mister Valentine?" he asked, not expecting me to respond. "I think you were involved in this somehow..."

His statement hit me like a ton of bricks. My head shot up like I had been smacked across the face.

No.

I opened my mouth to protest, but there was nothing in me to fire back.

"I think you were involved, but you freaked and ran...which is why we found your gym bag at the scene of the crime. There was blood found not far from the scene as well, and call it a whim but I'd be willing to bet my mother's life that blood belongs to you." He straightened up in his chair, very matter-of-factly. "The cuts on your hands and head...I also think that if we checked your phone records, there wouldn't in fact be any call to the police last night...as you claim there was..."

"N-No...No you're wrong."

Is he?

"Am I, Mister Valentine?" he asked, cocking his head to one side. "Or are you not so sure anymore, either?"

Detective Smith stood up from his chair, the sound of the chair scraping across the floor made me jump.

"If I had it my way, we'd book you right now, but lucky for you the evidence I have isn't enough to keep you at the moment."

An incredible rush of relief flowed through me, and I'm sure he could sense me visibly relax slightly. The detective moved towards the door and knocked on it in an S.O.S type pattern. As the door opened from the other side, Detective Smith turned to look at me once more before leaving.

"But..." he said, his dark eyes flashing in my direction, a look of satisfaction across his face, "...don't think about leaving town, Mister Valentine..."

Is that a warning or a threat?

"We'll be in touch. I've got your number."

And with that he was gone.

Chapter Seven

The taxi ride home was somewhat of a blur. After leaving the police station, I felt like I was watching everything happen from someone else's point of view. My limbs moved of their own accord and I was simply their host. My head felt heavy, weighed down with too many dark thoughts. I was exhausted, spent, despite only being awake a few hours. My whole body ached, mainly from shaking and trembling for so long. It was like my core was set to vibrate and despite battery power running low, it was going to be a long night.

Sitting in the back of the cab, the driver didn't dare attempt petty conversation, the look on my face telling him that I was far from in the mood for small talk. The outside world passed by, once again reminding me of passing images in a film. A horror film, where I was apparently the main star. People out the window carrying on their business, completely unaware of my situation.

I was battling with my head to try and remain somewhat calm. I felt that if I allowed my thoughts to wonder and realise the severity of my predicament that I would crumble under the pressure.

They think I did it. *They think I killed him.*

I castrated myself mentally for allowing my head to go there. I lifted my hand to my forehead and rubbed hard at my eyes. The sensation felt good, momentarily taking me away from all this pain, and soothing my nerves. But it didn't last long. The fear quickly returned, seeping through my veins and reaching all the way from my finger tips to my toes.

How the hell am I going to get through this?

There must be something I'm missing. Some detail that I can remember that will help prove I'm innocent.

*Why can't I remember what happened after I fell? Why did I run? Of course they think I did it. I fucking ran away from a dead body. The body of the man who I was on my way to meet. They have my gym bag and blood on the scene. I can't believe this is happening. Where the **fuck** is Tony?*

I fished into my pocket and pulled out my mobile. Unlocking it I frantically checked for any new calls.

Nothing.

I decided to ring Dale, again, for probably the hundredth time in the past hour. Putting the phone to my ear, it took seconds before the call went straight to voicemail. Dale's beautiful voice met my ear and swam around inside my head.

"Hey it's Dale, sorry I missed ya, leave one…"

I hung up before the beep.

Fuck, where the hell are you?

The silence inside the taxi was interrupted suddenly by the sound of my stomach grumbling.

Have I eaten at all today?

I felt ill. When I considered it, I couldn't tell if I was in fact hungry or not. Gut rot was making it hard to think, and the bumps in the road were making me nauseous. I closed my eyes and let the sensation pass, breathing in sharply between clenched teeth and squeezing the arm rest of the taxi for support until my knuckles turned white.

"What was the number on King's Road, mate?" came the taxi driver's voice from the front seat.

The sudden interruption in the silence made me jump. I looked up to meet his eyes staring back at me from the rear view mirror.

"Uhhh, sorry?"

"Your house number?"

"Oh, sorry…Yeah it's number, uh 145," I answered slightly caught off guard.

I surveyed the outside through the taxi window, the surroundings becoming increasingly familiar. I suddenly felt very anxious. Almost like I didn't want to be at home just then. The thought of being alone in my flat was almost too much to bear all of a sudden.

I didn't have time to give into my growing anxiety as the car pulled up outside my building a few moments early causing me to snap back into reality. I paid the driver quickly and opened the door without looking behind me. Suddenly my ears were pierced with the sound of someone leaning on their car horn a few metres away. I whipped my head around just in time to see a gray sedan swerve to avoid me. The momentum of the passing car forced me back up against the taxi and my back connected hard with the cold metal practically knocking the air out of my lungs. I closed my eyes and clasped my hands over my heart to try and calm my racing pulse.

"You alright mate?" the Driver yelled, craning his neck to see me.

Jesus Dice, careful or its curtains for you.

I didn't respond, instead dashed around the back of the car and straight through the front door of my building, not even looking back to see if I'd left anything behind. I was at once filled with an overwhelming sense of agoraphobia, and needed to be off the street and locked up safely inside my house. As I climbed the stairs two at a time, tears were already spilling out my eyes and stinging my cheeks as they rolled down towards the floor.

Get home, get inside, everything will be alright.

I passed someone in the stairwell, but didn't stop long enough to even register their face. My chest was tight and I felt as if my heart was going to implode.

This was all too much.

When I finally reached my front door, my bandaged hands fumbled in my pockets for my keys. As the key struggled with the many locks, the sound of my heart beating like a drum reverberated so loudly in my ears that I was sure my ear drums were going to burst.

"Dammit," I mumbled under my breath, the words coming out were practically a sob. When the key finally turned and the heavy dead bolt slid out of place, I fell into the flat and slammed the door behind me. Instant relief flooded my body and I let myself fall back against the door, closing my eyes and sliding down to the floor, my feet giving out beneath me. As my bottom made contact with my cold hardwood floor, my head fell into my hands and the tears flowed more freely. I didn't try to stop them or wipe them away this time. There was no point. I didn't try to move. I just let the dark shadows of my empty flat swallow me up.

Chapter Eight

The familiar sound of seagulls woke me from a beautiful dream.

Time had turned back to a few nights ago and I was dancing again with Dale at the club. We were just finishing our tease, but this time as the curtains drew around us, we didn't pull away. Our eyes were locked on each other's. His green eyes exploring my blue. Our lips were parted and his hands were gently gripping my hips. The heat from his body radiating against my own was creating the most intense feeling of sensuality between us. I could almost taste the pheromones in the air. His hot breath smelled of cinnamon and his skin of mint. We were holding each other so tight that his erect nipples were grazing my smooth chest. Down south, I could feel his dick poking through the confines of his jock, hot and trembling, desperately seeking to be freed and tended to.

Kiss me.

I let my hands trace their way down his muscular back, worshipping the many grooves before stopping at the gentle curve of his lower back that bordered his ass cheeks. They paused there for a moment as his breathing hitched and his lips parted further, his tongue coming to the tip of his lips. I wanted to feel it in my mouth, lapping against my own, our saliva mixing up inside our mouths. Dale mimicked my touch and let his own hands leave my hips and reach around to the small of my back. I half nodded, giving him permission and urging him to do what I was hoping he would do. As if reading my thoughts his right hand carried on moving down and gripped itself across my ass, pulling my pelvis closer to his. The connection of our cocks against one another forced my head back. I closed my eyes and swam around in the sensation, my cock was so hard; its engorged head dying to be sucked. My left hand made its way under the elastic band of his jock strap and caressed his naked cheeks.

Dale let out a moan against my mouth as I dug my fingers into the tender skin of his behind. I tilted my head up again and looked into his eyes. They had darkened and his expression had turned serious, His brow was set in a firm line.

Kiss me.

Our faces were hovering mere inches from each other, both of us waiting and willing the other to make the move and finally kiss. The anticipation was electric, and I was afraid that if he didn't kiss me then and there that I would surely die. Once again as if reading my thoughts he leaned his head in the few inches, both of us now closing our eyes, until our lips connected…

That's when I opened my eyes and woke up.

I wasn't at the club. I was alone. In my flat. It took me a moment to come back down to earth. The anti-climax of the feeling that my dream had left me with slowly dissipated and in its place seeped in the all-to familiar feeling of fear and uncertainty. Dale was gone, or at least not answering my calls. We hadn't kissed. My alley cat was dead, and the police think I killed him.

In the space of 48 hours my life had become a complete and utter living nightmare. And the only thing I could think was how much I wanted to wake up from it.

Chapter Nine

There was a knock on my door. Four quick, sharp knocks in succession that woke me again from a deep sleep. My eyes fluttered open and immediately shot around the room, suddenly unaware of where they were. A bright sliver of sunlight was chasing away the shadows that crept around my bedroom.

How long have I been asleep?

I stilled once again and listened for another knock to confirm that I hadn't been dreaming. A few moments passed before, as if on cue, the knocking came again. Three more strong knocks that filled the silence of the flat and made my heart jump into my throat.

Who the hell could that be?

I peeled back the duvet and taking in my appearance realised that I was still dressed in yesterday's clothes. I swung my legs over the bed and stood up. My bare feet against the cool wooden floor boards sent a shiver up my body. I smoothed my white t-shirt over my chest and grabbed a dark oversized hoody which I pulled on for warmth.

Tip-toeing out of the bedroom and towards the front door, I strained my ears to listen for some clue as to who was at the door.

"Mister Valentine?" came a muffled voice from the other side of the door.

I stopped in my tracks as I realised it was the Detective.

Holy shit. Is he here to arrest me?

My head was still swimming with a lucid, dreamy feeling and every bone in my body felt like it had to crack. It was moments before my heart leapt into action and resumed its frantic irregular beating. My palms immediately felt sweaty, and I wasn't sure whether to answer it or to run.

"Mister Valentine, it's Detective Smith. Can you open the door please?"

I was trying to judge his tone of voice, but it was near impossible. Between the rising sense of panic that was gripping at my throat and the thumping of my heart in my ears, it was all I could do to stop myself from passing out. I grabbed at the wall for support and sucked a deep breath in through gritted teeth.

The persistent detective knocked again. Being closer to the door this time, the sound caused me to jump and nearly call out.

Just answer it.

I sucked in a deep breath and with a trembling hand pulled back the dead bolt and opened the door. As the door opened up, letting in the dim light from the hallway, I drank in the Detective's appearance.

He was even more beautiful than I remembered. He was casually resting one elbow at chest height against the doorframe; the other hand was tucked comfortably into his trouser pocket. My eyes were immediately drawn to his dark tousled hair, which looked even more raven coloured in the shadows than before. His strong jaw was still speckled with the same dusting of five o'clock shadow and his slightly wrinkled suit suggested he hadn't gotten much sleep. His navy shirt was unbuttoned a little bit too much to be considered professional, and as my eyes trailed south I could see the definition of his smooth, tanned pec muscles through the material.

I could tell he was taken off guard by the door opening and as his eyes met mine he quickly straightened his stance and cleared his throat.

I stared straight into his dark eyes which were like black pools of granite in the light. His skin was practically glowing and radiant looking despite the appearance of his suit. After staring each other down a moment too long, my eyes trailed down to the ruck sack at his feet.

My bag.

He saw where I was looking and spoke suddenly, disturbing the quiet.

"Uh, Mister Valentine," he stuttered, perhaps slightly unsure as to how to begin his conversation. "I, uh, didn't think you were in."

His tone was less official sounding as before and if I didn't know any better, I'd almost classify him as nervous.

As my eyes travelled up his frame they stilled on his large, tanned hands that were now knotted in front of him.

He is nervous.

My subconscious mind jumped into action and immediately took advantage of the situation. I straightened up as I stood in the door way and my expression darkened; from full of fear, to cocky and dominant in the flash of a second.

This is what I do, after all.

I didn't respond to his words. Instead just stood there and let the silence between us get wider. I put a hand on my hip and let a smile flicker across my lips. He just stared at me, perhaps half in awe and half unsure. The dominance between us had shifted and it was me who had more power in this instance.

My turf.

Detective Smith cleared his throat again and looked pained for a moment. "I, I'm sorry to intrude Mister Valentine," he stuttered, clearing his throat again, "I wanted to deliver your ruck sack."

"In person?" I said, tilting my head to one side coquettishly.

"Um…Well…"

"I thought you might send a courier," I shot back without giving him time to answer properly.

His eyes narrowed as he tried to decipher my tone.

Intrigued, are we?

"Does this mean I'm no longer a suspect, Detective Smith?" I cooed.

"Ahem, actually Mister Valentine, I wouldn't go that far."

Again there was a shift in the air, as if he was suddenly remembering the reason he had come here.

"At the moment Mister Valentine-"

"Dice."

"I'm sorry?" He asked, somewhat confused by my interruption.

"Please...Call me Dice."

A smile played with the corner of his mouth and he shyly looked away momentarily.

"Mister Valentine," he continued, "the lab is currently running tests on the DNA that was found at the scene and on the body, and if the results come up as a match for your own-"

"I'm sorry?" I interrupted again. "Did you say *on the body*?"

"Yes...Mister Valentine, there was blood found both a few yards from the scene of the crime as well as under the fingernails of the victim. The Coroner's lab is running both samples as we speak, and well I'm thinking they'll both belong to the same person."

Under his nails?

"But, Detective...That's impossible..."

Now it was my turn to look down and away from his piercing dark eyes.

"Impossible, Mister Valentine?"

He shifted his weight to the other foot and replaced his arm on the door frame, straightening up so that he once again towered over me.

"I, I thought yesterday you said that there was blood on the ground."

"Yes, and upon further analysis the victim turned out to have dried blood caked under most of his finger nails."

I swallowed hard.

"Care to venture a guess as to who's it might be, Mister Valentine?"

There was that twitch of a smile again. The tone of his voice was tantalising, mocking even. I narrowed my eyes at him this time, glaring with all my might and my blood beginning to flare inside my veins.

Play it cool, mate.

"Sounds like you already have a good idea Detective, why don't you enlighten me?" I shot back, taking half a step closer to where he stood, defensively.

He didn't take the bait. Instead he remained rooted to the spot, his expression playful.

"Are you antagonising me, Mister Valentine?" With this he met me half way and took a small step towards me.

There we were, man to man, inches from each other. So close, I could smell his aftershave. It was intoxicating, like a heady mix of cinnamon and musk. I was trying desperately to keep my eyes fixed on his, but they were aching to explore his face up close; the soft skin around his collar, his stubble that so artfully graced his beautiful, strong face. I let my lips part, the moment between us playing with my insides, clenching the muscles in my stomach and those between my legs. His gaze was strong, paralytic almost, squeezing me in its grip. I could feel the heat resonating off his body and see the rise and fall of his chest as he breathed in the same air as I. I could feel myself begin to tremble slightly.

Fuck, he's sexy.

I think I half-expected him to do something, make a move. My eyes dropped to his mouth of their own accord. I could do nothing to stop them, they were suddenly filled with the urge to kiss him. They took in the sight of his plump red lips; glossy, slightly parted and waiting.

Cock sucking lips.

But the moment fizzled as quickly as it had begun as he let out a soft grunt and stepped away from our showdown, the trance broken.

"Nice to see you again, Mister Valentine," he said casually.

And with that he turned on his back heel and walked slowly down the hall, hands in pockets, and a smug smirk plastered across his face.

Chapter Ten

After he left, my head was spinning. I shut the door behind him and leaned against it, facing my empty flat. The throbbing behind my eyes was back again, and I had to close them to try to drown out the incessant ringing that I was hearing in my head.

Blood on the body? But, how?

The Detective's words already seemed like something from a nightmare.

Was it my blood on the body? How could it be? Who else's could it be? Holy fuck, how did this happen?

I rubbed my temples frantically, in an attempt to clear my head and focus on the other night.

I saw the body. Did I touch it? No, no I didn't get anywhere near it. You screamed and ran, mate. I did…Didn't I? Think Dice, THINK.

I opened my eyes for a second and it suddenly felt like the walls of my flat were slowly closing in on me. I couldn't breathe. I couldn't think. My skin was crawling and I had the creepiest feeling, like I had just walked through a spider's web. My hands brushed at my bare arms and it was everything I could do not to scream out in frustration. I felt sick. Nauseous. Empty and completely hollow. It was then that I realised that I was about to really freak out and do something rash.

I've got to get out of here.

I wasn't thinking rationally anymore. This whole situation was insane, and I just needed to be out of my house and with other people; otherwise, I was afraid I might just stop breathing and drop dead right then and there.

I stepped into a pair of flip-flops, grabbed at my keys that lay on the end table by the door and launched myself out of the flat and down the hallway of my building. My subconscious was propelling me forward. I wasn't even aware of what direction my feet were taking me. I was just happy to be on the move.

Go see Joe. He'll know what to do.

***

I don't know how long it took me to get to Joe's place. Even as I stood outside his door, I wasn't sure how I actually got there. My mind was on auto-pilot, and the feeling of being outside my own body and watching this whole nightmare happen to someone else, had returned. How safe I felt; watching this hellish situation unravel on someone else's shoulders. Like a horror film, I was loving being sat safely in the audience, knowing that it wasn't real and that when the credits rolled I could return to my little haven and be grateful for my easy, mess-free, life.

But it didn't take long before the harsh truth came crashing down upon me like an angry wave on a stormy sea. This was happening to *me*. It was me who was starring in this freakish film, and they think I did it. And if I didn't do something about it, then I was gonna fry.

This last thought jarred me and I shook my head violently in an attempt to dismiss the thought.

Get a grip, Dice.

With that I lifted my heavy limbs and knocked feverishly on Joe's front door. Joe lived on the other side of town a few blocks up from the seafront. I had been to his place a few times since working at the club. Mainly on happy occassions; usually afterhours, with a bunch of the other guys and usually involving lots and lots of drugs. I felt a sudden warmth wash through me at the memory of being care-free.

I didn't give him time to answer, knocking quickly again this time with the palm of my hand. My heart rate quickened with each passing second that I stood there, inching me closer and closer to the breaking point. Small beads of sweat began to materialise on my forehead and the feeling of warmth that had filled me moments ago had now cooled, and I began to shiver there on the spot as I waited for Joe to pull himself away from whatever the fuck he was doing and answer his door.

"*Joe!*" I called out in desperation, moving towards the window adjacent to the door and putting my hand to the glass, peered in. "*Joe, where are you?*"

Returning to the door, I knocked again frantically. On the third knock the door swung open and a 'pissed off Joe' stood in front of me, completely naked except for a white terry-cloth towel wrapped around his waist to cover his modesty.

"*Dice?* What the fuck, mate?" he called, obviously furious at having been disturbed.

Without my permission, my eyes trailed themselves down Joe's glistening chest. I could feel my mouth drop open slightly, despite myself, as I marveled at his sculpted arms.

Jesus.

I always knew Joe was broad and built; he always wore tight t-shirts that left very little to the imagination, but seeing him practically in the buff, still wet from the shower, drops of water reflecting the light off his rounded pecks, made my dick stir inside my trousers.

Fuck, I haven't gotten off in days.

I couldn't help but admire his bronzed smooth skin and treasure trail of dark hairs that were running away from his abs.

"Dice?" he called.

I suddenly felt like a pervy frat guy who'd just been caught staring at a chick's boobs. I flinched at the sound of my own name and peeled my eyes away from his nipples.

"Joe…Thank Christ," I pushed past him and let myself into his flat.

"Uh, come on in?" he said sarcastically.

Once inside the flat, I paused, letting my eyes adjust to the sudden shadows.

I had forgotten how nice this place was.

Joe had impeccable taste and the money to support it. His flat could be described as nothing but chic minimalism at its best. Everything was black except for the walls, which were painted a pearly shade of white. I always felt like a lost little child inside Joe's place; with his posh leather furniture and polished surfaces, I was afraid to touch anything for fear of breaking something. As my eyes adjusted to the abnormal darkness they surveyed the paintings on the walls. Joe was an enormous Lichtenstein fan and had spent thousands upon thousands of pounds in search of originals and now they were proudly displayed on the walls of his house. Some say Joe had more money than brains. I just always thought he went for what he wanted. The sound of his voice behind me made me turn around to once again drink in the sight of him standing half-naked before me.

"I take it, this isn't a social visit," he said matter of factly standing proudly in front of me and making absolutely no attempt to cover himself up.

Damn, he was fit.

Once again I found myself avoiding eye contact and instead focusing on those little 'v' muscles below his abs. He really was statuesque. I should have known; Joe practically lived in the gym. He prided himself on looking good, most club owners did, I suppose. But Joe's physique was different; just the right combination of muscle and definition. Not too muscular, but beautiful strong biceps and a tiny, narrowed waist. His taut skin rippled over the grooves of his six-pack. Suddenly, I felt my mind imagine my body pressed up against his.

How had I never really noticed, before?

"Dice!" he shouted, louder this time as if he knew what I was thinking. "What the fuck, mate? Are you alright?"

I realised that I had probably been standing in his lounge for a bit too long without saying something. I shook my head abruptly to clear it out.

"Sorry, mate…Fuck, I'm sorry to barge in on you like this."

Joe sighed heavily and looked away before moving into his kitchen area. His place was open plan and he carried on speaking as he moved over to the refrigerator and opened it.

"S'ok mate, I shoulda rang you after you left the club Saturday morning. I've been a bit of a wreck, to be honest," he said with his back turned to me. He was fiddling around in his enormous inset fridge.

"Tell me about it," I mumbled under my breath.

"Beer?" he offered, extending a green bottle in my direction.

"Cheers, Joe."

He cracked the bottle open and passed it to me. The bottle was cool to the touch and made me shiver despite the balmy temperature in the flat. I took a long swig from the bottle and relished the feeling of the frosty liquid as it stung the inside of my throat and filled me with warmth.

"Mate, what the fuck happened?"

"Joe, I-I'm freaking out …I don't know what to do."

I took my bottle and swivelled on my heel to practically launch myself onto Joe's sofa. I sat down, feeling deflated and defeated. I let out a heavy sigh as the leather of the sofa settled around me. "Joe, I think I'm in trouble…"

Joe continued to stare at me from the kitchen for a few moments before moving over to where I was sitting.

"Dice, you gotta tell me what happened the other night? What did you see? Why did they question you?"

He settled in next to me on the sofa, bringing with him a whiff of peppery aftershave. He tucked one of his legs underneath himself and turned so he was facing me, his left arm resting on the back of the sofa, the other weighing down on the taut white bath towel so as not to expose himself to me. I couldn't help but steal a glance of his slightly exposed inner thigh. My mind immediately wondered what his cock looked like.

I turned my head to see him looking directly into my eyes, a look of sincere worry blazoned across his beautiful features. He put out his hand and let it rest on my thigh, rubbing it affectionately.

"Shh," he cooed in a friendly and reassuring voice, "Just talk to me. It's going to be alright, Dice."

I looked down at his strong hand that lay on my right thigh, the feeling was electric. I knotted my hands in my lap, cracking my knuckles to distract myself from my stiffening dick in my pants.

"They think I did it, Joe."

I let my voice trail off, I couldn't think of what else to say. A thousand thoughts were swimming around inside my head; I felt afraid, worried, panic-ridden and horny all at the same time. I just needed to be close to someone, if I was with someone then I would be safe.

Safe from what?

"Dice, that's insane. Why? How could they think you had something to do with the murder?"

The tone of Joe's voice led me to believe that he actually believed what he was saying.

Thank Christ he's on my side.

I was suddenly filled with more emotion than I knew what to do with. The familiar prick of tears behind my eyes took over and I unknotted my hands to lay my head in them. And with that I began to sob. I couldn't hold them back any longer, I didn't want to hold them back anymore. Before I knew it, my shoulders were heaving as I let the tears stream down my face. This was unreal. A fuck buddy of mine was murdered and the police think I did it. Everything had happened so fast and I felt so out of my body.

"Dice, you need to calm down mate, this is going to be fine...You...You're innocent...right?"

Was that doubt in his voice?

My head shot up and met his dark eyes. "Of course I am...But it's..."

"It's what?"

"It's complicated..."

"Complicated how, Dice?"

I wasn't sure how to answer. How could I tell him what had happened without sounding like I had done it?

"I...I was the one. It was me who found the body."

I looked into his eyes and tried to figure out what he was thinking. Joe just stared back at me, his brow furrowed.

"You found the body?"

I nodded at him, my throat suddenly feeling swollen and closed up.

"Why didn't you fucking tell me, Dice?" He asked angrily, a deep crease appearing between his brows.

"Joe, it's not like that. You, you see."

"What? What Dice?"

"The guy...I was supposed to meet the guy last night...He was...We were..."

I felt so cheap. I couldn't even finish my sentence.

"You were seeing the guy who was killed?"

"Well...sort of..."

He leaned back in his chair and looked away, bringing a hand up to his own brow this time and rubbing it in a contemplative manner.

"Jesus..."

"Exactly...Joe, I'm sorry to do this to you."

He sighed heavily again, resting his elbows on his knees, head in hand.

"S'ok...So...Who...Who do you think..."

"I don't fuckin' no Joe…I…When I left the club that night…I heard someone inside…"

He quickly looked up at me again. "Someone inside?"

"Well, I think…I heard a noise."

"Did you tell that to the police? Who do you think it was?"

"I don't know, mate. I never actually saw them. I was shitting myself and bolted outta there as fast as I could. When I got outside…I…I ran into Tony."

"Wait…You don't think, Tony…"

"No, NO," I answered quickly, "Well, I don't think so…"

"What did he say to you?"

"Well that's the fucking weird thing…He…There was something up with him."

I was focusing on a spot on the floor, trying hard to remember exactly what happened. I was so afraid that if I didn't continue going over the whole shitshow in my head that I'd forget what really happened.

"What do you mean?"

"When I ran into him…He-he didn't say…Anything."

Joe just looked at me with a puzzled expression.

"I kept speaking to him, but he just…stared…"

"Stared?"

"Yeah…Like he was really outta it, or something."

"How did it end, then? What did he do?"

"He literally just…walked away."

"And you didn't think to follow him?"

"I-I was supposed to be meeting…him."

I swallowed hard, a violent shiver making me flinch.

"That's when I…"

I involuntarily let out a loud sob and bit the knuckles on my right hand to stop myself from losing it completely.

"It's ok, Dice…" Joe said, moving in closer to me and wrapping an arm around my shoulders and pulling me closer to him. I could do nothing but collapse into him, my cheek finding rest against Joe's bare shoulder. The peppery aftershave scent was stronger now, and his skin was still wet and fresh from his shower. I felt comforted from his closeness and the tears stopped falling as I took consolation in my friend. Suddenly I didn't feel so alone anymore, and the burden of this whole mess felt slightly less daunting. I held my breath so as to enjoy the feeling momentarily, wishing it to never fade away. For the first time in days I felt a pang of relief. A tiny glimpse of light amidst the shadowy events of the past few days.

"Shhhh, just try and relax Dice. Try and be calm. I'm here," he cooed over my head, rocking me slightly, "I'm here…It's going to be alright."

The soft rocking was soothing, and the sound of his voice mixed with the scent of his aftershave was intoxicating, filling me up and taking away the heaviness that I was feeling inside. I felt brighter with his arms around me, safe, cocooned despite the darkness I was fending off.

"It's alright."

Without being conscious of what I was doing, I lifted my head slightly to look into Joe's eyes. His arm withdrew slightly to allow me to come up to face him. He was looking down at me with a look of sincere concern, his eyes telling a story of condolence and worry for my greater good. With his free hand he gently wiped a lone tear that had escaped from my eye. The feeling of his thumb brushing across my flushed cheek, stirred something deep inside me. I could feel my insides respond to his touch and the muscles in my stomach clenched sweetly. I continued looking into his beautiful deep eyes and watched his expression change from one of worry to something hungrier and darker. His lips parted slightly and he pushed his tongue to the tip of his mouth. I began to tremble slightly, unsure as to where this was going or what was about to happen next. His left arm was still cradling me close and I could feel his skin begin to grow warmer as his heart rate picked up and his cheeks flushed slightly. I could hear his breathing begin to quicken to match the pace of my own that had also grown quick and shallow. None of us spoke a word. The tension between us was heavy and thick. I stole my eyes away from his own and took in the sight of his plump red lips that were parted and hungry.

All of a sudden I wanted nothing more than to kiss him. All rational thought had left me and I wasn't thinking any longer. I was nothing but instinct and feeling as my body took control of my head and overruled the thought that I shouldn't do what I was about to do. His lips looked so delicious, and I was overcome with the feeling that if I didn't kiss him at that moment that I might actually explode.

He looked like he was about to say something, but stopped and ran his tongue over his lips, moistening them so they glistened in the dim light of the flat. My hand reached up to his cheek and cradled the side of his face as I tilted my head further and gently placed my lips on his . The moment our mouths connected I felt alive once more. My limbs sprang to life as fresh heated blood coursed through my veins, electrifying my insides and causing my skin to sing out in reaction. I held my lips there for a moment, getting used to the sensation of being once again connected to someone else. I pulled away slightly at the same time he did. Joe opened his mouth, further this time.

"Dice, I…"

Before he could say another word, our eyes connected once more for a brief moment, mine on fire and his a smoldering pool of dark chocolate, before I closed mine and kissed him again, harder this time and brimming with intense, fiery heat. At first I could feel his hesitation, but after a moment of having my tongue probing against his, he seemed to give in to the feeling. Within seconds Joe was kissing me furiously, his tongue battling against my own, invading my mouth until all I could taste was his own breath. He reached both hands around and took hold of my head, steadying himself and forcing his tongue further inside me. I opened my eyes for a second to see that his were closed tightly, completely lost in ecstasy. His grip on my face was firm as his fingers knotted themselves in my hair. I kissed him back; hungry, desperate, brimming with white hot lust. I was craving this; yearning to be touched, my body invaded. I needed to be lost inside someone else, and in my own fantasy world.

Sex had always been an escape for me, a pleasure cruise out of my own head where my body ruled and instinct took over.

This is gonna be good.

As if on cue, my hands awoke from their slumber and went into overdrive; exploring Joe's neck, his broad shoulders, massaging and caressing their way down his biceps, squeezing his triceps and rubbing like mad. I pulled back from his kiss to judge his expression, seeking permission to carry on. When his eyes opened, they were like molten lava; alive and fiery and full of desire. He was breathing heavily now, completely taken by this all. His hands shot out and grabbed at the bottom of my t shirt, lifting it abruptly upwards. I lifted my arms and let him pull it off, exposing my smooth chest to his hungry eyes. He let them trail up and down my torso, devouring every detail visually before opening his mouth and pushing me backwards so I was half lying down on the sofa. He lowered himself down onto my pecks, licking and kissing and nibbling on and around my left nipple, taking it in his teeth and biting gently until I cried out from both pleasure and pain. My reaction only furred him on as his strong wide hands massaged my other nipple, all the while continuing his fevered licking. The sensation was unreal, a mixture of gentle sloppy lapping and frenzied bites. I arched my hips so that my pulsating crotch pressed up against his stomach. With every movement of his tongue my cock grew increasingly stiffer until it was battling against the rough material of my jeans. My hips began to rock of their own accord, dry humping his naked chest as he continued his endless worship of my round, smooth pecks.

"*Fffffuck*, Dice," he groaned through kisses, "You have no idea how long I've wanted to do this."

His filthy tone only turned me on more. I took his head in my hands and gently helped him move down further. His lips left my nipples and I could feel him trail his hot wet tongue down the center of my abs all the way to the waistline of my jeans before moving up again, pausing to worship the deep grooves of my six-pack and trace their outline. I arched my back further; a sign for him to continue his slow torturous descent on me. My skin felt rejuvenated and awakened, his tongue leaving behind a hot trail of saliva.

After a moment I felt his tongue withdraw. I pulled myself up onto my elbows and peered down to catch Joe looking back up at me, a cheeky devilish grin plastered across his face. He licked his lips and flashed me a set of pearly white teeth as he went to work on the bulge in my jeans. His towel that had so delicately covered his lower half had now come free and fallen to the floor, giving me a glimpse of his beautifully round, pert ass.

Like two scoops of butter pecan ice cream.

In seconds Joe had unbuckled my belt and worked my top button open. He paused again, the anticipation forcing my head to fall back and my eyes close.

I wanted him to suck me so badly I could have cried. When I looked up again he was admiring the size of my hard-on through my underwear.

"Jesus you're fucking sexy."

He pulled my jeans down slowly, revealing more and more of my hot pink Aussiebum briefs with every tug. When they were down to my knees he tugged harder, pulling my legs free in a quick movement. He tossed the jeans aside and returned to admire the sight that lay on his sofa before him. I was completely at his mercy as I lay there, dying to be sucked dry, cock trembling and wet with pre-cum.

"Is this what you want, baby?" he asked, his voice sultry and raspy.

"Oh fuck, Joe…"

It was all I could say. If I spoke I was afraid I might cum right then and there. He slipped both thumbs into the waist band of my briefs and pulled them down slowly. The strain on my dick was almost too much to bear. I groaned at the sensation of my cock bending back before being released and bouncing gently back up against my stomach. Joe didn't waste any time, sensing my excitement. He took my shaft in his right hand and stroked me adoringly, up and down, working the foreskin back and forth, finding a rhythm that seemed to work for me. I spied his left hand descend on his own cock. I strained my neck to get a look at his size, and let out a deep moan when I saw how hung he was. Joe was entirely smooth down below to match the smoothness of his muscular chest. He was completely bare, which only served to make his smooth shaft appear even longer. His grip on his own dick matched the speed he was working me with, and he closed his eyes as he got used to the feeling of having a cock in each of his hands.

Suck me.

As if reading my thoughts, Joe opened his eyes again and licking his lips, opened his mouth wide and took the head of my dick in his mouth. The sensation was luscious. My cock went from feeling exposed to suddenly being devoured by his lips. His mouth went to work on me, his plump red lips shielded his teeth and he worked my shaft up and down, sucking hard and taking as much of me into his mouth as he could. The feeling of his lips enveloping my cock and his tongue caressing the underside of my long, smooth shaft almost made me lose consciousness. My breathing was quick and shallow, my heart furiously pumping blood to my dick keeping it throbbing and rock hard. My hands shot up to my chest and I let them work away at my nipples gently; tweaking them between my thumb and forefinger, sending added waves of pleasure rippling through my core. His hot mouth carried on bobbing up and down on my cock; with each slow lift and descent of his head I could feel his throat relax further, allowing my length to dip deeper inside him. I looked down at his arm and observed him jerk himself off, taking note of how he liked to be gripped and how shallow his movements were.

I couldn't wait to get my hands all over him.

I moved my hands slowly away from my nipples and let them trail over my abs, leaving the skin tingling and alive. My fingertips found Joe's head and gently began massaging his shaved scalp before taking control and forcing his head to move up and down at a faster pace. The quickened bobbing mixed with his intense suction made my hips want to join in on the action. I began thrusting my pelvis and fucking his face, feeling his mouth go up and down, up and down on my shaft. I could feel him swallowing every now and then, drinking my juices and increasing the intensity of my pleasure, his lips working me over like a hoover.

Baby, stop or I'm gonna blow it right here.

I lifted my head once more and pulled myself up onto my elbows, inspecting the situation. The sight of Joe; muscular, all brawn and bulk, sucking me off was almost too much for me to handle.

Fuck, I wish I coulda filmed this.

My cock was telling me he had had enough of this; he wanted to get this man on all fours.

I reached down and taking his head in my hands, eased Joe off of my cock. He looked up at me, somewhat puzzled he searched my face for an explanation. With his mouth wide, and lips glistening with my pre-cum, he looked fucking sexier than I had ever seen him look. A cheeky grin from me reassured him that I was far from finished. I sat back on my elbows, inviting him to climb up on top. He quickly obliged and climbed up my frame like a hungry tiger, a look of lust having quickly replaced his confusion. When his head was level with mine, he leaned in slowly for a kiss.

Not so fast.

Before he could connect, I turned my cheek and wrapping my right leg around his, flipped him over onto his back and rolled on top of him, straddling him between my legs. I sat back a bit so that his cock was standing at attention just in front of mine. I used my legs to pin his together, making it difficult for him to squirm, and took ahold of his girth in my right hand. My left hand found my own dick and began a slow, torturous pumping action, both fists working in unison. Joe's head immediately tilted back against the sofa while his hands rubbed at my thighs that were holding him hostage. The feeling of his meat in my grip was lush. He wasn't so much thick as he was long; my closed fist barely covering half of his length. Joe let out a deep moan from between clenched teeth, giving me the impression he liked what I was doing.

Not wanting him to get too comfortable, I abruptly stopped my masturbation forcing his eyes to shoot open, a pleading look in his eyes.

Don't worry, mate. The best is yet to come.

A devilish look flashed in my eye as I released his right leg and wedged my left leg between both of his so that my knee was inches from his balls. I took his right leg and used it as leverage to flip him over once more so that he was face down on the black sofa. The rest of his body could do nothing but oblige and before he could protest he had a mouth full of leather. I took his hips in both my hands and pulled him into a kneeling position, his ass in the air and perfectly level with my crotch. I stayed like that motionless for a few moments, getting him used to the idea of how it would feel if I fucked him like this. As a silent response, Joe leaned down so his elbows rested on the sofa seat, the angle forcing his perky round ass further up into the air.

Fuck yes.

The sight of his asshole perfectly on display for me to play with at my will made my cock grow even harder. Without hesitation I spread his cheeks and bending down spat as much saliva as I could onto his smooth exposed hole. The action made him jump slightly, but he didn't pull away. Instead he pushed his hips back even further and I willingly met the action with my tongue. I thrust my tongue out as far as I could and tickled his asshole with its tip. Joe flinched at first, but relaxed quickly and began thrusting his ass further and further into my face, meeting my elongated tongue. He moaned again, longer this time, the sensation of being tossed off obviously sending him closer and closer to orgasm. I couldn't resist pleasuring myself at the same time, and reached one hand down to take hold of my own cock and began pumping furiously. My tongue caught up with my arm and quickened its technique, licking all around his taught hole, up and down between his ass cheeks, lathering up the area and getting it primed for what was to come.

"*Uuuuhhh*," he moaned, completely lost in the moment. My tongue fucked his ass, and switched from short pumps to long licks, starting at the crack of his ass and continuing all the way down to his balls. Once at his balls I paused for a moment and took one in my mouth and sucked gently, licking gently and bobbing it up and down on my tongue.

"Fuck, Dice...Oh Jesus..."

I moaned back, mirroring how turned on he was. My fist jerked my cock off faster and faster until I knew that if I didn't wrap a condom on it soon I'd cum right there.

It took everything in me to stop tonguing him then. I wanted nothing more than to make him cum with my mouth. But I knew there was something else more rewarding in store for us both.

I didn't waste a second getting up behind him again, his hips resting at a level so the tip of my dick was lined up perfectly with his asshole. Joe turned his head around to look at me.

"In the jar...On the coffee table."

It took me a second to realise what he meant. I leaned over to the table and opened up the lid of a black onyx jar, which was obviously not just for ornamentation. Inside were a dozen or so brightly coloured condoms. I grabbed the first one I saw and using my teeth, tore the package open and spit out the remnants. Releasing his hips only for a second, I rolled the condom over my erect cock until it sheathed my entire length to the bottom of my shaft. As I lined it up with Joe's perfectly primed hole, it twitched in anticipation.

I took Joe's hips in my hands and gently eased him closer to me so that the tip of my penis was just grazing his entry. I could feel his warmth on the end of my dick. I could feel him clench the muscles in his sphincter and then unclench them in an effort to further relax his hole. I closed my eyes for a moment and enjoyed the excitement that was running through my veins, knowing full-well what was to come.

I want this so badly.

Joe craned his neck once again and peered over his left shoulder at me. He gave me a brief imperceptible nod, as if to signal he was ready. His brow was already furrowed; he was already imagining what it was going to feel like to ride my long schlong.

"You ready for this?" I breathed.

"Yeah," he signaled back to me.

Applying a bit more pressure on his hips I lifted my pelvis while pulling him further back onto me. My cock fought against his tight asshole for a moment, aching to penetrate him and be inside. I closed my eyes again and opened my mouth wide as all the nerve endings in the head of my cock screamed out in ecstasy; the pressure being applied was so intense, I had to bite down on my tongue to stop from crying out. I lifted my hips even further and at once his ass gave in and I could feel my cock begin to slide up into his anus, slowly disappearing further and further up inside him. Colours danced inside my eyelids as I took in the feeling of being inside another man. I hadn't been on top of a guy in ages, and it was taking all my strength not to start ploughing away at Joe right now.

After I was about half way in, I eased off and paused for a moment, letting Joe's muscles inside begin to relax and adjust to my girth. I opened my eyes to look at him and saw his hands clawing at the sofa beneath, his eyes squeezed tightly shut and his teeth gritted.

"You okay?"

He nodded in response and let out a deep, slow moan as I pulled my hips back until I had almost completely withdrawn, leaving just the tip of my cock still buried inside him.

"*Ffffuck*," I moaned letting my head relax again as the skin on his ass acted as a suction cup around my cock, jerking me off as I pulled slowly out. I was shaking now, itching to fuck him hard, desperate to pump away at his ass until I came all over it. I wanted to forget about everything. Bury myself deep inside a man and just fuck away my troubles the best way I knew how. My hips must have agreed because the moment I was practically out they sprung to life and thrust themselves sharply, forcing my cock deep up inside of Joe so far that I felt my balls slap against his ass.

"Aaaah," he cried out, half from shock and half from pleasure, "Yeah, mate, come on…"

The sound of his deep, husky voice asking me to carry on was enough to send me over the edge. I hesitated for a moment when I opened up my eyes, when I saw Joe, my boss, naked and on all fours on his sofa, begging me to fuck him.

Should I be doing this?

I quickly dismissed the thought. No turning back now, I'm afraid. After all, I was already inside him. I smiled cheekily, despite myself before returning to the moment.

"You want me to fuck you?" I teased, a smirk appearing across my lips when I realised the power I had right now. I was lost inside him. He was completely at my whim. Vulnerable. Naked. My very essence invading him.

Just like I had been the other night in the alley...

No. Don't think like that. Then I began to thrust before quickly pulling myself completely out. Joe relaxed as I withdrew and moaned at the feeling of my cock exiting his ass.

"More?" I teased further.

"Yeah, do it, Dice. Fuck me!"

The dirty feeling returned to my core, and my instincts took over. I was filled with a sense of primal urgency as I gave Joe what he wanted. Having no mercy, I began pounding away at his ass, thrusting once, twice, and then again and again. Each time pulling out further than the last so the entire inside of his anus was being stimulated. His ass stretched further and further as my thick cock forced it to constrict. We were into a rhythm now; he was even beginning to bounce on my dick and meet it half way as I thrust inside of him. With each thrust and slap of my ball sack against his ass, our moans and groans began to twist and intertwine in the air around us.

This is so hot.

Our voices grew louder and steadily more intense as each rock and pound brought us closer and closer to release. I could feel my blood heat up inside me and my face got more and more flush as I could feel my body approaching orgasm.

I fucked him, more and more, deeper and deeper, each time trying to bury more of myself inside him, desperate for closeness and release. There was nothing quite like the suction and tightness of being inside another man, and Joe's beautiful and perky ass was no exception. I peered down at his smooth, tanned, muscular back, the muscles moving and reacting inside his skin as they took the brunt of my thrusts.

Joe steadied himself on his knees and left arm, while his right reached around to his own cock and began furiously jerking himself off. He was close and so was I. His breathing was short and coming through gritted teeth in short bursts. I admired his flexed biceps in his right arm as he worked his foreskin up and down.

"JESUS, Dice, I'm gonna cum…"

"Yeah, Joe, come for me baby…" I urged him on, my lips curled into a type of sex snarl around my teeth. I closed my eyes once more and let my cock do the talking, pumping away again and again, harder and harder until I could feel the cum inside ready to explode.

"Come inside me."

His words were what did it to me. As soon as he murmured that sentence I exploded inside him, my juices filling the condom and my body shuddering with every pump of cum. I pumped and pumped, thrusting again and again, emptying every last drop of cum into him. My neck and body instantly began to relax, the stress and tension dissolving as I bathed in the after effects of orgasm.

Joe wasn't far behind me and as soon as he sensed my release, let himself go, a loud sexy moan signaling he had come. He jerked and shuddered as he carried on pumping slowly at his cock, again and again, completely lost in the moment and relishing the sweet release of his orgasm. His eyes were closed and his mouth was wide and jaw relaxed. He held his cock in his hand adoringly, the sticky cloudy mess oozing out from his closed fist and dripping onto the leather below.

I stayed inside him, thrusting my hips one last time, the movement causing Joe to flinch suddenly as if torn from his dream-like state. He moaned sharply, his ass being reawakened. I pulled out slowly and felt his muscles tighten around my girth one last time as they released me. I pulled off the condom and let it flop to the floor. It landed with a wet sounding smack.

We were spent. Exhausted. Satisfied. Momentarily distracted from what we were both going through. At that exact moment I felt safe, hidden away almost. Invincible, even. Certainly not the murder suspect that the rest of the world believed me to be.

Not wanting my head to go down that path, I fell back against the sofa, let my eyes softly close, and gently drifted away from where I was.

Chapter Eleven

When I awoke the house was filled with darkness. The only sound was a gentle humming coming from the refrigerator. The open blinds let in sporadic slivers of light from passing cars on the street that danced across the walls and then disappeared as quickly as they had arrived. My sleepy eyes surveyed the room around me. Nothing seemed to stir.

I felt disoriented and a little out of sorts, as if I had been sleeping for days instead of hours.

You're at Joe's.

The stickiness I felt in my underwear when I shifted on the sofa was a stiff reminder of last night's…*today's*…events.

I looked around the room once more, now with a better understanding of where I was, but I was alone. No Joe to be seen. I craned my neck to see into the open bedroom door at the far end of the hall, but from what I could tell the bed remained untouched.

I stood slowly, every muscle in my body feeling achy and in desperate need of a stretch. My knees cracked as they took the brunt of my weight. I looked down to inspect my situation. I was still naked, apart from my dirty underwear. Shadows splayed themselves across my smooth, nearly naked frame. I looked around the floor to find my clothes that had been carelessly discarded.

I dressed quickly and tiptoed around the room looking for signs of life. But there weren't any. As far as I could tell I was completely alone.

Where the hell was Joe?

I made my way across the room and down the long hall that led to his bedroom. With each step I took, flashes of our encounter played in my head. His muscular body, the feeling of his mouth around my cock, how it felt to be inside him. I shook my head slightly and stopped in my tracks.

I was all at once filled with a heavy sense of dread. My thoughts shifted from the pleasures of having had sex with Joe and turned to the events of late.

Why isn't Joe here? If he left, then why didn't he wake me? Or why didn't I hear him go?

I shuddered as if a breeze had just swept through the room. The hairs on the back of my neck stood on end and the air in the house turned suddenly. I no longer felt safe here. I felt eerily confined and alone.

What if something had happened to Joe? Just like what happened to...

I gritted my teeth and balled my hands into fists at my sides. I had a choice; I could turn and run the hell out of this place, or I could look into Joe's bedroom and make sure he wasn't in there somewhere.

What if someone else is in there?

"Fuck," I whispered to myself.

Get a grip, Dice. When did I get so paranoid?

I strained my eyes to see into the bedroom without taking another step. Everything appeared sullen inside. I don't know why I felt so on edge at that moment, but it was as if I could feel a set of eyes on me somewhere, watching me and waiting for me to make a move. From where I was standing, rooted to the spot, I could make out the bottom of the dark duvet that covered the bed. A TV was mounted on the far wall and a tall wardrobe stood against another.

This is stupid. Just fuckin' look.

I took another step closer to the open door, tip toeing ever so carefully as if I was walking through a lion's den trying desperately not to wake one. I was inches away from the door frame. All I had to do was reach around and feel for the light switch on the wall. I squeezed my eyes shut tight and with a trembling hand, reached around the door and felt blindly for the switch. I fumbled for what felt like ages as the feeling that I was being watched, washed over me. I wanted to scream as I stood there vulnerable on the spot, my paranoid mind getting the better of me.

My fingers finally made contact with the switch and flicked it up quickly. The sudden flood of bright light made me jump and squint as my eyes surveyed the now well-lit inside of the room.

I bit down on my bottom lip as I prepared myself for something to jump out at me like in the movies…but nothing did.

I drew in a deep breath as Joe's empty bedroom stared back at me. My shoulders unclenched themselves and I exhaled slowly, feeling relief cascade from my head to my toes.

Jesus Christ, mate. What is happening to you?

Joe's bedroom was decorated in the same monochrome décor as the rest of the house. It was minimal to say the least; the only furniture being his enormous steel four-poster bed, mounted television and lone wardrobe.

The bed lay completely untouched; duvet unruffled and pillows carefully stacked at the top. No clothing lay on the floor, even the wardrobe doors were firmly shut. The room appeared utterly undisturbed.

I sighed as the initial comfort of finding the bedroom empty slowly faded away. If the room was empty and unoccupied, then the mystery of where the hell Joe had gone only intensified.

The electric feeling in the air returned, setting the little hairs on end all over my body. I needed to get out of there.

I turned quickly on my heel and flicked the switch off at the same time. As I turned to face the front door at the end of the hall, my eyes quickly caught sight of a dark figure standing on the other side of the front door, his hands raised to his face as if trying to see better through the glass.

I let out a yelp and held up a hand to my breast bone at the sight. I must have caught the person off guard because as the sound of my yell filled the emptiness of the flat, the figure turned and bolted away from the house. I felt like I had been suddenly shot through the chest as blistering fear took hold of me and I had to fight to stay conscious as my heart fluttered in reaction to seeing this dark person outside.

"*Jesus fuckin' Christ,*" I muttered, my voice filled with crackling hysteria.

I stood rooted to the spot for a moment, unsure as to whether or not I should run after the person outside or hide under the bed.

Who the fuck was that? How long were they standing there? Were they watching me?

My feet took over and without me being totally sure of their intention, took off in the direction of the front door to the house. When I reached the end of the hall, I peered outside and let my eyes search blindly for the figure.

Nothing.

I pressed my head against the glass door and cupped my hands around my face to get a clearer look.

Whoever it was had left.. Either they didn't expect anyone to be in the flat, or simply got spooked when I screamed, and ran. Either way, I was outta there.

I took one last look around the house, picked up my phone and quickly threw on my green Adidas trainers.

Getoutgetoutgetoutgetout.

With a quivering hand I reached to unbolt the lock before realising that it was already unlocked. I froze for a second and considered it.

The door's unlocked…meaning that either Joe left in a hurry or someone else was inside who didn't have keys. Maybe someone was still inside…

The thought sent my skin crawling away with itself. I looked back again into the dark flat, my eyes squinting to see anything moving amongst the shadows.

"Fuck this," I muttered to no one in particular. I turned the knob and swung the heavy glass door open and slammed it shut behind me.

And with that, I was off. Where to, of that, I was unsure. I just needed to get the hell away from there.

The night was young and fresh. My eyes looked towards the seafront and saw a slight glimmer of passing daylight still alive on the horizon. I crossed my arms over my chest to protect my bare skin from the chill in the air. I turned my head to look behind me, sheer paranoia running through my veins. People walked nonchalantly all around me, heads down and thoughts occupied with their own situations. A dog barked from inside a flat across the road making me jump slightly. I hugged myself tighter as I reached the end of the road across from the sea front. Without thinking I turned right, heading in the direction of the police station. Whether it was a conscious thought or not, it was where my guts told me to head. I stole another quick glance behind me just before turning off the road and nearly lost my footing as I caught sight of something out of the corner of my eye. .

I stopped and turned around completely. My arms dropped to their sides as I made out someone, something, a few yards behind me. I struggled and squinted to make out more details than their outline in the darkening night sky, but it was useless. They too, stopped in their spot when I stopped in mine.

It's him. He's following me…

The realisation that this dark figure was in fact after me and not simply a figure of my imagination, made me suddenly feel completely exposed and vulnerable as I stood on the side walk. My eyes were locked on the dark stranger before me, waiting for him to make a move. I decided it was a 'him', as I stood studying his outline from afar. His shoulders were too wide and stalky to belong to a woman. He wore what looked like a heavy dark overcoat, despite the late August weather, and a simple black hat on his head, making it difficult to note any more distinguishing features. His face was bathed in shadows, but the more I stared at the shadow where his face would be, I swore I could see a glimmer in his dark eyes, almost as if they were glowing back at me.

Fuck this, shit.

I decided to fake this fucker out and moved slightly to the left as if I was about to bolt from where I stood. The man in the shadows mimicked my own movement and took a quick step to his right as if he was prepared to chase me if I ran.

His sudden quick movement made my heart hammer inside my chest. *Jesus.*

"Hey," I called out into the night air, my voice echoing around the surrounding buildings. "*WHO THE FUCK'S THERE?*"

I was met with silence as my words came back to me, reverberating into the vastness of the early evening.

"I'm not fucking around, mate. Who are you?"

Feeling slightly more brave than I should have, I took a step towards the stranger, who in turn took a step back from me.

"Hey, mate I'm talking to you…"

I took another step in his direction, my hands uncrossing from across my chest and balling into fists at my sides. All of a sudden I was filled with a sense of utter fury at being toyed with like this.

I wasn't the type of person to sit back and let themselves get harassed like this. I have never played the victim in my life, and I wasn't about to let this dipshit be the first one to make me cower and run.

Anger surged through me as I made the conscious decision to take this situation in my own hands and with a deep breath, took another step in his direction. Whoever it was, took his hands out of his coat pockets and straightened up slightly, as if he was trying to make himself seem as tall and intimidating as possible. This time I mirrored his actions and prepared myself to run after him if he bolted.

I opened my mouth to speak but stopped as I watched the figure reach into his coat pocket once more and pull something out slowly. My heart went into overdrive as I considered the possibilities.

What if he's got a gun, Dice?

Bracing myself, I dug my finger nails into the palms of my hands so hard I was sure I would draw blood. Whatever he pulled out of his pocket suddenly lit up in his hand casting an eerie bright glow on his torso. I strained my eyes to make out his face which was illuminated for a brief second.

It's a phone.

My brow furrowed as I considered this.

Why's he got-

Before I could finish my thought I felt something vibrate in the back pocket of my jeans and the familiar muffled sound of my ringtone found my ears. I jumped again at the sound and instinctually tore my eyes away the figure before me and yanked the mobile out of my back pocket and frantically turned it over in my hands to inspect the number on the screen.

I don't know how long I looked at the name and number flashing across my iPhone, but I'm sure I stopped breathing then and there and began a slow tumble into confusion. I suddenly felt like I was falling, slow and steady as my head became filled with a light airy feeling that swirled around and almost made me lose my balance.

No. It couldn't be.

Tony...

I felt paralysed from the neck down. My phone began to appear like a foreign object I'd never seen before. Nothing made sense anymore.

Tony...But...How? Tony was...

My mind was screaming *answer it*, but my gut was telling me to throw it down and run. At that moment I lifted my head back up to look at the dark shadowed man in front of me...But he was gone.

He's g- …Where did he…

Despite the persistent ringing from the apparent 'beyond' coming from my hand, my eyes searched the surrounding area for any signs of the man who stood in front of me a mere moment ago, but found nothing. A car driving slowly down the road towards the lights made me squint as his headlights flashed a bit too brightly. A couple on the other side of the road chattered and giggled at something unbeknownst to me and faded as they rounded the corner disappearing into the night. I brought a hand up to my head and ran it through my hair, trying desperately to make sense of what was happening.

A thousand questions raced through my brain, each one more confusing than the last. I searched the blackness around me, completely unaware as to how he had completely disappeared into the night so quickly.

He was just right fucking here…Where did he…

When I finally looked back at the mobile phone in my hand, the screen had returned to its previous black and had become silent once more.

"Fuck," I muttered at having missed the call completely. Nearing a state of panic I unlocked the screen and checked for a voicemail, but there was nothing. I found the missed call from Tony's mobile and immediately pressed 'return call'. Pressing the phone to my ear I listened intently, plugging my other ear with my other hand to block out the oncoming traffic around me.

Within moments the phone went straight to voicemail without ringing. I heard Tony's rough voice recording on the other end telling me to leave a message.

I tore the phone away from my ear and stared at it in complete disbelief. I scoffed in utter confusion as tears began to prick behind my eyes, blurring my vision and making the outline of my phone fuzz before me.

Was that Tony just then? Standing in front of me? If not, then how the hell did whoever it was get ahold of Tony's phone? Fuck, this is insane.

My other hand shot up to my head to meet the other and squeezed my skull, the pressure keeping me from passing out on the spot. My teeth were grinding so badly they were emitting a horrid crunching sound and I could feel a layer of sweat begin to laminate the skin on my back. I looked around frantically, searching for something, anything that might help shed some light on what the hell was going on.

And just like that, there suddenly seemed like nothing else to do but run.

Run…Run…But run to **where?**

I swung around again and took off around the corner in a sprint. Each time my foot connected with the pavement, a shockwave went up my leg from my heel to my knee.

Jesus, my cuts.

But I ignored the pain, the most important thing was that I kept up my speed. The needed to get as far away from that spot as possible. The sea wind whipping against my face provided a sobering effect. I ran past various people scattered along my route, each chatting and laughing, completely unaware of my situation.

How lucky and carefree they all seemed. How I yearned to feel carefree again. My heart was thudding loudly inside my chest and I could feel my pulse reverberating in my ear drum, pounding away like a marching band in my head.

I welcomed the sound. It was a pleasant distraction from the dark thoughts that had taken control of my brain. My legs picked up speed and my sprint became a full-fledged run as my feet sped away down the road. The lights on the buildings and the pier ahead of me were like beacons in the night sky.

It took me a few moments to realise that my feet were heading me in the direction of my flat.

Chapter Twelve

My mobile was ringing.

Am I dreaming?

I felt heavy. Weary. Exhausted, like I'd been up all night partying. My eyelids felt like they had sandbags attached to them, weighing them down and making it incredibly difficult to open.

Where am I?

My mobile was still ringing. Vibrating and singing incessantly from somewhere across the room.

Answer it.

I willed my eyes to open, but they resisted. I was happy where I was. I felt comfortable and safe. My body felt cozy, all wrapped up in a warm blanket of assuredness. My limbs felt unattached from my body. I tried focusing my mind in on my arms, my legs, my feet, but I couldn't register them.

This is nice…

I was floating in between reality and a translucent state where my problems were nonexistent, and it felt wonderful. In my head I searched for strength; reached out for a hint of reality in this blurry dream world where I lay, but came up with nothing. It took too much effort to think. Stress only made me feel heavier and brought an achy feeling to my head and core.

Give in.

Behind my eyelids I saw a white light that was growing larger and brighter by the second. It was so bright, yet appeared soft and welcoming at the same time. I felt so peaceful as the light grew steadily more intense and gradually took over my senses, stilling them to the point of numbness. As it grew bigger and bigger, the calmness I felt before began to melt away and was instantly replaced with the familiar feeling of sheer panic that had claimed my insides as of late.

It was so big now that I could see nothing else from behind my closed eyes. Slowly I became aware of my arms again, the feeling returning to my fingers and biceps, the screaming in my muscles bringing me out of my dreamy sleep. My legs were waking up too, the blood returning to their veins and pumping furiously again. I could feel my brow furrowing as the white light was too bright now it was hurting my eyes. Squeezing them tighter and tighter, my heart begged them to open.

Wake up. Wake up.

I willed myself awake, the feeling of panic in my chest growing to the point of boiling over.

And with that my lids shot open, and I bolted upright to a sitting position, my body awakening a little too quickly as if hit by an electrical shock.

My eyes took a moment to refocus on their surroundings. Colours blurred and edges blended together, shapes swimming in front of me before settling and becoming clearer.

I was sitting up in bed.

My bed?

Yes, I was in my flat. Naked. In my bed. I looked down at my body, half inspecting to see myself missing a limb or something. But aside from the cuts on my bare legs, everything seemed normal.

How did I get-

My thoughts stopped in their tracks as if they couldn't bear to finish themselves. I didn't think I could take any more questions that I couldn't answer. If I let myself consider my situation, even for a second, I was afraid my brain would implode.

My mobile's still ringing. Who the fuck is that?

I sat up further in bed and ran both my hands through my disheveled hair. I turned my head to inspect my reflection in the mirror opposite. I cringed when I saw the shadow of the man I once was staring back at me. Squinting to get a closer look I saw that the dark circles under my eyes had reappeared, skirting my cloudy blue eyes and casting menacing shadows over my high cheek bones. My long blonde hair was so tangled it resembled matted dreadlocks on top of my head. I looked thin and withdrawn.

When did you last eat, mate?

All at once the ringing from my mobile stopped and deathly silence filled the air. It was so quiet my ears popped as if the pressure in the flat had suddenly dropped. I swallowed hard, my throat feeling dry and rough like sandpaper.

I held my breath for a moment, the silence casting an eerie glow to the room around me. I waited for the sound to reappear. But nothing. I heaved a heavy sigh, my body filled with tension and anxiety.

Carefully, I swung my legs over the bed and dared to put weight on my feet. The floor was cold on my bare skin and I flinched as I made contact with the stripped wood. I steadied myself with my right hand and stood up tall for the first time in what felt like days.

Staring at my mobile, I inched myself closer to where it lay on the dresser across the room, my eyes never leaving it for fear it would disappear.

I huffed at the thought, but I wasn't taking any bets anymore. Not the way the last few days had gone. If the past few days had taught me anything, it was that all bets were fucking off.

The mobile phone was still. Silent and unnerving. I stopped moving when I was about a foot away from it and with a shaking hand reached over to pick it up. When my hand was inches away from it, the screen suddenly lit and the phone came to life, screaming and vibrating its alerting tone so loudly I jumped back from it as if it had just caught fire.

I let out a yelp, frightened at the unexpected sound and quickly grabbed it up and inspected the caller ID.

"Fuck this shit," I mumbled as I took in the unknown Brighton number.

Do I even want to know who it is?

I considered the repercussions for a second before sliding my finger across the screen, instantly thwarting the ringing. I waited for a moment before putting the phone to my ear and listening. There was silence on the other end for a second, before a man's voice broke through.

"Mister Valentine?"

I recognised the cocky tone immediately. Oozing with authority as my name slid off his tongue. I swallowed hard in an attempt to steady myself and regain some of my long lost composure. I breathed deeply before speaking into the mouth piece.

"Um," I stuttered before clearing my throat and trying again, "yes...Detective?"

"Mister Valentine...Did I wake you?"

I paused, not knowing how to answer his question.

What time *was* it?

I wasn't sure it was or wasn't an appropriate time to be waking up. I turned around to face the drawn blinds, checking for a sign of daylight.

"Umm, sort of..." I stammered, giving up completely, "Detective...What can I do for you?"

I decided on a direct approach. We were well beyond formalities at this point, and any sort of delay would only further my insecurities at this stage.

"Mister Valentine I'm actually calling from outside your flat," he said matter-of-factly, pausing to allow me to react. My silent response was probably exactly what he was hoping for, and I swore I heard him snicker on the other end of the line.

"I'm afraid we're going to have to ask you to come with us, Mister Valentine; the DNA results have come back from our lab on the blood found on the body and we have some more questions for you."

My heart began its irregular thumping and the flat seemed to heat up around me.

"You're…here? Now?"

I was stalling. Trying to get my head to catch up with what was happening.

Fuck, fuck, fuck. What am I going to do?

"Yes, Mister Valentine, can you buzz us up please?" He asked, more of a command than a question.

"Uh, y-yes…H-hang on a second Detective…"

I turned and pressed the button to release the downstairs door. I heard a loud buzz come through my phone and shuffling of feet as the Detective and whoever else was with him, came into the building.

"We're in Mister Valentine, thank you. We'll be right up."

That's what I'm afraid of, I thought.

I ended the call abruptly and dashed into the bedroom in search of something to put on. They'd be upstairs and at my front door within seconds.

Shit, I can't believe this is happening.

I stood motionless in the center of my bedroom, panic rising in my throat and my feet planted to the floor.

The DNA tests are back. They're here to take me back to the station. The tests must show it was my blood on the body. But how? Fuck, why can't I remember what happened.

I looked around the room for anything incriminating that might explain what happened last night or cast doubt on my innocence. Everything appeared in order. Well, as 'in order' as things could be considering. I stole another glance into the mirror and ran a hand through my unruly blonde locks in an attempt to smooth them to my head. I tucked the long hair behind my ears and licked my fingers and smoothed it further, detangling some of the knots I had somehow given myself.

There was a knock at my door. Loud and forceful, four times in sequence to announce their arrival, as if I could have forgotten about them already.

"Fuck," I muttered under my breath, searching for my underwear which were nowhere to be seen. In the end I grabbed a bath towel that was slung over the bedroom door, and wrapping it around my waist secured it tightly. I smoothed the terry-cloth material over my cock and willed myself not to get a boner in my state of undress.

Might as well give him a show as he's here.

I hurried to the front door and taking a deep breath to try and calm my expression, pulled back the dead bolt and swung the door open. As the outside air hit my naked chest and face I blinked as I took in the sight of the beautiful Detective Smith and his apparent partner, who was equally as stunning. Both men appeared slightly taken aback with my appearance, and I saw Detective Smith's mouth drop open ever so slightly. He recovered quickly and straightened up his stance.

"Ahem, Mister Valentine," he said clearing his throat at the same time.

I let a slight cheeky smile dance across my lips at having made him feel uncomfortable and let my eyes wander to the other man at my door. Detective Smith's partner looked less than impressed with me already. He wore a stern look on his face and his composure didn't have the same likeability factor as Mr. Smith. He didn't appear uncomfortable in the slightest, rather impeccably annoyed and rather put out by the whole ordeal. He didn't flinch or look me over as I opened the door, but instead let out a soft sigh.

Of annoyance?

He stood just as tall as Detective Smith, but not as muscularly built. His hair was cropped quite close to his head, military style, which only added to his attractiveness. His skin was mysteriously as tanned as his partner's and his suit was the epitome of put together cool.

Fuck, do these two tan and shop together? Bloody hell.

Detective Smith cleared his throat for a second time and shifted his weight nervously from one foot to the next.

"Mister Valentine, this is my partner Detective King," he looked to his partner who didn't extend his hand for me to shake, "Mister Valentine, I'm afraid we're going to have to ask you to come with us," he said repeating his words from before.

I turned my gaze from Detective King to Detective Smith and flashed him my best-award-winning-shit-eating grin. Through batted eyelashes I said, "Why, whatever for, officers?"

Detective King sighed again, louder this time, announcing his disdain in case I didn't catch wind of it before.

"Mister Valentine," Detective King started, "you need to get dressed immediately and accompany us to the station, if you refuse to cooperate we will be forced to read you your rights and use force."

Definitely not gay.

"Mister Valentine we have to inform you that you have the right to have an attorney present during questioning-"

"An attorney?" I asked surprised.

"Uh, yes…If you cannot afford an attorney then one will be provided for you," continued Detective King.

"Do I need one?" I asked again, completely ignoring his partner and focusing solely on Detective Smith.

Detective Smith stared back at me, eyes searching and trying desperately to read my thoughts. A flicker of a smile flashed across my face before quickly fading away.

"Only if you have something to hide, Mister Valentine."

Without tearing my eyes away from Mister Smith, I stepped back from the front door to allow both men to enter my flat, the flirty look in my eyes slowly disappearing and being replaced with one much colder.

"Loud and clear, officers. Please, come in. I won't be a moment."

I didn't wait for the men to move into the room, instead left them standing at the door. Turning my back to them I sauntered back towards my bedroom, being sure to sway my bubble butt back and forth as seductively as possible.

"Make yourselves comfortable while I get dressed," I said from over my shoulder, not making eye contact with either men. When I got to the door of the bedroom, I paused for a second too long and let the towel fall to the floor, making sure to give Detective Smith a glimpse of my naked ass.

I ain't going down without a fight, Detective.

I peered behind me quickly just in time to catch his eyes staring at my frame before I disappeared behind the door in search of something to wear.

***

For the second time in as many days, I found myself sitting in the back seat of a police car, being driven to the station to defend myself against a crime that I couldn't remember.

How many cop shows had Dale and I watched over the years? Sitting there in the comfort of our own homes, watching someone else's story unfold before our very eyes, laughing judgmentally at their expense. How ironic it all seemed now that I was in their spot. Driving down the A road, my future suddenly so uncertain.

I shivered in the back seat. Not necessarily from the temperature but more from the feeling of dread that had impregnated my stomach. Looking out the window at the bright, sun-lit horizon in the distance I still couldn't find a silver lining to my own situation. I felt so alone. Completely desolate and utterly left behind. My best friend in the world had deserted me, my boss ran screaming for the hills after I made the mistake of sleeping with him, and the man I'd been fucking…a man whose name I didn't even know until yesterday, had been found dead…

And I was the last one to see him, and I can't remember what happened…

A voice from the front of the car jarred me from my dark thoughts.

"You alright, Mister Valentine?" asked Detective Smith, meeting my eyes in the rear view mirror.

I scoffed at his question and stared back at him with a look that said 'are you kidding?'

Detective Smith returned his eyes to the road for a moment, but as I anticipated they found their way back to me, staring and studying my expression. I looked back at him through the mirror, my gaze unflinching; his eyes were so dark, yet so alive, wide, deep and inviting. I felt like I could swim around in them for hours if he'd let me carry on studying them.

Damn me for being such a sucker for sexy eyes.

Detective Smith caught me staring and I detected a soft laugh escape from his lips, making his eyes crinkle slightly in the mirror.

"You look shaken up, Mister Valentine," he asked rhetorically.

"You could say that," I scoffed back turning away from his probing stare.

"If you're innocent as you say you are, then you have nothing to worry about Mister Valentine."

His words made it seem so easy to believe.

Then why don't I feel reassured…

I turned my eyes back to where he sat and studied his outline from the back seat. His shoulders were rounded and I couldn't get over how broad they were; filling up the driver's seat and spilling out seductively over the edges. I studied his big strong tanned hands that gripped the steering wheel casually near the bottom. I looked to his ring finger.

Ringless.

I smiled slightly, despite myself.

No matter what your situation, always a fuckin' flirt Dicey.

I had never been with a man with such masculine hands before. My mind wandered and fantasised as I sat in the back of the police car, the bumps in the road not helping my predicament.

His hands all over me. Rubbing and worshipping his muscles. I wonder how his mouth would feel.

"Would you like a cigarette, Mister Valentine?" Detective Smith offered, extending a pack of Marlboro's in my direction, his eyes intently focused on the road.

I'd really love a fuckin' line actually, mate. Got any blow?

I don't normally smoke without cocktails, but this situation seemed to call for one. I reached for a cigarette from the white package and put it immediately to my lips. The sweet smell of nicotine already ripe to my nostrils. Detective King reached around with a lighter which he held at arm's length. I leaned forward as he lit the end, and sucked in deeply as I sat back in my seat.

The sharp sting of the smoke burned my throat as it travelled down and filled my lungs with its exhilarating poison. I held the smoke in my lungs for a moment and tilted my head back and shut my eyes, momentarily escaping from my ordeal. Slowly, I exhaled the dark smoke in a steady stream through perched lips, feeling immediately more at ease as the head rush took over.

"Thanks," I said, taking another drag off the cigarette. "So, what else can you tell me about this case? Do you have any new leads?" I asked, hoping to further ease some of my anxiety by asking questions.

"Straight to the point, are we?" Detective Smith said, half-jokingly perhaps. He exchanged all-knowing glances with his partner.

"Don't feel I have much to lose, to be honest," I quipped taking another drag and blowing the smoke in their direction. Catching them off guard, Detective King spluttered and shot me a glance from over his shoulder.

"Then why don't you tell us, Mister Valentine. What do you think we've found out?" said Detective Smith, the sparkle in his dark eyes returning.

"I asked you first, Detective," I shot back, a sly smile playing with the corner of my lips.

He snickered to himself and narrowed his eyes at me, trying to suss out my position.

"You like to play games, Mister Valentine?"

The flirtatiousness in his voice was so obvious I almost blushed.

"Games, Detective Smith?" I asked coquettishly, "Why do you ask?"

"Just a hunch I'm getting," he lifted a perfectly manicured eyebrow up at me, "or perhaps it's chances you like to take…" his voice trailed off.

"Chances?" I pondered, unsure of where he was going.

"Yes…Mr. Dice Valentine…"

I rolled my eyes slightly at him and returned my gaze out the window, taking another long, slow haul on the cigarette, my head rush dissipating. I wasn't about to indulge him as he made insinuations about my name.

"I don't take chances Detective, I can assure you."

He looked at me through the mirror, his gaze lingering a little too long, "Good…because this game isn't worth playing, Mister Valentine."

His tone changed slightly, becoming more intense and serious. His brow settled into a fine line, accentuating a deep groove above the bridge of his nose. I can only imagine he was talking about the case and not my involvement with *him*.

Chapter Thirteen

I was escorted into the police interrogation room, again, and found myself sitting alone on the cold chair biting my nails. The air was chilly and uninviting. They obviously didn't want you getting too comfortable while you waited. My foot tapped away relentlessly on the floor, partly from anxiety, partly from nervousness.

My head turned slightly and caught a glimpse of my reflection in the mirrored glass beside me. I stared hard at the person in the glass. Although the contouring dark circles around the eyes had faded, thanks to last night's beauty sleep, he still looked worn and spent. My blonde hair hung listlessly against my face and my skin didn't have its usual glow. My shoulders looked hunched as I sat forward on the chair with my arms resting on the table in front of me. I had decided on a baby blue polo shirt, a pair of faded blue jeans and flip flops on my feet. I sighed when I took in my defeated appearance. Even my eyes looked less vibrant than normal.

You're stronger than this.

I took in a deep breath and straightened up quickly. I ran a hand through my hair, shook it out so it looked healthier, and rubbed at my tired eyes to wake them up a bit.

You can do this.

Standing up and running my tongue over my lips, I gave myself a little mental pep talk to boost my confidence. The detective was right, if I was indeed innocent, than I had nothing to worry about.

I just wish that would calm my nerves.

The door knob turned and made me jump back from the mirror, catching me off guard and making me flinch. My face immediately grew hot as if I had been caught with my hands down my pants or something.

I inched away from where I was standing with my eyes down and sat quickly back in the chair. Even without looking I could tell it was Detective Smith who had entered the room first. When I did venture a look, I realised it wasn't his partner who accompanied him, but another officer. This one wore a police uniform instead of a suit like the Detectives and carried a manila folder tucked under his arm. His features were set in a hard line, and his face reminded me of granite; firm, weathered and worn. The look in his eye was one of 'take-no-prisoners'.

"Mister Valentine, this is Officer Hunter," Detective Smith said, motioning to the man who came in with him.

I nodded in their general direction and swallowed hard, licking my lips once again in an attempt to get rid of my sudden dry-mouth. Officer Hunt neither smiled nor extended his hand for me to shake. He simply stared in my direction, his eyes burning into me from across the table.

"Detective Smith tells me you have waived your right to have an attorney present during questioning."

"Is that a statement or a question, Officer Hunt?" I asked, staring him down with as much power as I could muster into my eyes.

"Why have you waived your right to an attorney?" he asked, rewording his statement.

"I didn't think I would need one, officer…" I retorted, looking from one officer to the other, trying my best to remain cool, "As I told Detective Smith, I have nothing to hide…"

Both Detectives stared blankly at me for a moment too long before Detective Smith coughed quietly and broke the trance.

"Before we begin, I'd like to inform you that our session will be recorded."

"I assumed," I answered, half smiling. I was putting on a front. A rough exterior to hide how absolutely terrified I was. I felt that if I exuded confidence then I could hide behind it. I clasped my trembling hands together in front of me on the table; the only give-away to how I really felt.

Both men stared at me for a moment before Detective Smith began.

"I know this may sound like you're being asked to repeat yourself, Mister Valentine, but would you mind beginning by explaining your relationship with the deceased, David Adams."

I sighed heavily, "He was a, client, at the club where I worked…"

"When you say 'client', can you be more specific?"

There was something about the way Officer Hunt used the word 'client' that made my skin crawl. I shot him a defensive look that spoke volumes.

"I'm a stripper, Officer Hunt, and he was a regular at the club." I responded curtly in my best attempt to make both men feel as uncomfortable as possible. The more uncomfortable they felt, the more at ease it put me.

"And can you tell us the name of the club where you work?"

I stared dumbfounded at both men before me.

This is such a fucking waste of time.

"Mister Valentine, the more you cooperate with us, the smoother this will go for you…"

I couldn't decide if his words were a warning or a threat.

I sighed heavily again, "I work at The Lumberyard. But you already know that…"

"How many times had you seen David Adams at the club?"

"I don't know… a few, I guess…"

"How did you first meet?" Detective Smith asked.

"Well, he ordered a lap dance from me once…Which I don't normally do." My mind began to wander, back to that first night when I met him.

"Why's that?"

"It's just not something I was ever into. Some dancers don't like it. Too intimate."

"*Intimate?*" Officer Hunt asked, obviously mocking my choice of words.

I glared at him, narrowing my eyes.

"I prefer it on stage. Makes me feel safer. In control."

I don't know why I felt like I had to explain myself or my actions. I have never answered to anyone before in my life, and I certainly wasn't going to begin with these two.

"Can you tell us about that night when you first made contact with David Adams?"

My eyes found a spot on the far wall and suddenly became transfixed on it, staring intently until my vision blurred and the walls of the police station morphed and changed and faded away.

"I remember it like it was yesterday…"

For a moment I was completely lost in my head, swirling and tumbling in a mass of memories shooting and flaring in my mind at an incredible speed, before settling on the one it was searching for.

That night.

***

He had chosen me out of all the other guys at the club. I remember dancing to a hard song. Something rocky. Motley Crue, I think. He must have liked it, because just after leaving the stage I remember Tony coming back to find me…

"Dice, you got a request."

"Mate, you know I don't do those…" I had said.

"Said he'd pay top rates," Tony had fired back, giving me a side-ways grin.

I remember pausing to think it over for a second.

"Is he a creep?"

Tony had shrugged off my question. Typical straight guy. "Dunno. Seemed alright to me…" his voice had trailed off.

I sighed and looked out into the faceless crowd, expressions blurred by the spot-lights still illuminating the stage.

"He's by the bar. Dark haired guy, tall. Think you'll like him."

I remember thinking I could really use the money. Things had been slow as of late.

"Tell him it's £500…Not a penny less…I'll be in the Playroom waiting for him. Three knocks then let him in, yah?"

***

"£500? For a lapdance?" Detective Smith scoffed at me, bringing me out of my head and back into the room.

I stared into his dark-unbelieving-eyes and tilted my head to one side. "Not a penny less, Detective…"

He continued to stare at me, disbelievingly, until Officer Hunt cut the tension.

"And what happened when you met him?"

I looked at the mirrored glass for a moment and pondered.

"I danced for him…"

"And?" Officer Hunt urged.

"And he was…nice."

"I'm sorry, *nice?*"

"Yeah…Nice…A complete…gentleman…"

***

The knocks came…Three of them in succession. I took it as my cue to turn my back and prepare for his entrance. The music started up on cue as the door opened and the client walked into the room. I could smell him before I saw him. He smelled of citrus, like he had just freshly showered. I breathed in deeply, the smell almost intoxicating. I heard his footsteps come to a halt. I imagined him standing there, waiting for my instruction. I imagined what his face would look like. I always did; I liked to create a fantasy of my own, liked to fantasise that my client was the hottest thing on two legs. What can I say, it helped me get off. Why should the client have all the fun, anyway?

Without turning around to look at him yet and still facing the mirrored wall in front of me, I pointed my long muscular arm behind me at the single plush velvet chair that sat in the center of the room.

"Sit," I ordered in my most sexy yet commandeering tone.

I could sense him oblige me as the chair legs scraped against the floor. I was wearing short little white booty shorts that showed off my muscular thighs perfectly, and a simple white mesh tank top. On my feet I wore my black lace-up military style boots, laces undone and open. My tousled blonde hair hung perfectly around my face and my body felt toned and pumped up from this morning's gym session.

I felt sexy.

The soft sexy house music oozed from the speakers in the corners of the room, making my hips instantly come to life. With my back still to the client and my hands on my hips, I began to sway slightly from side to side, bending my knees and slowly coming all the way down to the ground, making sure to stick my ass out to give the guy a nice view of my round, perky ass cheeks.

Makes them think of fucking me…

My hands rested on the floor and with my knees wide and ass still in the air, I bounced gently up and down, gyrating my hips and thrusting my pelvis forwards and backwards and then in a circular movement in time to the music. Using all the strength in my legs I slowly straightened them out and keeping myself bent at the waist, peered at my client from between my legs.

It was such a hot move, and showcased my ass perfectly. What I saw when I finally got a glimpse of the man sitting casually in the chair behind me, almost threw me off track.

He was… beautiful…

Even from upside down I could make out the contours of his muscles from beneath his snug-fitting v-neck shirt. Despite the darkness of the room I could tell his hair was short and dark but the rest of his features were hidden in shadow.

It wasn't so much his masculine appearance that took me for a loop though. It was the way he sat there on the chair; relaxed and completely at ease. His legs were apart and elbows resting on the arms of the chair. His hands were loose and his head slightly tilted to one side. He seemed…chilled…

***

"What do you mean, 'chilled,'" Detective Smith asked.

His sudden interruption stirred me from my reminiscent state.

"I'm sorry?" I asked, completely having missed the question.

"You said David Adams appeared 'chilled'. What was so out of the ordinary about that?"

"Have you ever paid for a private dance, Detective Smith?" I asked.

Detective Smith stared at me with wide eyes, completely taken-aback.

"Normally when I've done private dances in the past, the guys come in a big bundle of nerves…All hunched over and drooling, they never come in all chilled out and relaxed. Takes usually the whole dance for them to loosen up."

"And why do you think that this David Adams, was more at ease than other clients?"

"I dunno to be honest. In fact, it kind of made *me* feel nervous." I sat back in my chair, enjoying this little walk down memory lane. "Yah, he threw me right away, this guy. This guy was…different."

***

I tore my eyes away from him and hinched myself up from the hips to a standing position. I was feeling the base now as it pounded through my bones. Music always took control of me when I danced, steering my movements and taking over my mind. I was no longer ruled by thought, but pure unadulterated instinct.

I turned on my heel to finally face my client. When my eyes laid themselves on his dark features, it was as if someone had read every fantasy that I had ever had about my perfect man and created a superhuman in his exact image.

He almost took my breath away.

When I caught sight of his beautiful shape I'm sure I tripped over my boot. There was such an aura around him as he sat there, cool and collected in The Playroom, his dark eyes completely transfixed on my body, and a slight smile twitching at the corner of his mouth.

I chastised myself mentally for losing my footing and quickly regained my composure, getting back into character and forcing my eyes away from his beautifully shaped face. Looking down at my feet, I dropped my head and as the deep house music picked up slightly, took at a bit of material from my mesh top in each of my hands and just as the base broke, tore the material away in a swift rip. The fragile shirt tore easily away from my chest, exposing the dark smooth skin beneath. I peered up at him through my hair and saw him shift position in the chair, one hand moving down to tug at the tightening crotch of his jeans.

Excellent.

Letting the material drop to the floor around me, my hands reached up to pinch at my nipples until they stood at attention, round and hard under my touch. I let my head tilt back and parted my lips slightly, as the feeling of having my nipples tweaked was incredible. I let one hand tangle itself in my long shaggy blonde hair while the other trailed south and found the protruding contour of my package being held so neatly in my thong. I squeezed gently, my own touch making my dick begin to show itself more and more inside my shorts.

The man in the chair bent his right elbow and began to chew on his thumb nail, while straightening up in his chair.

Do it, baby.

I took a step closer to him, naked except for my tiny shorts and boots. One hand still lost in my hair, bicep flexed to show off my muscle definition, the other dipping slightly into the waist band of my short shorts, seeking and teasing as it inched further and further, disappearing into the material and reaching for my thick meat which was begging and screaming out for attention. I took another step closer to him until I was about a foot away from his legs. I spread my legs and turned away again until my back was to him. With my back arched and ass jutting out I eased myself down until I connected with his bent legs, straining my thigh muscles and holding myself in the air, just enough to graze the material of his jeans with my ass. I swayed from side to side, creating friction as I rubbed my ass against his legs.

He flinched when I touched him and I could feel his hands suddenly grip the arms of the chair. I let my head fall back and shook my hair out of my face . Leaning my hands back I gripped the arms of the chair just in front of where his hands were resting, and eased my back down further so that we were almost spooning in the chair; me almost resting directly on top of him, all the while rotating my hips in a circular motion and keeping the movement going as I inched myself further up his legs until my butt was perfectly in line with his crotch.

When we were in line with each other, I turned my head to the left so that my nose was just tickling his cheek and he could feel my breath on his face. I held myself like that for a moment, all my weight being held up by my arms that continued to grip the chair beneath me. He shifted beneath me again, and I could feel him begin to harden in his jeans against my ass. My lips found his mouth and lingered just there, teasing him and making him begin to fantasise about kissing me.

He wanted desperately to touch me. I could tell by the sudden tenseness in his muscles as he sat there motionless under my weight. My arm muscles were on fire, screaming out for me to stand up again. He parted his lips slightly and brought his tongue to the front of his mouth, dying to lick me, but held back. Air escaped from between his lips in the form of a low moan as he let his head fall back slightly, relishing the feeling of having me gyrating on top of him.

Abruptly I pushed up and away from the chair until I was back in a standing position in front of him, my back still facing him. I could see his reflection in the mirrored wall before me; he ran a hand through his short hair and straightened up further, quickly adjusting his boner in his jeans.

I reached down to the button of my booty shorts and flicked it open, unzipped them quickly and began easing them frustratingly slowly down over my bubble butt, exposing to him the back of my black satin thong which left little to the imagination, barely covering up my hole.

Behind me I could hear him moan quietly as his eyes appreciated and bathed in the sight of my near-naked behind. My shorts struggled over the bulge in my thong, the thickness filling up the soft black material around it. I looked to the ceiling as I let the shorts slide down my muscular thighs until they landed on the floor softly, making the movement drip with eroticism. Stepping out of them I hitched from the waist again and bent all the way down, flat back, reaching both hands down and over to my right foot, giving him a full moon view of my ass, nothing but a thin piece of material covering up my modesty. I snuck a peak over at him; he had caved and allowed his right hand to rest and cradle the hard-on in his jeans. He squeezed it gently, giving it the attention it so desired.

A smile crossed my lips as I decided to put him out of his misery and show him what he came here for. I bent my knees again and came into a squat, ass still extended in the air behind me, and mimicked bouncing up and down on a cock.

Yeah, baby.

Finally I stood up straight and turned to face him once more, my cock pitching an obscene tent in my thong and facing slightly upwards. I met his eyes which were wide and lustful. His mouth was hanging open now and he ran his tongue over his lips which only served to make me harder. I could feel the tip of my cock begin to moisten with precum and I knew if I were to service it even in the slightest, I could easily cum right then and there.

Hold it back, baby.

I held his stare and inched myself closer to him again. Spreading my legs wide, I wasted no time in straddling him where he sat. I rested one hand on my hips and the other shot up to my hair, flexing my bicep again to guarantee him a perfect view of my muscular frame. As the song began to wind to a close, I moved my pelvis in a circular motion once more, in line with his hard-on beneath me. With only a few beats left I knew I had to pick up my pace to get the job done.

My hips dry-humped him hard, pressing down against the massive bulge in his jeans and gyrating continuously up and down, faster and faster until the movement mimicked getting fucked. Underneath me I could feel him begin to pulse his own hips to meet my ass when I came down. The feeling of his cock pressing up through his jeans against my hole was orgasmic, as I humped him through the rough material.

Again and again, each movement sent me closer and closer to coming on top of him. He was gripping the arms of the chair so firmly, to keep from reaching out and grabbing my bare skin.

Even though it was against the rules to touch a dancer, part of me was so turned on that I was dying to feel his hands all over me. Every time my hole connected with his crotch I felt a jolt of electricity shoot through my body.

I was so close, and so was he. He was full on thrusting now, harder and harder he pressed himself up to meet me, the look in his eye one of utter desperation to fuck me. Harder and harder, faster and faster, I wanted more. I shut my eyes and imagined him inside me, fucking me for dear life and pushing me till I came all over his chest. His hands caressing my pecks and massaging my arms as he fucked away at my hole with his big dick.

My body had had enough and with one last press against my hole I felt myself boil over and release itself right there. My hand shot down to my cock, connecting with the tip and cradling my erection. At once, he came with me, his body tensing and heaving as he came hard in his jeans. Our bodies jolted together as each thrust forced us to come again and again, our ejaculations pounding out of our cocks, pooling in the material that confined them.

A thin layer of sweat coated my whole body. My breathing was shallow and erratic as I came down from my orgasm and realised at once where I was. Immediately I was beyond embarrassed.

Fuck.

I looked away quickly from his pleading face, utterly furious that I had let this dance go this far. I bit my tongue in utter shame that I had broken my cardinal rule of coming with a client during a dance. I would have been shocked if he hadn't of come, but I always found the strength, always, no matter how into it I was, to pull back and never orgasm during a dance.

How did this happen?

I was so ashamed. I stood quickly and turned away from him just as the music finished and died out, the room filling quickly with a heavy silence. The air in there was thick and damp and probably reeked of sex. I reached down for my discarded shorts and quickly slipped them on, all the while keeping my back to the client. As I buttoned them up, I heard him clear his throat and stand, his footsteps leading him to the door.

Just as I was about to turn around, I looked up and he caught my eye in the reflection in the mirror. I froze, paralyzed by his look and waited as neither of us spoke, each perhaps searching for the proper thing to say, but both coming up with blanks.

After a moment, he broke the connection, turned and quickly disappeared out the door, leaving me in a warm yet shaky, orgasm-induced state alone.

***

The two policemen exchanged all-knowing glances with each other then returned their stares to me.

Officer Hunt looked mildly uncomfortable and I swear I could detect a faint blush to Detective Smith's cheeks. To be honest, I was feeling slightly self-conscious as well, for a change. It wasn't often that anyone, or anything, could make me feel raw and exposed, considering my line of work, but sitting here…Admitting details to two strangers about how I lived my life…Somehow this was different. And not in a good way.

I turned my eyes down to my knotted hands that were resting on the cold, linoleum table. I picked at the skin from around my thumb nail, another nervous habit of mine. Detective Smith cleared his throat again before speaking.

"Mister Valentine, how did your contact with David Adams progress after that night?"

"After that night, I was sure I wouldn't see him again..."

"How do you mean?" asked Officer Hunt.

"Well, I just thought he had had his fill. If you know what I mean..."

"His fill?"

"Yah...I dunno...Why would I expect to see him again after that night? I thought it was probably just a one time thing..."

"But it wasn't, Mister Valentine, was it?" Detective Smith implored.

Fucking in the alley. His dick pounding away at my ass.

"No...No it wasn't." I paused, not wanting to willingly give up too much information without being asked the right questions.

"Mister Valentine, did you have an affair with David Adams?"

I flinched slightly, his question hitting me harder than it should have.

I looked him straight in the eye, drips of my self-confidence returning

Does he sound turned on by the idea?

"The next night...at the club...the very next night, he was there," I started, remembering seeing him in the crowd. The shape of his chest and shoulders and shortly cropped hair unmistakable even in the darkness of the club. Same table. Same cocktail glass. Always alone.

"Did he order another dance?"

"No...Not another dance...He was just...there."

"Can you be more specific, Mister Valentine?"

"He was just in the crowd."

"Did you speak to him?"

I could tell they were getting antsy; they weren't getting the answers they were looking for.

"Not exactly..."

***

I made my way off the stage and headed for the backstage dressing room.

Was that him in the crowd? Far left hand table. Long cocktail glass. So cool and so confident. Enjoying the sights. Did he raise his glass to me?

Fuck, I want to see him again. Maybe he'll ask for me again. Maybe he felt it too.

I shook my head and pinched the bridge of my nose in annoyance with myself. What the hell was happening to me?

When I spotted him while I was dancing I swear I almost fell off the stage. This is not me. I've never been put off by someone in the crowd. Not by the hecklers and certainly not by some hotshot who flashes cash around the club like he's James fuckin' Dean.

Jesus, Dice. Get a grip.

Probably wasn't even him. Why would he be back a second night in a row, anyway?

"Nice dance, hot stuff!" Tim called as he past me in the corridor.

I half-turned to him as we brushed past each other and gave his ass a playful slap.

"Thanks mate. I'm here to please," I shot back as I continued towards my dressing table. I chuckled to myself, half-ashamed that I was feeling this way.

Don't shit where you eat, Dice.

I turned the corner and walked into the brightly lit back room. It was a slow night tonight, only Tim, me and three other guys were in, two of which were about to go on. Sitting down at my dressing table I took a long hard look at myself in the mirror, staring at my reflection, studying each and every small detail in my freshly Botoxed face. My bright blue eyes, vibrant and alive after the thrill of being on stage. My tanned skin and plump red pouty lips.

Damn, you're fine.

My narcissistic admiration session was interrupted by Tony turning the corner and giving a shy knock on the door to the dressing room.

"Knock, knock" he added for emphasis.

I turned to see him standing there with a huge shit-eating grin spread across his face. In his hands he held a single long-stem red rose and a small white envelope.

"Well, hello there, handsome," I cooed knowing that compliments embarrassed him.

"Apparently someone thinks **you** *are,"* he responded coming over to where I was sitting. *"These are for you."*

I reached out and took the rose and card, immediately putting the rose to my nose and breathing in the sweet scented nectar.

"Seriously? Who from?" I questioned, putting the rose down and tearing open the envelope.

Tony shrugged, *"Dunno mate, found them on an empty table and your name was on the card, so…"*

He turned to leave, *"Wait, wait! So, you didn't see who left them?"*

"Nope… 'fraid not."

"What table?"

"Sorry?"

"What table did you find them on?"

"Oh, uh, back of the main room…next to the bar. Why?"

"It's not important. Thanks T," I said, staring hard at the small card.

In small handwriting written across the card read the words:

> "Thanks for the dance last night. Want to see you again, meet me
> behind the club when you get off.
> -D"

I could feel my face grow hot as I reread the words over and over again, my pulse quickening and my cock twinging inside my shorts at the thought of what the note suggested.

It **was** him…He came back.

I smiled despite myself and put the card down and looked to the rose once more. What to do, what to do…

***

"That's how it all started," I finished.

"For the record, Mister Valentine, can you confirm for us how long you had relations with Mister Adams?" asked Officer Hunt, at the same time riffling through the manila envelope he had brought with him.

"Umm, I'm not sure exactly. A few weeks I…"

"A few weeks?" He repeated my words back to me.

"Um, yeah…a few weeks, I guess."

"Were you seen in public, Mister Valentine?"

"Together?"

"Yes, together. Did you go out on dates?"

"No. No, it wasn't like that."

"How was it then, Mister Valentine?" Detective Smith implored.

I opened my mouth to answer but before I could finish Officer Hunt took out several A4 size pieces of thick paper and just as I was about to continue, thrust them out on the table nonchalantly in front of me.

My breath hitched in my throat when I recognised the sheets as crime scene photos. My hands shot up to cover my mouth as I realised who the body in the pictures was.

Black and white pictures of David Adams from numerous angles, some up close of the wounds, others taken from further back, different parts of his body all covered in dark splatters of blood, the walls and parts of the alley.

I clasped my eyes tightly shut and forced myself to look away.

"Jesus Christ…" I murmured, in complete shock.

"Officer Hunt!" Detective Smith yelled, obviously unimpressed by his shock tactics.

"I guess your little *fuck-buddy fairytale* didn't work out though, did it?" Officer Hunt spat at me.

"*Hunt*, back down," Detective Smith warned.

"Why'd you do it, huh? Was it jealousy?" he continued, his voice filled with hatred.

My eyes shot open to stare in awe at the Officers in front of me. I was at a loss for words and without wanting to, took another look at the grisly photographs on the table. Seeing him in front of me like this made my stomach twist and churn.

"I-I, no. *Stop,*" I pleaded with my hand tightly clasped over my mouth.

"Were you in love with him?"

"What? What do you-"

"Was he fucking someone else too? Did he try and end it, is that why you did it?" he accused, standing up suddenly causing his chair to scrape loudly across the floor.

"Officer Hunt, *stop!*" Detective Smith shouted, standing up and taking Officer Hunt's shoulders in each of his hands as if to hold him back.

"Then how do you explain him going from meeting you in the alley for a quick shag to getting his head bashed in?" Hunt shouted.

His words were like slaps across the face, each one stinging more than the last.

"I-I-I don't know…I" I stuttered.

"*You* what?"

"Hunt, that's enough…This is not how I work," Detective Smith's voice grew louder and more forceful, "back down *now* or I'll have you removed from this case."

Officer Hunt tore his wide angry eyes from my face and looked directly at Smith, completely taken aback by his sudden threat.

"*What?* Come on Smith, he's just wasting our time. Telling us tales of back alley smut…I've had enough."

"*Now,*" was all he had to say. Detective Smith's voice was firm with authority. He was obviously in charge of this investigation. As strange as it may seem, I felt a slight twinge of hope that he might actually believe that I was innocent.

"Mister Valentine," Detective Smith started more calmly than before, "the DNA tests came back from the blood we found at the scene. It *was* your blood we found not far from the body…as we suspected."

I blinked hard at this news.

"And the victim had your blood underneath his finger nails."

His last sentence stunned me into silence. I felt like I had been sucker-punched in the gut, knocking the wind right out of my chest. I looked up from the spot on the table on which I had been focusing and stared wide-eyed at him sat across from me. I could feel my mouth gape open slightly as my brain processed what he had said.

But…how?

"I don't…I don't understand…"

"We found traces of skin under David Adams' fingernails as well as blood not far from the scene. Upon analysis, the tests came back as two positive matches for your DNA."

I was shaking my head now. Part of me not wanting to acknowledge what was happening, as if my nervous system was shutting itself down slowly in an attempt at self-preservation.

"Mister Valentine…I don't know if you're aware of the implications this has on the case. You were having an affair with the deceased and we have you placed at the scene the night of the murder. We also have your blood on the scene and skin cells under the victims nails."

Both men returned to their seats. Officer Hunt crossed his arms and covered his eyes with his right hand, rubbing slowly at his temples and letting out heavy sighs from his nose.

"This isn't possible," I pleaded, my voice coming out like strangled cries. "I didn't…I didn't do this."

I mimicked Officer Hunt's actions and put my head in both my hands, running them through my tangled hair and squeezing my skull for comfort.

"Mister Valentine, what happened that night in the alley? This is your chance to tell us your side."

"I, I already told y-you…" I was shaking now, trembling from the top of my head to my toes. "You have to *believe* me."

I looked up at both men again, feeling the warm sting of tears drizzle out my eyes and down my flaming cheeks. My panicked eyes shot from one man to the other. I felt so drained. Terrified and exhausted. My body felt like it was on the brink of shutting down. I didn't know how much more of this I could take before I gave in to the urge to either just close my eyes and pass out or run screaming.

"Previously you said that you were supposed to meet him that night…" His tone was soft and comforting, despite the fever-pitch feeling in the room. I met his eyes. Soft, large and enticing.

Maybe he does believe me.

"Take yourself back there and tell us what happened."

"I-I don't know if…"

Every time I opened my eyes I could see *him*…Dead, bleeding.

This is all my fault.

"Focus Mister Valentine. Tell us what happened."

I drew in a shallow sharp breath, careful not to release the sob that was threatening to escape if I let it.

"You said you were the last to leave the club."

"I left the club. It was deserted. I was the last to leave."

I squeezed my eyes shut tightly, trying to bring myself back to that night, and desperately remember what the hell had *actually* happened. Everything seemed so foggy. So uncertain, like there was a black curtain that was hanging in my head and keeping details of that night from me.

"I heard a noise. I was so scared, I, I just ran…"

"Did you see anyone else around?" Smith asked, his eyes focusing hard on my expression.

"Tony…"

"Tony Matthews," Detective Smith said, more to Officer Hunt than anyone else.

"In your previous statement Mister Valentine, you said that when you saw Mister Matthews you believed him to be under the influence of narcotics."

"Well, I don't know. He was just…strange."

"Strange, how?" Officer Hunt asked abruptly.

I considered what I was about to say, trying hard to remember exactly how he was acting.

"He was just staring at me…Not speaking, just staring."

"Did you ask him if he was alright?" Smith asked.

"I…I did…But he just stared at me…Almost *through* me, like he didn't even recognise me."

When I looked up at the two officers, I was struck with the realisation that what I was saying, this whole story, my entire defense… sounded completely and utterly *crazy*.

"Mister Valentine, why didn't you follow Mister Matthews? If you were concerned for him, why didn't you take care of him? Put him in a cab?" Detective Smith implored.

"I dunno…I dunno, he just kind of walked off."

"And you didn't follow because you had better things to do, right?" Officer Hunt stated sarcastically.

"Listen, I know this sounds fucked up, but I swear to you he just left.I don't know why I didn't follow."

Detective Smith riffled through some papers in the folder on the table. Choosing one he continued, "the police have been unable to locate a Mister Matthews…Any idea where he might have gone that night?"

"I…I don't, I'm not sure…"

Where the hell was Tony? Where could he have gone?

Then a dark and twisted thought seeped into my stomach like a cancer.

What if he's…no, no he can't be.

I shook my head quickly, not allowing the thought to take over like it was threatening to do.

"So, after Mister Matthews walked away, what happened next?"

I stared off again, my vision blurring in and out of focus.

I went to meet…him.

"That's when, I…"

Both men were looking at me intently.

"The alley isn't far from where I found Tony…"

"Mister Valentine, was Tony coming from the alley when you saw him?"

"Sorry?" I asked, not sure I had heard him correctly.

"Was he coming from behind the building when you ran into him?"

"I don't know…I guess, maybe he could have been."

My eyes widened when I realised what the officers were implying.

"You don't think…"

The officers exchanged looks once again.

I shook my head in their direction, "No…No, Tony…Not Tony. Why would…"

My eyes searched for an answer to my unanswered question, looking down at the floor and thinking hard.

Tony? Would Tony ever? No. He couldn't have. Why would he? It couldn't have been Tony.

"Mister Valentine, would you describe Mister Matthews as a violent man?"

"Violent?"

"Yes. Do you know him to be prone to acts of violence? Outbursts? He *is* the club's bouncer, is it not possible that he might in fact be responsible for the murder of David Adams?"

I opened my mouth to speak, then reconsidered.

Tony? He was always so kind. Sweet. He'd never do something like this. Would he?

"How well do you know Mister Matthews?"

"He's a…friend…I guess."

"Did you ever sleep with him?"

"Tony?" I asked quickly, my voice ripe with surprise, "Tony's straight, Detective…"

"Are you sure about that?" Smith asked quickly.

"I…Well…" But I couldn't finish my sentence.

I'm sure he's straight…Wasn't he?

Both men cleared their throats at my hesitation.

"Did he ever make a pass at you?" Smith enquired.

"Did Tony ever hit on me?" A slight giggle escaping my lips.

"Isn't it possible that he perhaps had feelings for you, Mister Valentine, and got a little jealous of David Adams?"

I could do nothing but stare wide-eyed and slack-jawed at both men. I shook my head slightly and closed my mouth quickly to hide my reaction to their ridiculous insinuation.

"He was *there*, Mister Valentine," Officer Hunt's voice trailed off, his tone making me uncomfortable.

"When you found the body…" Smith interjected, throwing me off my train of thought. "What did you do?"

I took a moment to gather myself, the icy cold feeling of being back in that alley, returning and infecting my bones. Flashes of dark memories appearing like photographs behind my eyes.

The alley. Dark. Dreary.

If I let myself focus for too long, it was like I was back there, rounding the bend and stumbling across the body.

His body.

Blood soaked and lying awkwardly. Waiting for me.

I squeezed my eyes shut tightly in an attempt to rid my mind of the sight.

"Mister Valentine?"

"Oh God…" I muttered under my breath, sucking in a sharp breath through my gritted teeth.

"Mister Valentine, what did you do when you found the body?"

"When I got to the alley…" I began, swallowing the lump in my throat, "he…I saw…I saw him…"

"Did you touch the body, Mister Valentine?"

"No…I…I don't think so…" I furrowed my brow as I tried to remember if I *had*.

"Try and remember…Did you run up and check if he was breathing? Did you disturb anything at the scene? Touch anything at all?"

Think, Dice. Think.

"He was just…lying there. I remember not recognising him at first."

"Go on," Smith urged, scribbling something in black ink on a piece of paper from the manila envelope.

"I got closer and…and when I saw that it was…that it was *him*…I think I was sick."

"Mister Valentine, did you **touch** anything," the annoyance in his voice slightly accentuated.

"No….No, I…When I saw he was…dead…" I swallowed again, the bile in my stomach rising by the second, "I remember…r …"

"You ran, Mister Valentine?"

"Yes, I ran…I was so freaked that I ran. But that's when I tripped…I…"

"You tripped? Are you kidding me?" Officer Hunt asked, thinking my statement trivial.

"That's why I was so cut up. That's why you found blood on the scene."

I held up both my scraped hands for the men to inspect. Their eyes wavered for a moment before returning to focus on my face.

"Yes, Mister Valentine, our lab tests we conducted on the blood found…" He checked his notes, "Fifty feet from the scene of the crime came up as a match for you. That part of your story checks out. Care to enlighten us with your version of how your blood *also* managed to get onto the body?"

He was mocking me now. I could almost sense his inward laughter emanating from his pours. They both thought they had me pegged; that this was an open and shut case and that it was only a matter of time before they got me to confess. But as I stared back at the men sitting opposite of me, there was something not quite right. Almost like there was a slither of doubt behind their hard expressions; like they were missing a piece of the puzzle. My eyes searched their expressions for a glimmer of hope. I couldn't put my finger on it, but my gut told me that this wasn't over.

They're missing something. They're trying to back me into a corner and pin this on me. But they don't have all the facts. If they did, they would have arrested me by now. They're searching for something else. And they're not going to find it. I didn't do this. I'm sure of it.

But my head knew better than to be so self-assured, because in the pit of my stomach, a seed of doubt was slowly growing inside of me as well. It was sewing itself into my veins and threatening to reveal itself if I wavered in the slightest or showed any sign of weakness. If I let my guard down, even for a second, it would reveal the truth. The scary, harsh truth that I didn't even want to acknowledge existed. The truth was…that I wasn't sure of much beyond this point…

Because I couldn't remember.

With every passing second I was beginning to feel more and more exhausted. My heart ached and even my bones yearned for this all to be over with. My head was so tired of trying, and was throbbing slightly from trying so desperately to remember what happened that night. If I told them that I couldn't remember what happened; that after I fell the rest of the night was a blur; that the next thing I remember was waking up in my bed, unsure as to how I actually got home or what had happened…that would be the end of me. They'd lock me up right then and there and charge me with a murder I *was sure* I didn't commit.

I was beginning to feel overwhelmed with frustration. Partly directed at the officers and partly at myself. The fact that there were gaps in my memory of that night only served to stoke the feeling of panic that I had been trying to suppress for days now.

I sighed heavily. It felt nice to let out a deep sigh. I imagined my stress and frustrations going out with my breath, expelling them from my insides.

Just admit defeat, Dice.

But as alluring as that thought was, how freeing it would be to just let it all go and stop fighting…I knew that that wasn't who I was.

You're not a quitter, mate.

I willed myself to stand up for myself, but it was as if I just couldn't find the words.

"I don't know…"

It wasn't quite defeat, but it certainly wasn't an alibi. My words acted like quite the conversation halter. Both officers seemed stumped all of a sudden, and mirrored my actions by letting out a deep sigh of their own. Detective Smith shifted in his seat, never taking his deep, penetrating eyes off of me. He stole a quick glance at Officer Hunt who gave him a slight nod and swiped a hand across the table, scooping up the police photos that he'd strewn across a few moments earlier.

Smith cleared his throat before speaking again, "Well, Mister Valentine, as much as it pains me to say this, it seems that the law is on your side…" he paused waiting for me to respond.

"Excuse me?" My heart did a little flutter at the mention of the word 'lucky'.

He flexed his jaw, defining his strong facial structure once more. I couldn't help but stare. "Regardless of the fact that we have evidence of your DNA across the scene of the crime, DNA fingerprints are not ideally used as the sole piece of evidence in a case…"

It was taking all of my might to focus and make sense of what he was saying.

"UK law states that DNA fingerprints must be presented in conjunction with other evidence to be admissable in court."

I shook my head in an effort to clear it.

"Namely a motive.""

He narrowed his eyes at me, studying me intensely and trying to judge my somewhat confused expression.

"A motive?" I repeated.

"Yes…a motive…a reason **why** would you murder the man you were sleeping with, in cold blood, in the exact spot you planned to meet him that night…"

Detective Smith seemed to be thinking out loud, more to himself than to anyone else. "Almost seems a little too easy, doesn't it Mister Valentine?"

"Easy, Detective?"

"But don't worry Mister Valentine. If there's a motive to be discovered, I'll find it."

His words made me shudder in my seat. They were more of a promise than a threat that carried so much weight they frightened me.

"You seem sure of yourself, Detective."

"Oh, I am," He stated confidently, his eyes burning into me and his assuredness making me stiffen slightly in my jeans. "I never start a game I can't finish."

Chapter Fourteen

Detective Smith offered to give me a ride back to my flat, since he could no longer hold me after my questioning was over. There was something off about the way he walked me to his car, almost as if he was enjoying this whole scenario.

As I watched him lead the way to the car, his stride struck me as a bit too sure of himself. He carried himself confidently and even his walk was cocky. I stayed close to him, admiring the view of his backside, despite the horror of what I had just endured. I couldn't help but feel somewhat hopeful as I walked out of the police station. Almost rejuvenated as I realised that I might just have a chance to clear myself of this shit, now that they couldn't hold me any longer.

Smith's perky ass was distracting me from my thoughts and I inwardly chastised myself for letting my cock lead me astray. I closed my eyes tightly and tried to focus. Every second I had needed to be spent thinking of how the hell I was going to prove I had nothing to do with this.

How, is right…

When we got to the unmarked police car, Smith turned to face me.

"Do you want to ride in the back, or…" His voice trailed off and I swear I could see a small smile play with the corner of his beautifully shaped lips.

His obvious flirtatious innuendo caught me off guard and stirred me out of my head for a moment. I shifted my weight onto one leg and puffed out my chest slightly. My eyes met his and I blinked coquettishly, urging him to go on and finish his sentence.

"Or what Detective?" I offered.

Smith swallowed and opened his lips to speak, then reconsidered. Not giving him a chance to finish, I moved around to the other side of the car without breaking our eye contact. As I reached the front passenger side I opened the door smoothly and lowered myself into the seat without saying a word.

Two can play at that game, Detective.

I put on my belt and stared straight ahead as Detective Smith got into the car as well and started it up. He looked over at me for a moment. I could feel his eyes looking me over, but I resisted meeting them, instead keeping mine focused on the empty car park. Smith let out a small sound that was almost a quiet giggle, and put the car into reverse and headed out the car park.

I studied him out of the corner of my eye. The way he gripped the gear shift with his large tanned hands; the way his legs rested, spread open at a nonchalantly sexy angle; the way the material of his trousers strained against his taught leg muscles.

As we drove a few minutes in silence, the air between us began to thicken with pheromones. There was no denying the attraction between us both and sitting here so close to him, and not being able to even look at him, was utter torture. I yearned to steal a glance at him; to take in his strong frame. But I had to imagine instead. I let my vision blur and lost myself in thoughts of what he might look like out of his suit. How his trousers framed the bulge in his pants as he sat there next to me.

I couldn't believe I was feeling this way towards the man who was trying to pin a murder investigation on me. But as much as my head tried to fight these feelings, it only stoked the fire I was feeling in my loins. I bit my tongue and turned my head to look out the window and deter myself from the sexual thoughts that were running through my head.

"Are you alright, Mister Valentine?" Smith asked, his voice jarring me further.

"Am I alright?" I repeated his question back to him.

"You look a little uncomfortable."

I turned my head in disbelief at what he was saying. "Uncomfortable?"

He looked from the road to me and then back again without saying anything further.

"Wouldn't you be?" I asked rhetorically.

He swallowed again and flexed his jaw muscles in that way he had earlier.

Oh god, that's sexy.

I turned away again in an effort to shift my wayward thoughts.

"I suppose I would," he said thoughtfully.

At that moment, there was something about his tone of voice that drew my attention back to his face. He sounded almost...heartfelt. I felt something in my belly stir and when I looked in his direction again it was as if I was seeing him for the first time. His eyes looked somehow softer and his expression a bit more compassionate as if he were considering how I must have been feeling and putting himself in my fucked-up shoes. He continued to stare straight ahead, focusing on the road, the look not leaving his features.

I couldn't help but stare, but the more I stared the more I began to weaken, and the more I lost sight of his role in this whole nightmare. But I couldn't help it, and at that moment I didn't care. The sight of him sitting next to me, so soft and considerate, was such a turn from how he had appeared not twenty minutes ago at the police station, and it had me in his grip. Smith opened his lips to speak, turned to look at me and then stopped. His dark eyes had warmed and lightened in colour to a milky shade of brown and even the muscles in his face seemed more relaxed all of a sudden.

"Mister Valentine..."

The way he spoke my name all of a sudden sent a warm rush through my bones, heating my veins and whipping my hormones into a frenzy. My eyes willed him to finish his sentence, fantasising of what he might say. It was as if we both had completely forgotten what was happening and got lost in a moment where we regarded each other in a different light temporarily.

"Detective, I-"

But before I could say another word, we both caught something out of the corner of our eye in the rear-view mirror. I looked up just in time to see a car speeding towards the back of our vehicle. Before either of us could react, we felt ourselves being propelled forward as our car was hit brutally hard from behind, sending us both jerking forwards so suddenly that my forehead was a mere inch from smashing itself against the dashboard. My seatbelt locked and held me firmly in place as our car shot forwards.

"What the fuck!" Smith shouted as we both realised that we'd just been rear-ended. Instinctually, Smith's left hand shot out to protect me in the passenger seat.

We both spun our heads around to look out the back window just in time to see the driver in the car behind us speed up again and smash himself a second time into our rear.

"Jesus!," I spat out as I was whipped forward again. The seatbelt caught me again, this time knocking the breath right out of my chest as it held me in place. My neck snapped forward and then back again hard before my head connected with the seat's head rest. I stole a glance behind us to try and make sense of what was happening.

"Detective, what the fuck?"

The car behind us was sleek and black with tinted windows, making it impossible to make out who the driver was.

I looked to Smith with a frenzied expression and saw that the kindness of his eyes had been replaced with a sterner look. His eyes were narrowed and full of fury and his mouth was fixed in a thin firm line.

"He's trying to hit us," he said in a low voice that made me flinch at the implication, "Hang on, Dice."

I blinked hard, momentarily thrown by hearing him use my first name. I recovered quickly and gripped the door handle as I was told, bracing myself for whatever was coming next.

Smith kept his eye focused on the car as seen from his rear view mirror, and not missing a beat laid his foot down on the gas pedal. Our car propelled forward from the sudden shock of speed and quickly moved along down the road, speeding up and away from our attacker. I looked in my door's side mirror and saw the black car behind us slowly become smaller as we sped ahead.

My fingers clawed at the seat and door like I might be ejected from my seat if I let go. My neck felt immediately stiff and I could feel my jaw clench down so hard I was afraid my teeth might shatter.

"Are you alright, Dice?" Smith asked authoritatively. "Are you hurt?"

I couldn't answer. My body felt paralised with fear. I shook my head in response and kept both hands locked in position.

"W-who is..." I stuttered.

"I don't know, do you recognise the car?"

His voice was loud and direct.

I stole another look behind me.

"Oh fuck, here he comes again," I whispered wide-eyed when I made out the black car coming closer into view and gaining on us again. "What are we gonna do?" I asked feverishly.

"Hang on, alright? I got this fucker," he stated, his jaw fixed in a hard line.

Our car raced down the long road ahead of us. We were nearing the town center and traffic was getting worse. We swerved in and out of the cars on the road, narrowly avoiding collisions at every second. Smith was a precise driver, and his actions led me to believe that I was safe. The car jerked left and then right, moving in and out of the passing lane, and jeering into oncoming traffic. The sound of blaring horns filled the air as manic drivers shouted obscenities at us as we narrowly avoided clipping them as we sped by.

I felt like I was in a movie; being chased by some crazed criminal who was trying to force us off the road. I squeezed my eyes shut as we moved into the wrong lane and sped straight on in the direction of an oncoming car.

"Holy F-"

My breath was caught in my throat and I brought both my hands up to shield my face in preparation for impact. But Smith swerved us hard again and back into the proper lane, narrowly missing being swiped by the car. We both looked behind us again and saw that the black car was still hot on our tail.

"How the hell is he keeping up with us? Who the fuck is it?" I screamed over the roar of the passing cars.

"My guess," Smith began calmly, "is it's the fucking killer!"

I couldn't believe my ears. I turned to look at him slack-jawed.

"What?" I asked, momentarily forgetting the fact that we were in a full-on car chase.

"Know of anyone else who might want you dead?"

He met my eyes for a brief second and I saw a flash of the warmth that had disappeared before we were first hit.

"You-You mean…"

I turned away and considered this for a second. Flashes of that night at the club. The noise I heard. The stranger at Joe's apartment door. The man in the street who was following me.

"But…But who?"

The car swerved again hard, only this time I was suddenly deafened by the sound of scraping metal as Smith's driver side made contact with a passing car.

"Fuck, watch out!" I screamed a little too late. I jumped practically out of my seat as we were lurched abruptly sideways from the slight collision.

Smith reached around to try and grab something from the back seat.

"Grab the wheel for a sec, will ya?" he shouted at me.

Without even thinking I grabbed the wheel with a sweaty hand and half-ass attempted to veer us back on track as we continued to speed down the road.

"What are you…"

Smith pulled out what looked like a police light from behind his seat and in a quick motion, rolled down his window and stuck the now-flashing light on top of the car. Instantly the siren came to life and screeched out its warning to oncoming traffic.

My hands let go of the wheel and shielded my ears from the piercing sound.

As soon as cars heard the siren, they immediately made way for our speeding car, freeing up the road and clearing a path. I looked behind me once more to see our follower not far behind.

"What are we gonna do?" I whispered through clenched teeth.

"We're gonna box him in."

"Where?"

"The Marina."

I looked out to my right and saw the great wall of the Marina Village coming into view through the misty sea air.

"But…but the Marina's bound to be heaving."

"Exactly."

As we sped down the coastline the traffic thinned until we were practically the only two cars on the road. The signs for the Village appeared and I held on tighter to whatever I could as we took a hard right onto the road leading to the coastline village.

"You alright? Hang on tight, k?"

Without giving me time to answer, Smith turned the wheel sharply to the right, forcing the car to spin 180 degrees suddenly. The wheels squealed and I closed my eyes and braced myself as the smell of burning rubber assaulted our nostrils and smoke rose up from the ground as the car came to an abrupt halt, facing the direction we had just come.

"What the hell?" I screamed through gritted teeth.

When the car was finally still, I peeled my eyes open to inspect the damage. Looking towards Smith I saw that his face had returned to a state of deep concentration; features set in a hard line and eyes narrowed on the open road ahead of us. He tightened both hands on the steering wheel, gripping it so hard his knuckles had gone white.

"Come on…" he whispered to no one in particular.

I followed his gaze to the road in front of us. We were but fifty metres from where we had turned right to enter the village and any car that turned down it would be suddenly faced with our car that was stopped in the middle of the road and facing them full-on.

It was a matter of seconds before I heard the sound of an approaching car speeding towards the turn-off.

It's him.

My heart leapt up into my throat as the sleek black car appeared from around the bend and squealed around the corner before regaining his speed and racing towards us.

"Get out of the car!" Smith screamed at me, unbuckling his own belt and brandishing his gun from his hip holster as he bolted from the car.

I sprang into action and unbuckled my belt, launching myself from the car in a quick movement and heading for cover on the grassy bank on the side. I turned my head at the sound of the black car speeding up and aiming itself at the cop car.

Smith held his gun at arm's length and without shouting a warning, opened fire on the oncoming car. The sound of the first gunshot was like a firework going off inside my head. Suddenly it was as if the scene had slowed down and everything was moving in slow motion. I watched as the bullet hit the black car's tinted windshield creating a spider crack in the darkened glass, but not shattering it completely. Immediately another sonic explosion pierced my ear drum as another bullet was fired, connecting mere inches from the first. This shot had more of an impact but still didn't slow the driver from pursuing ahead at full speed.

When the black car was but a few metres from where he stood, Smith dove for cover. He flew through the air, arms stretched in front of him preparing for contact with the ground and body twisting while in flight to brace the impact. I watched in shock and amazement as the black car suddenly clipped the nose of the cop car with a deafening smash of scraping metal and shattering glass. Smith landed inches out of the danger zone as the cop car was sent spinning away at an alarming speed, the force of the impact sending broken shards of glass showering through the air. I spun my head around and shielded my own eyes from the collision as the black vehicle continued straight ahead, apparently not slowed by the smash up. The cop car came to a hault in the far lane of the road, its bonnet completely obliterated from the crash and resting at an odd angle away from us.

The sound of another bullet exploding from the gun and sailing through the air forced my eyes open once more and in the direction of Smith. I turned to see him standing up, completely recovered from his fall and firing two, then three more rounds of bullets at the driver. The third shot hit the money spot as the sound of a popping tire filled the air and the black car jutted forward then slumped slightly to the left side. Sparks littered the pavement as the axle of the car connected with the road creating a sound like nails on a chalk board.

I stared wide-eyed in horror as the car continued down the road and disappeared around the corner, apparently not slowed by the flat.

It took me a second to realise that I was holding my breath, completely shocked and dazed by what had just happened. My hands were clutching my face and my throat felt taught and constricted. For a moment I thought I might have gone deaf as the only sound I could make out was a dull ringing from inside my head.

Out of instinct I drew in a deep and shaky breath that made my chest ache as it filled my burning lungs with air. The next few breaths were more ragged, as if I had just come up for air after being submerged in water. My shoulders heaved as I collapsed in convulsions, salty hot tears burning my cheeks as they sailed down my face. I relished the feeling as it made me realise I was still alive despite the fact that I had almost been terrified to death.

I looked up to see Smith running towards me, holstering his pistol as he got closer. He kept one eye on the road where the black car had disappeared.

"Are you alright?" he asked, slight panic starting to show in his tone. He put a hand on both of my shoulders and squeezed, his eyes searching me for any sign that I was hurt or injured. "You okay?"

But I couldn't speak. My whole body shook and shivered violently, and I felt that if I opened my mouth I would begin to hyperventilate.

"Dice? Dice, look at me?" Smith was shaking me now, moving his head to be in my peripheral vision so I would be forced to make eye contact with him. "Dice, can you hear me?"

After a moment, I met his eyes and at once could feel his empathy and concern for me. Back was the kindness and warmth I had glimpsed only a few minutes before and it was this warmth that moved me back to life. I flinched as the feeling came back to my bones and I became once again aware of my body and surroundings.

"Dice? You're alright. You're safe, now."

And with that he quickly removed his suit jacket and draped it around my shoulders. As the material touched my skin, I felt instantly safe, as if the coat was a blanket that could ease all my fears away. The faint smell of his aftershave hit my nose and I breathed in its intoxicating scent, letting it roll over me and relieve all my pains.

"You're okay," he repeated as he moved himself around to my side and sat down beside me, his right arm around my shoulders. My head tilted itself of its own accord to rest on his muscular shoulder.

I don't know how long we stayed like that, gently rocking back and forth, letting the shock of the attack subside and the ringing in my head become quiet. I closed my eyes to block out the world, and just let myself fall. The rocking of our bodies soothed my head. I imagined myself far, far away from here. In another world, in another life. One where I was safe and free from danger. I was happy there. Safe, and not alone. I liked it there. The feeling was so alluring and I let it wrap me in a shield of tender release, closing my eyes shut tighter and praying for my safety.

Chapter Fifteen

Within minutes we were on the move again. Having abandoned the car, Smith and I carried on by foot. Each step I took seemed more surreal than the last. I felt like I was watching this all happening to someone else. Or maybe that was just what I was hoping was happening.

Maybe this is all a dream. Maybe I'm safe at home in my flat...lying in bed. Warm. Safe.

But that was just wishful thinking. No matter how hard I wished for this all to be a giant nightmare, I knew it wasn't. This was for real. This is what my life had become, and the idea that sometime soon everything might actually return to a somewhat state of normalcy, was beginning to seem far off and doubtful.

We were rushing now. Smith had an arm behind me, gently leading me and protecting me, ready to catch me if I were to fall over and crumble from the shock that was inevitably building and bubbling up inside me. Every few yards I would stumble, my own feet betraying me and alluding to how fucking freaked out I was.

I almost died back there.

I shuddered at the thought. Every time I closed my eyes I saw the black car racing towards me. I heard the sickening sound of crunching metal and smashing glass. And every time it made my stomach churn to the point where I thought I would be sick.

Whoever it was in that car wants me dead.

My subconscious was failing me. No matter how hard I willed myself to be strong and to stay focused and get through this, I wanted nothing more than to just lie down and let it all surpass me.

How I longed to be back at work. Dancing on that stage. How I wanted everything to be back to normal. How I desired to be back in control of my life. Calling the shots. Giving men what they wanted. Thrilling strangers for cash. How far away it all seemed now.

My life will never be the same again…

Smith suddenly tugged at my side, probably to pull me back and keep me from falling off the sidewalk. The feeling of his strong hand gripping my torso was like a warm cup of tea; comforting and reassuring.

Please don't leave me.

I could feel his eyes on me just then. How awful I must look. Scared. Shaken. Cold and beaten.

We continued walking away from the marina and towards the city centre. Smith continued looking around us; eyeing each and every stranger who passed us, closely. I could do nothing but stare at the ground, trying desperately not to fall by concentrating on every step I took.

"We're going to be fine, Dice."

His voice was like velvet, caressing my ears and making promises that he couldn't possibly keep.

Are we?

I must have shuddered again because he tightened his grip on my arm, digging his fingers into my bicep. The feeling reminded me that I was still alive and stirred me from the blackout that was threatening to envelop me if I let it.

I forced my eyes up to take in my surroundings and see exactly where we were.

What time was it?

Everything that used to matter to me suddenly felt so unimportant. Work. Food. It all seemed so trivial. The only thing on my mind was plain and utter survival.

Smith must have sensed what I was thinking and answered my un-asked question instinctually.

"I'm taking you back to mine. Your place isn't safe. At least not any-more."

His place?

"It's not far. Once we're there we can figure out what to do next. I'll ring the station and get back up. Right now, I just want you out of the open."

His tone made it all seem so simple. Something between us had shift-ed and there no longer seemed to be a barrier separating us from one another. Although the way he had his arm around me as we walked was confusing. He felt so protective; like I was his possession and he had a responsibility to keep me safe from harm.

He needs to protect me now. He's got to believe that I'm innocent now after that.

As we hurried along the seafront, one thought kept repeating itself inside my head.

Get out of the open air and everything will be fine.

As long as we were moving I felt better. I could imagine nothing worse right now than sitting still and waiting. If we were on the move, then my mind would be at ease.

Without warning, Smith changed direction and led me abruptly into the street, looking in both directions for oncoming traffic and practically picking me up to hurry me across the road. I let out a small gasp at our sudden change of speed and held my breath until we were safely back on the sidewalk again. One hand shot up to my throat and held it protective-ly.

I wasn't sure how much more of this I could take.

Chapter Sixteen

We arrived at Smith's house a few minutes later. I was surprised to see that he lived not too far from my own flat, just up from the seafront in a quaint little building down a hidden road I'd never noticed before.

When he opened his front door, I paused before entering. Almost like I was a vampire and needed to be invited first. He caught wind of my hesitation and stepped over the threshold first, regarding me carefully, a small smile twitching on his lips.

"It's okay. Really. Come in," he invited curtly. When I met his eyes I noticed that the warmth had returned to his cheeks and when he smiled I saw it reach his eyes for the first time. It felt genuine, and with a deep breath I stepped inside his house.

Once inside the doorway, all of a sudden I wasn't sure how to react. Completely out of my comfort zone, I could do nothing but stop and stare at my surroundings. His house wasn't anything like I expected. For some reason I expected it to seem somewhat cold and uninviting; monochrome and unloved. But to my surprise it was anything but.

As soon as I stepped in, I was greeted with a steep, winding staircase with the most beautiful black marble banister. The floors were stripped hard wood and the walls were painted a warm cappuccino colour. Peering around the corner I could see a lounge that seemed to hold an assortment of deep, dark brown comfy sofas and chairs and a heavy looking oak coffee table in the center. The scent of lemon and wood polish was everywhere, and I breathed in the heady smell, filling my lungs with the comforting aroma.

Smith stopped and turned to face me looking somewhat worried by my deer-in-headlights stance.

"You okay?" he asked carefully, taking a step closer to me.

His question caught me off guard, and I quickly looked to him then away again, casting my gaze down to my feet, embarrassed.

"Hey, don't worry. You're safe. Please, come in. You must be freezing."

He held out a hand to motion me further into his home. "What can I get you? Tea?"

I nodded, my eyes still studying my filthy stained feet. I allowed myself to follow him into his lounge and slowly lowered my bottom onto one of the chocolate brown sofas. Instantly, I sunk into the luscious material and didn't fight the feeling it gave of being wrapped in a cozy embrace. I sat there motionless for a few moments as Smith disappeared into the kitchen, busying himself with the hot drinks.

"My phone was fried back there. I'm gonna ring the station and get someone over here. They must be wondering where the hell we are," he shouted from out of sight. I suddenly thought about my own phone. Patting my pockets to no avail, I sighed as I realised that I too probably lost it back there.

This feels so strange. All that has happened. I owe my life to this man.

The thought of how close I came to being a shit stain on the street just earlier, made me shiver slightly.

I don't even know his first name.

Forcing the thought out of my head and willing my body to move, I craned my neck to inspect the rest of the room. The entire place reminded me of a cosy little cabin; the type you'd find in the woods, buried deep amongst the tall green trees. The earth tone décor reminded me of the countryside; all that was missing was a log fireplace and mounted antlers on the wall. The vegan in me shuddered at the thought.

Scanning the room further, I noticed that many of the walls were adorned with old photographs; some black and white portrait style pictures, others displaying memories from past holidays and events.

Curiosity got the best of me and before I knew it, I found myself standing and walking over to inspect the photos more closely.

Squinting in the dim light of the lounge, I gazed upon them; Smith holidaying in Paris, then again in Italy. Standing outside the Roman Coliseum and then lounging on the beach in some tropical locale. My eyes lingered over a particular photo of Smith, lying topless in the sand. I felt a twinge inside my underwear as I couldn't help but admire his sculpted physique.

Even better than I imagined.

I browsed further over some black and white portraits of a couple who were probably his parents. A smile appeared on my lips as I took in one of Smith grinning madly with two very straight looking young lads, arms around each other in front of a very large looking estate.

Brothers?

Next to that particular photo, I stumbled upon another of Smith with *another* very handsome, but not-so-straight looking man. It was a bit blurry, as if it had been taken whilst moving somehow. I was just bending over for a closer look when I felt a hand on my shoulder.

I spun around quickly, completely caught off guard.

"Jesus- You scared me…" I breathed, a hand shooting up to my chest.

Smith was standing a few feet in front of me, a steaming hot mug in one of his hands. His eyes looked forlorn, staring at nothing in particular, almost dazed like he was lost in his own thoughts.

"What are you looking at?"

His tone confused me. It wasn't quite angry, more…accusatory.

"Oh…uh…I'm sorry, I…" I stuttered, not quite sure how to respond. I searched in vain for words that wouldn't give away the slight guilt I was feeling at prying. "I was just looking at your pictures. Who's this in the…"

"It's not important, here, sit…" And with that he took my arm in his hand and pulled me over to the sofa. I could tell that he meant business, and the hard look in his eyes actually made me feel a little bit uncomfortable. I did as he said and left the wall of photos and took a seat cautiously on a caramel coloured sofa.

"Detective…I'm…"

"Please, you don't have to call me that anymore." His tone instantly lifted.

"What shall I call you then?" I asked light-heartedly.

"Call me Ace…"

My eyes widened at what he had just said.

"Ace…" I repeated back at him, momentarily stunned by his admission. He tilted his head to one side inquisitively. "Your name…You're…You're called *Ace Smith*?"

He blinked a few times at me, a puzzled look spread across his beautiful features.

"Never mind." I retorted, embarrassed. "Ace…"

He continued to stare at me hard for another few moments, his eyes apparently lost in my features. He grazed over my whole face, taking in every detail and making me feel completely self-conscious in a way that I never had before.

"Are you cold?"

I must have shuddered without realising and Ace reached out behind his sofa and pulled out a blanket.

"Yeah, sorta…"

"You've been through a lot today. Here, wrap this around you," he strained as he flapped the oatmeal coloured blanket around my shoulders, trying not to get too close.

I looked him square in the eye, silently questioning his gesture. He caught sight of my glower and froze in an instant.

"What? Did I…" He paused. "Did I…Are you alright?"

It was my turn to consider my response. I studied his face; the smooth skin around his eyes and expertly crafted cheek bones, his tanned colour and light dusting of stubble. It was as if he was two people; one hard and firm, the other passionate and caring. At that moment, I swear I could almost see the two at odds with one another, flashing across his face and vying for control. He was struggling, I could tell. The harsh exterior was melting away the longer he spent in my company, and the other side, the one who was obviously attracted to me, was beginning to materialise before my very eyes. I couldn't help but snicker slightly as I took in the fact that it felt like at that moment. I was meeting the real Ace Smith for the first time.

"Why are you being so nice to me?" I asked, my mouth running away with itself. "I mean earlier today you wouldn't have given a shit if I was even alive…and now…"

Ace stiffened in his seat on the sofa, his expression immediately hardening. He looked away swiftly and knotted his hands in his lap.

I jerked at his sudden withdrawal. "Am I wrong?"

He looked back up at me and met my stare. He opened his mouth to respond, but reconsidered, a war playing out behind his eyes.

"I'm sorry. You're right."

How was I right, though?

"Mister Val-"

"Stop…" I interrupted, cutting him off before he could finish. "It's Dice. You saved my fucking life, I think you can call me by my first name."

"I'm sorry. I'm sorry about all of this."

He looked like he was going to continue and I decided to let it play out before sticking my foot in my mouth once again.

"When I met you…a few days ago at the crime scene, I…I was sure…*I mean*…that you were…"

"And now?" I urged.

"And now...I think I was...I mean, I know I was...wrong..."

From deep inside, my heart began to beat again for what seemed like the first time in a week. Warm relief surged from it, heating my veins and bringing with it a rush of euphoria. Hearing him say those last words was like an end to my prison sentence.

He's on my side...

I blinked hard and looked away, afraid of letting my intense relief bubble over too much.

"Dice, whoever was in that car...he...she...they wanted you..."

Seeing him afraid of finishing his sentence, brought me back down to earth. My balloon popped and reality came crashing down upon my shoulders, my frown returning as my head finished his thought.

...Dead.

I could feel my expression sink slowly as my feet hit the ground. Whether Ace Smith was on my side or not, I wasn't out of the woods yet.

I still have to survive if I'm going to prove my innocence.

I assailed my eyes from his view, turning slightly away from him so as not to show him the tears that were bubbling up from behind my eyeballs.

"Hey, hey, listen. You're safe now."

He sounded so self-assured that I turned back to face him, desperately seeking to be filled with his same sense of reassurance. When I took in his face my heart immediately began to ache. I was once again filled with that all-to familiar sense of longing and desire to be protected. As I studied his appearance, I all at once noticed the deep groove between his eyebrows; almost like it had been carved into his beautiful skin from years of frowning compassionately for others. It was like seeing into his soul; his tough persona was simply a rough exterior, one that masked the sensitive soul that resided inside his heart. One glimpse of his pain-filled eyes and I couldn't help but mirror it back to him.

I held his gaze for a moment too long. I felt I must look horrid; tired, drawn and colourless. I wanted to look away, turn away and hide from this beautiful man that was sitting inches away from me. I was normally so confident, and at that very moment I felt like a shell of the man I once was; beaten and defeated. These last few days had certainly been a battle and it was beginning to look like I may never see the other side, and if I did I wasn't sure I'd ever fully recover.

But as my eyes continued to drink in his appearance, I realised that the look he was giving me wasn't one of repulsion at all. Rather one of longing as well. Being in his house, surrounded by his things. *Does he feel this too? Oh, God, I really want him. Now more than ever.*

I couldn't help my eyes from focusing on his full, red mouth. It was parted slightly and I could see his tongue hovering at the opening. It slipped out of his mouth for a moment to slick the surface of his plump lips before disappearing back inside.

I took a deep breath as I felt the muscles in my stomach clench at the sight.

I want to kiss his mouth so badly.

My vision started to blur slightly, and I could feel my eyes begin to close at their own accord. My lips opened hungrily as if I was about to bite down on something delicious. I moved my eyes from his mouth to his eyes quickly. They too were cloudy and warm looking, the colour a smoldering swirl of flaming chocolate.

Kiss me.

I knew it wasn't right, especially not now. If ever there was a more inappropriate time to be having such lustful thoughts towards the man who, only 24 hours earlier, wanted nothing more than to see me behind bars, this would have been it. But I couldn't help it. Blame it on the adrenaline that was pumping through my body, my only driving force at all these past few days, but every inch of me wanted nothing more than to feel his strong arms around me, coccooning me in a blanket of safety and assurance. I yearned with every pore of my skin to be protected. Through closeness I was sure I'd find what I was looking for and no longer be on the verge of panic. If I could only know what it felt like to have his skin caressing my own, then I was sure I would be alright and that things would return to normal. Human contact was the only thing that felt like it would cure me. I wanted him so badly at that moment that my skin felt almost electric.

My eyes were closed now, but my head stood paralysed in its place. My heart urged it to move in for a kiss, but my brain kept it still. I felt like the two were battling inside of me, each commanding the other to obey and almost tearing me in two.

Kiss him.

My thoughts were shouting out to him to make the move, for then I wouldn't have to be held responsible for what was going to happen next.

Kiss me.

Each second dragged by slower than the last. I wasn't sure how long I was sat there waiting for my sweet release, but I was beginning to feel like my half-assed attempt was in vain.

I opened my eyes slightly to look in his general direction, and what I saw was so far from what I wanted. Ace's head was turned away, and he was staring down at his hands that had become clasped together tightly in his lap. He was concentrating on them so hard that it looked like it was the only thing controlling them from reaching out to me. One wrong move and they might act of their own accord and reach out to touch and caress my face. His expression looked pained like he was searching for the correct words to describe how he was feeling.

Immediately I felt my cheeks grow hot when I realised that he wasn't anywhere near to returning the feelings that I'm sure were written across my face. Shame and embarrassment began to fill me up like a flood of dirty water. I quickly looked away, sure that I was about to crumble into a million little pieces.

Oh please ground, swallow me up.

Ace was the first to speak.

"I'm sorry. I can't."

It wasn't much, but it was enough. I lifted my eyes to take in his face. He looked deeply conflicted; perhaps he too was battling between his head and his heart. There was no denying the attraction between us. Add to that the immense intensity of the situation we had both just endured, and it was like a recipe for devastation.

I had to get out of there.

I picked myself up quickly from the sofa, my embarrassment slowly being replaced with an intense fury.

"Dice, wait!" he called as I turned on my heel and headed swiftly towards his front door. "*Dice,* stop!"

"I'm sorry. I can't be here," I muttered with my back to him. I could feel the tears threaten to well up from the pit of my stomach.

"Dice, stop for a second."

I reached the door and turned the knob and pulled. Ace was right behind me and put up a hand to shut the door abruptly before I was able to get it half-way open. It slammed loudly back into place, causing me to jump at his strength.

"It's not safe," he said matter-of-factly.

I stopped in my tracks and waited, my back still to him. I didn't try to open the door again. Ace was standing so close to me I could feel his breath as it tickled the back of my neck. There was something so seductive and dominating in the way he stopped me from leaving.

"Stay."

It was only a little word, but it held so much more. I couldn't turn around. I wasn't used to rejection and I wasn't sure how my body might react and betray me if I were to look him in the eye.

This wasn't me. I was so much stronger than this. I was so much more able to brush things off and rise above. But this was too much. This whole nightmare was too much to take in.

When I finally turned around to look at him, I wasn't sure what to expect. I sheepishly held my gaze down at my feet in an attempt to retain a small shred of dignity, but I could feel his emotions even before I looked up at his face. His genuine longing for me was practically resonating from his pours. When I finally laid eyes on his pained expression, his inner turmoil was so apparent that it grabbed me by the balls and hooked me in until the only thing I could think was how much I wanted to relieve this sadness and make him smile once again.

Our eyes locked in on each other, the heat between our bodies mixing together like a fine mist, heavy with pheromones. I studied the rise and fall of his beautifully broad chest with every breath he drew in. My eyes traced down the side of his body until they fell upon his left hand which was clenched tightly into a fist at his side, the muscles in his forearm flexing and releasing. Without thinking of the consequences, I reached up to touch the arm of his that was holding the door closed behind me. The feeling of our skin touching was almost electric as it sent the hairs on both of our arms standing on end. I sucked in a shallow breath between clenched teeth as I relished the exquisite sensation of his skin against my own. My eyes took in his reaction and I was immediately intrigued by how his whole body seemed to stiffen as my fingertips lightly grazed and tickled the dark hairs on his strong forearm. I drank in the sight of him before me, my eyes following the line up his arm and continuing up his thick neck, and across his strong jaw line which was still stubbled with a thickening layer of equally dark short hairs.

Gently, he let his eyes close as my fingers lightly danced their way up his arm, past the rolled up cuff of his shirt and around the deep grooves of his tricep muscles. I could feel myself begin to stiffen in my trousers, the delight of this slow tease working its magic on my insides.

I knew I shouldn't pursue, but I wasn't thinking straight anymore. It was as if my body had granted my head its recourse and I had officially given up caring about what was right or wrong anymore. I wasn't made up of rational thought anymore, but pure and utter instinct; carnal and almost feral in my desires. After all the shit of the past few days, I felt consumed with sensualism and a need for closeness.

As I looked up at Ace's constricted face, I suddenly felt the need to protect him; reassure him that I was here, that I would help keep *him* safe. I owed this man my life. If it wasn't for him I don't know what might have happened to me. I had to repay him in some way. I wanted to show him my gratitude in the best way I knew how, so badly it was beginning to hurt. The tenseness of his stance told me he felt the same but that he was terrified of letting go and losing control. I could practically see the debate between his gut and his cock playing out on his face.

My hand moved slowly away from his bicep and around the collar of his shirt, wrapping my fingers around the back of his neck and gently tugging at the hairs at the nape. His head tilted to one side heavily and his lips parted to let his tongue out to moisten them quickly. I became distracted momentarily by the sight of his wet tongue and suddenly was hit with the feeling of what it would be like to suck on it. I practically jolted at the thought, desire making me twinge beneath my clothes.

Ace shook his head gently from side to side, silently mouthing 'no' even though his body made no attempt to pull away. I took a step closer to him, closing the gap between our bodies to the point that if he were to flinch he would feel the hardness of my dick against his leg.

I tried to take in the reality of this situation, desperately trying to see through the fog that had materialised before my eyes. The tables had turned so quickly it felt like my head had been constantly spinning the last few days. Never in a million years would I have seen myself lusting after a cop who wanted me behind bars a mere few days ago. I wanted him so badly at that point that I felt if I didn't find release soon I might explode.

My head began to move in towards his, my eyes set firmly on his plump red lips. I stopped breathing, anticipation of his mouth on my own taking complete control of my bodily functions. As I closed in every inch between us, the smell of his body intoxicated me further until I felt like I was swimming rather than standing on my own two feet.

As our lips were about to touch, the alarming sound of a phone ringing exploded into the air causing us both to immediately jump practically out of our skin and instantly recoil as if we had both been burned by a searing hot poker. His eyes shot open, a look of regret smearing his perfect features as he sprang into action and turned his attention to the offending ringing.

I felt like I had been punched in the stomach, our connection broken as quickly as it had been formed. The sight of him turning his back on me and releasing me from the back of the door was like a kick to the balls, to the point where I almost doubled over in pain.

Fuck me.

I drew in a sharp breath and tried to lift my head which felt like it was now dragging across the floor. The momentary comfort that had filled me just then, shattered around my feet into a thousand pieces. I hugged myself to stifle the feeling of emptiness that was slowly taking its place. Watching him stride purposefully over to the kitchen table where his phone sat was making me irrationally angry. I felt angry that he had deserted me like that, and perhaps even more angry that I seemed to have no control over him in the slightest. As he picked the phone up and pressed it to his ear I realised that the real reason I was suddenly filled with such rage, was because he was completely and utterly unaffected by my 'charms'. I wasn't used to rejection like this; in the club I was Top Dog; King of the Hill; when I was in the mood, no man could resist Dice Valentine…And here, in his house, our adrenaline pumping after the attack…And nothing. Watching him, with his back to me as he picked up the telephone and held it tightly to his ear only added to the feeling of resentment in my stomach.

"Hello?" Ace asked into the phone. There was a silence that followed which gave me cue to leave when I had the chance. I turned once more towards the door and was about to turn the handle when I heard Ace put the phone on speaker. Immediately a gruff sounding voice filled the room, making me jump and instinctually spin around.

"You two look deep in thought. Don't even think about tracing this call, Detective," the caller threatened on the other end of the line.

He can see us.

I looked up at Ace, meeting his stare with wide eyes. I let go of the door and dashed over to where he stood, looking at the phone in astonishment as if it had just grown antlers. The hairs on the back of my neck stood on end as the sick realisation that we were being watched crept up on me.

"Who is this?" Ace asked firmly, his brow furrowed.

"You can't run much further. That was a lucky escape."

Ace looked to me expectantly as if to ask if I recognised the voice. I shook my head as black fear hit me like a ton of bricks and shook me from the inside out. I wrapped my arms even tighter around me to stop myself from trembling.

"Who the fuck is this?" Ace spat.

"I'm close, Detective Smith. Next time I won't miss."

And with that, the line went dead. I put my hands to my face and crumbled to the floor until I was crouched down, my bottom grazing the hard wood beneath my feet. I wrapped my arms around my legs until I was in a squatting fetal position, and rocked slightly back and forth.

Ace stayed standing for a few more moments, the two of us shocked into silence.

That voice. Did I recognise it?

Nothing made sense anymore. Who would want to hurt me?

Jesus, I just want to wake up. I wish this was all just a bad dream.

"That's it, we're out of here."

Ace bent down and with a firm movement, grabbed me by the arm and yanked me to standing. I let out a small yelp at his force and quickly found my footing.

"Jesus, Ace! What the fuck is going on?"

"We just need to get out of here; it isn't safe here either. Come on."

Before I knew it we were moving, out the door and into the street. The air had cooled considerably since we were last outside and I shivered as my skin broke out instantly in goose bumps. Ace's grip on my arm was stronger now than before; less protective and more aggressive. I stole a glance at his face which looked like it was carved out of marble. His lips were set in a thin line and his jaw muscles were clenched tightly. His eyes were narrowed and set on the street ahead of us, as they frantically searched our surroundings once we stepped foot outside.

My head was swimming with a million questions and my ears were ringing due to the heavy buzzing happening between them. As we sped down the side-street that had led us away from the seafront and towards Ace's house, the wind picked up, whipping the hair around my head and lashing out violently at my face. I wiped a tear from my eye with my free hand as I was dragged along like a rag doll down the street and out into the throngs of early evening people traffic. The last thing I wanted was to be out in public, and as we entered into the crowd of people who were parading up and down the busy street, Ace pulled me in closer to him, his fingers digging into the bare skin on my arm causing me to wince with pain.

"Wh-where are we going?"

My question became quickly lost in the wind as my eyes danced over the people in the faceless crowd. Everyone looked so caught up in their own lives, talking and laughing loudly, not a care in the world. I was sure that we stuck out amongst them; I was sure they could all detect the fear and paranoia that was contorting my features. But as we turned into them, their voices continued, apparently oblivious to the terror that I was sure was emanating from my pores.

"Ace? Please," I pleaded, my voice a strangled whisper muffled by the sounds of the busy street. The feeling that somewhere nearby there was someone watching us who wanted me dead, got progressively stronger with each hurried step I took. My head whipped from side to side, lingering on the faces of the passerbys, wondering if they were the one.

I don't know what I was looking for. I kept scanning everyone who we passed for some sign of evil or menace. But after a few blocks they all began to look the same. Men, women, children even. The more my gaze flitted from one face to the next, the more faceless they became until everyone I saw bore the same blank expression. I shook my head hard in an attempt to clear it and regain my focus. This wasn't the time to faze out; from somewhere deep inside I had the feeling that this whole nightmare was coming to a head. I felt it in my bones.

Then it was as if my vision freeze-framed on one face in particular. A man. Standing against the partition on the side of the walk. His arms were folded and he was staring straight at me, eyes blazing and with the most wicked smile across his lips. It was all I could do not to scream out in alarm. I locked eyes with him, his expression so creepy it was like something out of a horror film. I opened my mouth to speak and get Ace's attention when I collided full-on with an on-coming stranger. Our shoulders connected so sharply that it knocked the breath out of me momentarily. I reached up to touch my shoulder and spun my head around to see who it was that I hit, and immediately regretted it. The person had stopped dead in their tracks and turned to face me. The look on his face practically made my heart stop. He was staring straight at me;

arms folded, eyes eerily wide and mouth twisted up into that same freakishly wicked smile as the man before.

"What the f-" I stammered, "Jesus, Ace!"

I yanked my arm hard out of Ace's grip so that he would slow down and look at me. I turned my head for a second to face Ace, but when he turned around his firm look of concentration had been replaced with something else. Gone were his chiseled features and strong set jaw; on his face was the same look as the other two men; eyes fiery wide and smiling in that same demented way. I let out a shriek so loud that it didn't reach my ears. When I spun around again ready to run away, it was as if everything was freeze-framed. Everyone on the street, including people in their cars, had stopped and were now silently staring at me...Staring at me in that same way. Staring at me as if they were all in on it. Watching me. Waiting for me. Their arms folded...All smiling.

Then everything went black.

Chapter Seventeen

"Dice? Dice, can you hear me?"

My eyelids felt heavy. Heavier than I could ever remember them feeling before. Almost as if there were little weights attached to my eyelashes, keeping them firmly shut. It took all my effort to even get them to flutter.

When they did separate slightly, the probing light from something above my head was so blinding, I flinched at the brightness.

"Dice…Jesus…You're alright."

Was that a question?

I knew right away whose voice it was I was hearing, even before I fully opened my eyes. I'd grown accustomed to the sound over the past few days. What started out as something fearful and threatening, had developed and morphed into something quite the opposite. Instead it had become, he had become, my reassurance, my safety.

The sound of his soothing, velvety voice made me desperately want to open my eyes so that I could be greeted with the sight of his beautiful face to accompany his sounds.

"Don't try to move too much, Dice."

There it was again; that beautiful sound. So calming and full of promise. I stopped fighting for a moment, and swam around in the sound of his words, letting them wrap me up in their safety blanket. The feeling of knowing he was so close to me was intoxicating and filled me with a sense of warmth like a flannel blanket.

I was reminded of the feeling of being away on holiday; his voice was like the gentle lapping of the waves on the shore, relaxing me with every ripple that stemmed from the surface of the water. The light from above my head was like the sun, warming me and paralysing my movements until I gave in to their desire.

Where am I?

That one thought was enough to stir my imagination and tear me from my dream world.

Am I alright?

My attention was immediately drawn to my body. I could practically hear the synapses going off in my brain as I tried in vain to judge the state of my body.

Can I feel my legs? I feel so heavy. Oh, God. What happened to me?

Ace must have been able to tell what I was feeling by the look of strain on my face.

"Shhhh, it's okay," he cooed from somewhere on my left, "Don't try to move too much. You came down pretty hard there."

Pretty hard.

I stopped struggling for a moment and retreated back into my head to try and remember what had happened.

"Do you remember what happened?"

He asked, as if reading my thoughts once more. I struggled to think of the last thing I remembered.

We were walking…Running, actually…Away from…From where?

My thoughts were interrupted by the sound of approaching foot-steps. Their stride was purposeful, official somehow. I decided they belonged to a woman, judging by the sound the heel made as they crossed the floor towards where I lay.

"Doctor, hello," Ace said quickly. His tone of voice changed slightly as the stranger approached.

Doctor? Oh fuck, I'm in a hospital.

"Hello, detective," came a lady's voice, "How's the patient?"

Her voice was soft and feminine, and with the smallest touch of a Northern accent to it. Ace cleared his throat quickly before answering.

"Good, I think. He looks like he's trying to wake up."

"Oh, good!" She sounded genuinely pleased by the news. "Let's just check a few things here."

It was a moment before I could feel warm fingers pressing themselves against my neck. Instinct told me to flinch at the feeling, but the feeling of tiredness that had swept through my body prevented it.

There was silence for a minute or two as Ace waited for the diagnosis. Even I felt like I was holding my breath, eagerly anticipating the doctor's response.

"Everything seems good here," she responded cheerily, "I think we can rule out a possibly concussion, but he's going to have a nasty bump for a few days."

Concussion? Bump?

None of this made any sense. Then it was as if someone had flicked a switch inside my head, illuminating what was until now a very dark, shadowy room.

I passed out. Right there in the street. *But…why?*

"Breathing rate is normal," she stated, her tone dosed in concentration.

"Can we wake him?" Ace asked.

There was a pause, then a small sigh from the doctor.

"Please, doctor. This is important. His life could be…"

Could be, what?

"Doctor, I'm afraid our position here at the hospital could be compromised. I need to get him out of here as soon as possible. Please."

Ace's tone had once again shifted. Even with my eyes closed I could imagine the look on his face. It was as if he were two completely different people.

The officer and the gentleman.

One was full of compassion and sincerity, the other wasn't one you'd want to ever fuck with. The more I considered it as I lay there helpless on the bed, I wasn't sure which one turned me on more…

Another sigh from the doctor brought me back into the room.

"Please." Ace repeated.

"Let me see what I can do."

The doctor took a few steps out the door, the sound of her footsteps growing quieter as she disappeared down the hall.

This is so frustrating. Why can't I open my eyes?

Confusion coursed through my veins and the serenity I had felt mere moments before was now replaced with restlessness.

Ace shifted from where he sat and leaned in closer to where I layed. He leaned in closely and exhaled sharply so that I could feel his warm breath against my cheek. I inhaled as deeply as I could, breathing in his luscious scent until I could practically taste it.

"Come on, Dice. Wake up. I...I need you," he breathed. His voice was a whisper that gave me a thrill somewhere deep inside. Then I felt his hand gently brush the hair away from my forehead.

I need you, too.

His touch was so soft and sensual. His fingers traced the contours of my cheek and circled my chin before letting go, leaving the skin fiery and tingling in their wake.

Suddenly, the desperation to wake up was too much for me. I wanted to shout out and tell him how much I was beginning to need him too. How much I wanted him to hold me and touch me and reassure me that everything was going to be alright. Tell me that we were going to get through this and that he would keep me safe from whoever was trying to hurt me.

The echoing sound of footsteps announced the Doctor's return before I even heard her voice. I felt Ace stiffen and straighten up from where he sat.

"Doctor."

"This should do the trick."

There was the sound of something being unscrewed. I felt her extend her arm and then my senses were accosted by the smell of something incredibly strong and intrusive, like ammonia.

Suddenly I felt like I had just resurfaced from having been underwater and instinctually drew in an incredibly sharp breath that burned as it travelled down my throat and into my lungs. The smell was like an electric shock to my system that catapulted me instantly awake.

My eyes shot open as the feeling returned to my arms and legs. It was like an adrenaline shot to my heart which began to beat furiously against the confines of my chest.

As my vision blurred then focused, the beautiful sight of Ace's face came into view. His features were twisted with worry and concern mixed with shock and alarm. My eyes flitted from him to the female doctor in front of me with the extended arm. As I shot up in bed, her arm recoiled quickly. I looked in her hand and made out that she was holding a small brown jar tightly in her palm.

There was silence again as I took in another long breath, the feeling instantly relaxing me and calming my heart before it spiraled out of control again.

"Bloody hell," Ace blurted out, his hands clutching his own chest in a knee-jerk reaction.

"Smelling salts. Works every time," the doctor said, unphased by my sudden alertness. "I'll give you two a few minutes." She shot Ace a look of contempt before turning again and moving towards the open door. She shut it with a gentle click and took one more look in my direction through the small double-paned window before moving out of sight.

I turned my stare from the hospital room door to Ace, whose hands were held out in front of him as if he were about to pounce and tackle me.

"You okay?" he asked softly.

I stared into his eyes and could almost see myself reflected back in his pupils. I looked away briefly, mainly to self-assess my situation. I felt alright. Alert. Sore. I lifted a hand carefully to my right temple and let it hover an inch or so away from the skin.

"Careful there," Ace warned, "that's where you went down…"

"I…I fainted."

Ace nodded his head slightly, "You could say that. Gave me quite a scare. Thought you had been shot or something, I was…" He cut himself off abruptly.

His sentence caught my attention and I looked from the room to him quickly.

"You were what?" I urged him to go on, desperate for him to confirm what I was sure he was feeling towards me.

He opened his mouth to speak, but hesitated, biting his lower lip in a way that I had never noticed before. My eyes widened at his rebuttal, and pleaded for him to continue. But as quickly as the moment had appeared in his eyes, it dissolved completely.

"What do you last remember, Dice? Did you see something? Hear something?"

He was back in investigator mode.

This is the Ace I like the least.

I was sure my eyes were filled with pain and disappointment, but with a sigh I turned my attention to the matter at hand. Looking down at my hands which were still scabbed from *that night*, I racked my brain to try and remember what happened before I went down.

"God…I dunno…I…"

I stammered. I wasn't sure how much I wanted to tell him as I recalled what I saw; the looks on the people's faces, how scared I was. If I told him that I was seeing things, he'd think I was a fuckin' nutter. That was the last thing I needed. I'd only just convinced him that I was innocent; that would be a step in the total wrong direction. The more I thought about it, the closer I moved to breaking out in tears. My brow furrowed as I fought them back, sucking them back inside.

Ace could sense my inner struggle and took his cue to step in and reassure me as a lone tear bubbled over and slid down my cheek.

"Hey, hey, listen, don't worry. I'm here, ok?" He bent over to me to catch my eye. When I looked up at him, he flashed me a crooked smile that I had never seen him do before. The look on his face was infectious and made me let out a small giggle of a response. "I've got a plan; I've notified the station of our whereabouts. They want me to bring you into protective custody."

My smile faded and I studied his face. "Custody?"

"It's the best thing right now."

"But…I…I don't…"

I don't want to leave you.

I had to stop myself before I came off as a total twat.

"Listen…" he said, locking his deep brown eyes with mine, "I'm not going to leave you."

After a few moments of staring at him, I felt more sure. I gave him a small nod and then turned my focus to the hospital gown that I was adorning. He nodded back, understanding completely.

"Right, let's get you out of here."

Chapter 18

Twenty minutes later we were back on the street. As we walked out into the brisk morning air, it dawned on me that a whole night had passed. I looked up at the sky as if for reassurance. The sun was strong in the sky, announcing the time as early afternoon. There were a few scattered clouds around, but apart from that the blue hue of the sky reflected back at me making me squint in reaction. Looking about at my surroundings, I took in that we were at the Royal Sussex Hospital. People busied themselves through the large double doors from where we had emerged, their eyes covered with sunglasses, shielding themselves from the late summer weather. Ace took notice of my sudden confusion and disorientation and taking my hand in his, led me across the street to a line of awaiting taxis.

As we crossed, I noticed that colours seemed to be a little bit brighter than before, as if I was seeing everything through a technicolour lense.

Probably a side-effect of hitting your head again, mate.

Ace nodded in the direction of a waiting taxi and quickly opened the door for me to climb in. I lowered myself carefully into the car, and noticed for the first time how sore I was. My head ached like hell and it felt like the welt on my temple had its own pulse. As my back rounded I realised that the muscles all the way up my right side were angry and screaming out in pain.

Wincing, I clipped the belt around my chest tightly, and as the car sped off I lost myself in the scene unfolding outside my window. I cupped my entire forehead carefully, as if the touch of my fingertips would provide some ease to the throbbing pain.

I was so disappointed in my body. I was a dancer. Muscle aches and pain were part and partial to my eyeryday life. I was so out of practise and inwardly chastised myself for being such a pussy.

"145 Kings Road," Ace instructed the driver.

Recognition of my flat address caused me to whip my head around quickly in Ace's general direction. He looked at me and tilted his head to one side inquisitively.

"Why are we…" I asked, not needing to even finish my sentence.

"Just to get a few things of yours, then to the station."

"But, what about…"

It was if I could only speak in three or four word sentences before weariness took over and forced me into silence.

"Don't worry. I'm here."

With that he took my hand in his and squeezed gently, not taking his eyes off of mine. With my hand still safely cradled in his own, I returned my stare out the window and tried to focus on the passing seaside beyond the road…

***

I must have dozed off because moments later as the car slowed to a stop, we found ourselves parked outside my building. Ace and the driver exchanged pleasantries as he handed him a note, muttering something about keeping the change.

I kept my eyes locked on my building, eyeing the spot where I envisaged my lounge window to be. I expected to feel a sense of relief upon seeing my flat for the first time in a while, but instead found myself overwhelmed by a sense of dread. Before I knew it, Ace was at my side with an arm around me protectively.

"You okay?" he asked, clocking the concern across my face.

I looked to him and nodded, biting my bottom lip so as not to give away how scared I really was. He nodded back at me and moved me towards the front door to the building.

"Let's get you inside."

As we made our way up the front steps and through the foyer, Ace's phone set off an alert making me jump.

Fishing it out of his pocket, he swiped his finger across the screen to unlock it and silently read the message to himself. He released me from his grip long enough to type something into his mobile quickly before tucking it back into his jacket pocket.

"I thought your phone was fried," I mentioned to him.

"This is a spare," he responded, "Back-up is on its way. I told them to be here in an hour. Should be long enough to pack up some of your stuff."

I nodded again. Words seemed to be failing me lately as I found myself struggling to put a concrete sentence together. My attention was entirely focused on putting one foot in front of the other.

As we reached the lift, I realised that everything in the building seemed, off somehow. I looked up at the ceiling and studied the wallpaper around me as if seeing it for the first time. The ding of the door opening provided a welcome distraction from my wayward thoughts. Ace's hand on my lower back ushered me inside.

Once inside my flat, flashes of the last time I'd been there ran through my mind. It was with Ace. I had woken up inside my flat to the sound of my mobile ringing. Just after I was with Joe. After I was followed.

Such unhappy memories.

All I seemed to have lately were unhappy memories. I stood in the doorway of the place that I called home and shut my eyes as tight as I could. Ace passed me and went straight for what he presumed was my bedroom. I just stood there for a moment, taking it all in and trying to remember a happier time.

Dale. Think of Dale. Tony. Where are they?

My best friends. Dale. How I missed him. People always say that you don't realise how much someone means to you until they're gone.

That couldn't be more true right now.

The thought of him made my insides ache. Even worse was the thought that something may have happened to him. How I wanted nothing more than to have him here by my side, a familiar face to provide comfort through this storm. I squeezed my eyes together tighter and thought about us dancing together at the club that last night. There had been such electricity between us that night. Something I had not felt before. And then he was gone.

The pain was almost too much and I found myself doubling over slightly, grabbing at the wall for support. I opened my eyes for a moment to catch sight of Ace running over to me.

"Hey, hey, hey," he said quickly putting out both arms to catch me as I crumbled into him. "Dice, come on stick with me."

His shoulder caught my head and before I knew it I was crying into his shoulder. Heavy, silent tears poured from my eyes, dampening his jacket. My shoulders heaved as all the emotions and fears that had been plaguing me for the past few days erupted from my eyes.

Get ahold of yourself.

Ace put his arms around me in a half-supportive, half-hug and rested one hand on the back of my neck.

"It's alright, Dice. I'm here."

The feeling of his cool hand against my skin had an instant icy, calming effect. We remained like that for what seemed like eternity. Completely still, unmoving. It felt so strange, yet so familiar; like strangers who had known each other for years. With each passing minute that we remained entwined together I could sense my fears dissipating. With each tear that fell from my eyes, with it flushed more of my paranoia and confusion. I was beginning to feel empty and hollow, like I had nothing more to give of myself. My body relaxed and sagged in his arms.

As I began to go slack, Ace shrugged the shoulder that was maintaining my head so that I was forced to look up into his eyes and support my own weight. When I saw his pained expression, it only served to crush me more. Too often lately I was witness to this look; this emphatic look of compassion, that seeing it now only broke my heart further.

I pulled back further to better take in his appearance as he stood there before me, arms wrapped supportively around me. How close, yet how distant I felt towards this man. As I studied each and every pour and little line on his face it dawned on me just how different we both were; born into two very different worlds. Our daily lives were at odds with each other, serving different purposes and each with different goals. Yet as I continued to stare at him, unmoving and utterly vulnerable, none of these differences scared me away. In fact, they drew me in. My heart was desperate to close the distance between us, but was at the same time full of hesitation. Perhaps I was waiting for a sign from him, something, anything that would assure me that he was feeling this too. But beyond his heartfelt expression, his body gave nothing away. He was trembling slightly as if being so near to me was pushing him towards the brink of implosion. Yet he didn't pull away, and neither did I. God knows how much time had passed since we embraced, both of us relishing the moment; our bodies introducing themselves to each other.

Then something shifted between us. It was as if the temperature in the room had risen abruptly causing us both to flush and tremble even more. I was like a pot of boiling water about to bubble over. I had to do something before this desire peaked and I lost complete control.

Ace and I locked eyes for a second, and the feeling was like fireworks.

He's feeling it too. Do it, Dice.

I blinked once or twice and he mirrored my actions. It was like a silent signal, imperceptible to anyone else. One that spoke consent without saying a word. And with that I fell.

I leaned my head in and our mouths connected. As our lips touched it was like being kissed for the first time. At first we were a bit clumsy, lips everywhere, kissing and swallowing hungrily as if we couldn't get enough of the feeling. Then slowly we found our rhythm, our tongues connecting, gently lapping against each other, exchanging saliva and welcoming the exchange into our bodies.

I couldn't believe this was happening. Something, somewhere deep inside me was screaming out that this was wrong and that I should stop, but the blood pulsing through my cock had a stronger effect on my judgment. My head was swimming in this feeling of finally kissing him. Each time his hot wet mouth met mine, my knees got a bit weaker. I could have continued kissing him for hours. Once I found out what he liked, I let go and just enjoyed the loss of control.

Nibbling, pecking, sucking on his bottom lip, I rested my hands on his forearms and let my tongue work away at his own. His short stubble on his chin scratched at my own, but I didn't care. The more friction between us the better.

We were like teenagers who had just come out; kissing a man for the first time and letting our mouths explore what they liked. But like any normal teenager, after a moment the swelling in my trousers became too big to ignore. The way we were standing, legs parted with a small gap between our bodies, meant that only the tip of our bulges were touching. The sensation was such an exquisite tease and a foreshadowing of what was to come.

Something in Ace forced his eyes open and he pulled away slightly, eyes searching and probing my own. His full lips were even more red in hue than before and remained slightly parted. His ran his tongue gently and slowly over his top lip, leaving a glistening residue behind. I was instantly reminded of what I thought of his mouth the first time I had seen it.

Cock-sucking lips.

We stared into each other's eyes for another moment, drinking in the sight and enjoying the torture and the anticipation of what was to happen next. I was completely and totally entranced by him. Visions of what I imagined him to look like naked, danced in my head. I wanted to lick every inch of his body and let him taste my own.

I was the first to break the connection and let my eyes dip to the top button on his shirt. The collar was already undone so that I could see the little dip between his collar bone. My fingers moved with expert ease and slowly undid each button, revealing more and more of his dark, tanned flesh with each one. He dropped his own arms and pushed his chest out further, making his bulk seem even more broad and impressive. I tingled with nervous excitement as my desire to kiss his chest took control of my every move. When I reached the last button, I paused and looked up into his eyes again. They had clouded over and were radiating lust. He nodded his head slightly in approval as I reached my hands up to the collar once more and as if in slow motion, peeled the material in opposite directions off of his shoulders. My eyes trailed down and appreciated the slow reveal of his chest. The material slid off his body, straining slightly over his biceps before falling to the floor at his feet. Ace stood there, half-naked, not moving and with eyes so lustful I thought for a second that if given the chance he might bite into me.

The reveal was even more amazing than I had imagined. Ace's chest was completely void of even the lightest dusting of hair. He was definitely more defined than I was; his pecs were perfectly round like dinner plates that jutted out and above the rest of his chest. His nipples were much darker than the rest of his skin and their erectness immediately drew my attention. With each shallow breath he drew in, his pecs rose even higher. He was the picture of perfection, an Adonis of a male, chiseled from the finest marble and mine for the worshipping. My hands tingled with pins and needles but with whatever self-control I had left I kept them at bay for as long as I could before unleashing them on his skin. I lifted them slowly and let my fingertips caress the satiny smoothness of his peck muscles. Ace let his head tip back, enjoying the feeling of my touch on his skin. His breath hitched in his throat as my expert hands licked up and down his muscles, teasing and squeezing before finding his nipples and running my thumbs over and around, tracing their contours gently with the pad of my thumb.

A low throaty moan escaped from between his lips whose sound only hardened me further. I lowered my head and opened my mouth and kissed each nipple once adoringly. Ace flinched as I licked and sucked slightly at the left one before raising my head once more and laying my mouth on his, kissing him deeper this time and letting my tongue linger inside his mouth for a moment.

I groaned as he gave into temptation and wrapped his arms around my back, closing the space between our bodies so that his beautiful erect nipples were now pressed up against the material of my top. His arms were like a vice around my torso, our heads tilting to the left and then to the right as we continued kissing. I put a hand on each of his cheeks and pressed my face against his even tighter.

We were no longer two different people. Instead we were just limbs and loins, desperate for satisfaction and release. Moving, touching, caressing, rubbing. Ace moved his hands up the back of my top and let them explore the smooth contours of my back muscles before moving back around to the tight skin at my sides. His fingers traced the lines from my hips sending small intense shivers up the rest o of my core. I let my hands fall to my sides and enjoyed the sensation of him taking control. Without warning he grabbed the material of my top and pulled it carefully northwards. I closed my eyes and lifted my arms in compliance as he fully removed the polo over my head and discarded it on the floor. When I opened my eyes again, the look on his face was far from innocent. He reminded me of a feral animal, hungry and ready to pounce.

I wanted him so badly it hurt. I took his left hand in mine and led him down the hall and towards my bedroom. The curtains were open and were letting in the midday sun. Shards of bright light illuminated the room, leaving only the corners in shadow. The effect was beautiful and as I turned towards him again, the sight of his half-naked body bathed in the rays of sunlight, was enough to take my breath away. We didn't waste another second apart. He stepped closer to me again and placed his mouth on mine, and with a hand on my lower back and one for himself, he lowered me onto the bed. I spread my legs and let him climb on top. Keeping one arm free to support his weight he lowered his head again and continued his slow seduction on me with his mouth. His other hand moved down my torso, pausing momentarily on my abdominals and running his fingers along the deep grooves of my six-pack. His fingertips worshipped my stomach as if they were paint brushes conducting long strokes on a canvas. The feeling sent butterflies through me and I kissed him deeper as a response.

My groans and moans got progressively louder as the same hand that had worked my abs now trailed ever so slightly more towards my crotch, grazing my boner just enough to send me into convulsions.

The sex fiend inside me wanted him to grab my cock and squeeze it until I came, but I knew this was going to be different. He wasn't here for a quick fuck, like all the other men before…He was here for something different. Something sweeter and gentler. And I was going to enjoy every second.

Still on my back, I let my hands wander up and run themselves over the strong muscles of his back. Tugging him closer and harder into me, and relishing the feeling of his hard-on rubbing up against my own. Once again I was reminded of being a horny teenager; furiously dry-humping away at a boyfriend, losing myself in the feeling of my dick pressing up against the denim of my jeans, knowing that he wanted me just as badly as I wanted him and that in a moment we were going to be completely naked and fucking our brains out.

Ace was the one to sit up this time; back on his heels so that his torso was once again on exquisite display for me to feast my eyes upon. Without breaking eye contact, his large hands unclasped his own belt buckle, the muscles in his chest moving in compliance as he pulled the leather free from its clasp and unbuttoned his trousers. He hesitated for a moment and I jumped at the chance to unzip them. His eyes slid back into his head as the thought of me sucking on his cock ran through his head. I sat up the best that I could with him pinning my legs down and with all my might pushed him backwards so that he fell back on the bed, instantly putting me on top. He lifted his ass off the bed so that I would be able to pull his trousers completely off. I broke our eye connection for a moment to take in the sight of his underwear. He wore black satin boxers that felt amazing as my hands brushed against them while pulling his trousers down slowly. Underneath, his dick revealed the extent of its length as it stood at attention, pointing skywards and pitching a black satin tent inside the constraints of the material. I was sure that if I stood there staring at him like this, vulnerable and sexy and aroused to the max, that I would cum within seconds.

To distract myself, I quickly stood and unbuttoned my own jeans. I paused only for a second, a stripper to the core, to let him stare and appreciate the reveal of my own girth. I stole a glance at my own pants to see what I was wearing before letting my jeans struggle then fall over my white with red tubing Aussie Bum's. Ace sat up on his elbows to get a full view of my show. I stood up right, my cock rock hard inside my underwear and already feeling moist with precum. I closed my eyes, picturing I was on stage, as I hooked both my thumbs inside the elastic waistband of my pants and slowly pulled them down. Even without looking, I knew that Ace's eyes were glued to my body. I could feel them linger over my abs, enjoying the slow reveal of my treasure trail which led down to a neatly trimmed patch of pubic hair that surrounded my long, pink, erect cock.

I was primed and ready, twitching and throbbing as it stood there begging for attention. Ace quickly moved and removed his boxers in one swift movement. I was caught off guard for a second when I finally saw his dick for the first time. I was sure I gasped and my asshole twitched when my eyes took in his width. He laid back again, one hand resting on his hip for a moment before letting it slide down over the length of his member, squeezing it gently at the tip, getting it ready. The sight of him touching himself with his hand moving slowly up and down over his shaft made my mouth water.

I wasn't sure what was going to happen next, until Ace spread his legs further and laid back, bringing his knees up into the air a little and exposing his hole slightly. My libido did a little dance in reaction. I took my cock in my right hand and gave it a little stroke, enjoying the pleasure of sliding my hand up and down my long shaft slowly, pausing to cup the head in my palm and tugging gently, awakening the pleasure principles in the tip.

Ace's knees, which were now pointing to the ceiling, quivered slightly as I inched myself closer to the edge of the bed. Looking down upon him, I took a knee in each of my hands and parted them a bit more, before sliding my hands down his thighs. His legs were hairy and just as muscular as you would have expected. He wrapped his legs around me slightly, crossing his feet at the ankles and resting them on my buttocks. When I gripped his hips, I pulled him closer to the edge of the bed so that his exposed hole was level with the tip of my dick.

I grabbed his cock for the first time and jerked it up and down a few times, watching his foreskin move up and down as it stretched over his glistening mushroom head. Ace stiffened and jerked his head up to look me in the eye. His expression was that of caution, as if to say if I continued that motion this would be over before it had begun.

I took his signal and let his thick member rest back against his stomach. He lifted his pelvis and moved himself closer to me until we both felt the connection of my cock and his hole. Ace's head fell back against the bed and he stretched his arms up above his head, grasping the metal bed frame behind him. He tightened his grip as if to brace himself, making his incredible biceps flex and show off their definition to perfection.

This was it. I had to have him. I wasn't going to last long as it stood. It didn't take much; a small easy thrust of my hips pushed the head of my cock through the threshold of his anus. My head fell back at the sensation. I could practically hear his hole stretching as it fought against the girth of my manhood.

I was going to take it nice and easy. Let him relax and enjoy every sensation, every thrust, every muscle flex of my body as I entered him inch by inch.

I groaned deeply like an animal and he mirrored it right back. I could feel his whole body stiffen more and more as I slowly pushed myself deeper and deeper into him. I looked up at his hands which were gripping the bed frame so tightly, his knuckles had gone white. His face was contorted in a mask of pleasure and pain and he was baring his gritted teeth, sucking air through the tight gaps.

I was almost completely buried inside him when suddenly his eyes shot open and his head tilted forward as I hit his g-spot from deep inside. The act made me smile as I stayed still like that inside him for a moment. The muscles in his sphincter relaxed around my penis and it wasn't long before our bodies began to feel like one organ whose connection was intensely strong. I drew in a breath for the first time in what felt like ages. As my lungs expanded, pleasure ran through my very bones, exciting everything in its wake. And with that I began to move again.

My hips were like a well-oiled machine. As I retreated back out of him, my dick slid easier this time. I pulled all the way out and watched his face closely as my large head expanded his lower anus before exiting completely. The feeling was insane and it showed on Ace's face. I stayed outside of him for a moment, long enough for him to meet my eyes with a furrowed brow, silently begging me to do that again. I happily obliged and slowly thrust myself forward again, the head of my cock penetrating him easier this time and pushing all the way into him until we both heard the gentle slap of my ball sack up against his ass. The feeling of deeply penetrating him sent his back arching off of the bed and allowed me to sink deeper still inside of him. He let out a sharp grunt as I hit his prostate again. One hand was in his hair now, massaging his own scalp in ecstasy while the other held onto the bed frame as if for dear life.

I pulled out all the way for a second time before immediately ramming myself inside him, harder this time and with more force. Once in all the way, I circled my hips as best I could, waving my cock around inside him and making sure my head traced the wall of his anus, hitting every pleasure principle and sending us both reeling at the feeling. Ace's other hand shot to his head and tangled itself in his hair before both his hands slid down to his torso and began rubbing his chest. He tweaked his nipples and massaged his pecks as I pulled out a third time before *gently* pushing back inside again.

He groaned again, pinching and pulling at his nipples and letting his head roll around on the bed as I began a more rhythmic motion with my hips.

I was all sensation now. Letting my eyes close, my hips did all the work; thrusting forwards and then pulling back, circling, dipping, pushing up and then down, exploring his insides to the utmost and bringing us both closer and closer to orgasm. The feeling was more intense and colourful than I had ever felt before. It was as if our bodies were pieces of a puzzle that fit together perfectly. His ass was made for my dick and we moved together seamlessly. My thoughts were lost. All memories of the past few days temporarily erased. I felt like I was myself again; sex and candy and the irrepressable urge to tease. This was so primal, so instinctual. This was life to me; hedonism, the seeking of pleasure. It was how I lived my life, and now I was experiencing it with someone I actually felt something towards. It was new and familiar all at the same time, and the idea that it might possibly come to an end was enough to knock the air right out of my lungs.

I stopped pumping for a moment and opened my eyes. At my sudden stall, Ace opened his eyes too and peered at me quizzically. My cock throbbed inside of him; our link was as strong as ever. But it wasn't enough. I wanted to feel more. I wanted to deepen our connection and experience it in as many different ways as possible. So I pulled out. Quickly this time, not for pleasure but because I wanted to shift. He flinched as I withdrew more forcefully and purposefully than before. Ace quickly sat up on his elbows again, spread-eagle with his own erect cock girating for more. I climbed up next to him on the bed and positioned myself on my hands and knees, my perky ass in the air.

I want him inside **me**. *I need him inside me.*

I turned my head to him and locked eyes with him once more. I could feel my pained expression; one of longing that was all too familiar to myself now. The insatiable need for comfort and protection had spilled over into the act of love making now, and I wanted to relinquish all the control I had over this and just become a slave to my body again. Having someone take *me* was the ultimate antithesis to what I did on the stage. There, I was the one in control. People did what I wanted. I made them feel what I wanted them to feel. But here…now…I didn't want to drive. Giving myself over completely to Ace…this beautiful man to whom I owed my life…would be my unravelling. And I couldn't be more ready for it.

The expression on Ace's face assured me that he understood what I wanted. He quickly composed himself and rolled over on his side and quickly mounted up behind me on the bed. He took my hips in his hands and without a moment's hesitation, spat on my exposed hole. The feeling of his saliva hitting me made me grunt and nearly topple over. If I or he were to touch my cock now I was sure I would explode right then and there. I resisted the urge to finish myself off and tried to focus all my concentration on what he was about to do.

I closed my eyes and could feel his index and middle finger locate my anus. With a gentle touch, he probed me once, then twice, swirling his two fingers around in a circular motion inside me, getting me used to having something foreign shoved up my sphincter. When he withdrew I knew that I'd only last a couple of thrusts before I let myself go completely. There was about ten seconds of silence, and I bit down on my lower lip in anticipation. Then I felt him connect with me. First, the tip of his cock, then a tiny bit more. He was taking it easy, but I just wanted him inside me as quickly as possible.

He must have read my thoughts because without warning he plunged himself inside me as deep as he could go. I cried out in shock, as pain shot up my spine. He stayed like that for a moment, and then slid one of his hands up my back, grabbed at my hair and pulled until my face was pointing towards the ceiling. Eyes closed, I let out another yelp as the movement forced him further up inside me. He thrust his hips into me again without withdrawing. At once I saw stars as his penis massaged my prostate. Again he thrust his hips hitting that sweet spot again. Again and again, his cock still deep inside me. It was like pounding an alarm inside my body that sent wave after wave of pure ecstasy coursing through my body. His penis was like a hammer that kept hitting something inside me again and again.

I was orgasming and he could tell. My body spasmed and my back arched as I spewed my load all over the bed without even a hint of manual stimulation. Ace was coming too and quickly started pumping away at me as he blew his load inside my body. We orgasmed together, wave after wave of cum shooting out of my cock and all over the bed, his hips grinding into my backside until every last drop of his sticky mess was inside me. It took me a second to realise that the screams I was hearing were coming from us. Pleasure moans and groans bounced off my bedroom walls as my g-spot orgasm climaxed over and over to the point where I was sure I'd not sit for a week.

Then he stopped. Still inside me, his cock driven up inside my anus, he slowly began his withdrawal. My back rounded as he slid the last inch out of me and I collapsed onto the bed in a heavy, sweaty heap. My own cock still throbbed as the blood slowly left it, deflating softly like the air from a balloon. I felt Ace's lips on my back, kissing me softly as you would your greatest possession before he dismounted completely and collapsed next to me on the bed.

I didn't try looking at him. I didn't need to. I felt fulfilled. Satisfied. Spent. My craving had been met, my itch had been scratched. I begged for this feeling to never fade. I wished that I could remain like this forever. Shielded from the outside world. For that moment, I felt safe, and I let myself drift away on a silver cloud.

Chapter Nineteen

I heard a chime outside my window that startled me awake. I felt bleary-eyed as I stirred in the bed. For a moment I was disoriented as I looked around the dark room, wondering where I was now.

It was becoming the norm for me as of late; waking up somewhere I didn't remember going. Wondering what time or even what day it was. As my eyes adjusted to the darkness, I began to make out the shapes of my bedroom. My vanity mirror in the corner. The tall black velvet drapes.

You're at home. In bed. With...

It was then that I looked to my left at the still shape next to me.

Ace.

I smiled despite myself as the memories of our encounter replayed themselves before my eyes like a dirty movie.

I stole my stare from the beautiful man, peacefully asleep lying next to me and looked back towards the sheathed windows once more. I was looking for a sign of daylight beneath the heavy black material.

But I saw nothing.

Have we been asleep all day?

I looked to my bedside table in search of my mobile phone. I blindly picked up what I thought was my phone and pressed the circular button on the bottom of the iPhone. Instantly the screen sprang to life, displaying the time.

8:05 pm. My God.

I looked back to Ace and watched him for a few moments. The rise and fall of his back as he breathed. I admired the curve of his bottom. How he looked so peaceful lying there next to me. My savior. I owed him so much. I just hoped I would have the chance to truly pay him back...

I swung my legs carefully off the side of the bed, being careful not to wake him. As my feet hit the floor, something clicked in my head as I remembered Ace's words upon arriving back at my flat.

"Back-up is on its way. I told them to be here in an hour. Should be long enough to pack up some of your stuff."

My body froze for a second.

What the hell happened to the cops?

I padded over to the window and peered behind the drape to check that it was in fact nighttime. Outside the street was cast entirely in shadow. Street lamps illuminated small patches of sidewalk, making the rest of the area around them appear even more dark. Everything seemed so deserted. I struggled to see across the street, scanning the road for any signs of life. But nothing moved. In the distance I heard a siren, screeching as it sped off in search of some evil in the night.

Replacing the curtain I turned around again to admire the sleeping man in my bed. He hadn't moved. A small sound escaped his lips when he exhaled. Heavy breaths signaled a deep sleep.

Fuck, I'd really love a cigarette.

Tip-toeing around the room I carefully opened the bedroom door and went out into the lounge. I must have left a light on for as I stepped out into the cold hallway I had to squint to protect my eyes from the accosting light above my head.

Shutting the door behind me I went in search of Ace's jacket, hoping and praying that he still had that pack of cigarettes from the other day. Being inside my flat gave me a strange feeling. I felt creeped out; almost like I shouldn't be here, as if I were a trespasser in my own home. Even looking around the room, everything looked foreign to me, like the belongings that filled the shelves were objects from someone else's life. Wrapping my arms around myself, I rubbed my bare flesh in an effort to warm myself up.

On the floor I spotted my polo shirt and faded blue jeans from earlier. Slipping them on I found Ace's suit jacket discarded by my feet. Picking it up, I held it up to my nose and breathed in deeply. The material smelt like him; I let the scent intoxicate me for a moment, instantly relaxing me again.

Even his smell has a catalytic effect on me.

I patted the jacket carefully and felt a small box in the right hand pocket. Searching for the pocket I shook the jacket a few times.

"Where the…"

I tipped the coat upside down and continued shaking until all the pocketed items fell out and dropped to the ground with a clatter.

What appeared to be Ace's wallet, landed open on the floor along with a slightly crumpled box of Marlboro Lights. I sighed heavily upon seeing the cigarettes, and bent down to pick them up when something caught my eye.

What looked like the corner of a photograph stuck out of the main part of Ace's wallet. I paused for a moment and considered.

I'm snooping again.

I bit my lower lip as I thought about what I was about to do. I thought about how I'd feel if he were to go through my private belongings. It felt wrong, but curiosity got the better of me and I grabbed the picture between my thumb and index finger.

Standing up I rubbed sleep from my eyes and stared at my discovery.

What I saw in my hands made my heart stop. I dropped the packet of cigarettes and stared dumbfounded at the picture I was holding.

No.

My jaw slacked and I immediately began to tremble. The hairs on the back of my neck and all up and down my arms stood on end and my entire nervous system seemed to shut down for a moment as shock seeped into my veins and paralysed me slowly from the inside out.

No. It can't be.

My eyes stared down at the picture in my hands. I gripped it tightly now. Staring down at it expectantly, as if it might change. The more I stared, the more truth began to hit me. I felt sick. Bile began to rise from the pit of my stomach up my throat. Immediately, I cupped a hand over my mouth as the two people in the picture came in and out of focus.

I didn't want to believe my eyes. But there was no denying it. The picture was of two men; arms around each other adoringly. Happy smiles plastered across their faces. Their skin was tanned and the background images seemed to suggest that the picture had been snapped whilst away on holiday. So much emotion radiated from the two men in the picture that it was obvious to anyone seeing it for the first time, that the two people were deeply in love. The man on the left was without a doubt Ace.

But the other man…

My eyes trailed from one figure to the next and then back again. Tears began to blur my eyes and my skin began to crawl to the point where I almost wanted to scratch it off. The second man in the picture, who Ace had his arm around was…

"David Adams," came a voice from behind me.

The words were like something out of a nightmare, piercing the air around me like an eerie whisper. I yelped as I spun around dazed to see the shadowy outline of Ace standing inside the bedroom doorway.

"Ace…"I said, my voice a choked whisper.

He took a step out of the shadows. His face was blank and calm.

"David Adams," he repeated confirming what I knew he had already said.

Confusion and uncertainty danced about in my head.

David Adams. **My David***…From the alley…But…*

"Ace, I…"

My brow furrowed as a million different explanations sped through my brain. David Adams.

"He was my husband."

I felt like I had been punched in the stomach. I lurched forward a little and wrapped my arms around my middle protectively.

His husband?

Then it dawned on me. The sick truth behind this whole nightmare.

Ace and David.

"Ace, I don't...understand..."

"Oh, but you do, don't you?" his question was tinged with mockery and caught me off guard. Something had changed in his tone. He took another step closer towards me, and I instinctually took one away. "He was my husband...a cop...like me."

"A cop?"

"We met on a case eight years ago."

Another step closer. His hands were balled into fists and hung tensely at his sides. He was topless still but had dressed in his dark suit trousers. He appeared casual, yet there was something darker about the way he carried himself now.

"Fuck, I loved him...So much. You know, we were partners? On the squad. Our Captain said we were two of his best men." His eyes shifted up to the ceiling as if he was living out a pleasant memory.

Like pieces of a puzzle, things started to shift into place as he spoke.

The pictures on the wall in his house.

They were of Ace and...David.

That's why he freaked when I tried to look.

I swallowed hard, my throat feeling tighter and like sandpaper.

Oh fuck...

"But he had secrets..."

Oh God, please no...

"Secrets...So many secrets..."

In my head I begged him not to go on, because I knew where this was going, and I wasn't sure I could bear to hear him finish.

"Secrets I found out about a little too late…" His voice trailed off as he returned his gaze to me. His brown eyes, that once held such passion, had gone darker. Black almost, as if completely devoid of any sort of hue whatsoever.

I shivered again at the sight of his menacing expression.

"Seemed he had a thing for *strippers.*"

"Ace…" My voice quivered as his name escaped my lips, "I'm…I'm so-"

"So, what?" He interrupted quickly as he took another step closer. I retreated a bit further as adrenaline began to furiously course through my veins.

What is he going to do?

I put up both hands in front of me as if waving a white flag in front of his eyes. "Ace, I didn't know…I didn't know who he…"

That whole time. That whole time we had been together in the alley. He had a…

"I put two and two together after a while. Being a cop I already had a suspicious mind. Looking for clues, it's what I do, right?"

He took another step towards me, fists still gathered at his sides as if ready to strike at any time.

My brain immediately went into defense mode. What the fuck was I going to do? I started running through all possible scenarios. Fear had been creeping up my spine slowly ever since he appeared out of the bedroom.

He's going to kill me.

I shook my head at the thought, straightening up and trying desperately to gather my wits about me.

Think, mate. THINK. How am I going to get out of here…

"I followed him to the club one night…Your club…"

Stop talking, please.

"That's when I first saw you…"

He stopped moving and stared straight at me. He suddenly looked so sad, so torn, so full of lament.

"He seemed quite taken by you."

I've got to stall him. Keep him talking. Isn't that what they do in the movies?

"Ace, listen to me. Please. I had no idea David was…"

Ace's head twitched slightly at the mention of David's name, making me flinch slightly at the sight. I put my hands up again in front of me, as if to defend myself somehow. "He didn't mean…"

"Anything?"

His eyes welled up suddenly, glistening over with tears. He sniffed them back and quickly rubbed them away so as to destroy all sign of apparent weakness. He straightened up as well, making himself seem so much taller.

Before I knew it, I was backed up against a wall. My front door. I felt behind me blindly until my fingers grazed the door knob.

Keep him talking.

"I waited after the club closed that first night…"

Oh God.

"I followed David…My David…To that alley…"

He paused and looked down, lifting a hand to his eyes and began rubbing them furiously. His voice cracked as he continued.

"Ace, please…"

"I watched…"

"Don't do this…"

"I fucking WATCHED…as he fucked you…"

"Let's just stop for a second…"

"I was so…*angry*…"

I swallowed again, the tears beginning to prick behind my own eyes at what I was hearing.

Guilt and sheer terror were running through my bones. I didn't know what to say.

"If I had known…Ace…I would never have…"

"I hoped it was a one-time thing. I really did. Fuck, was I stupid…"

"You're not stupid."

"After, I pretended like everything was normal…If it was only once, then I thought…Maybe…Maybe I'd be ok with it…I loved him so…So much…"

Reach out to him.

"Ace, let's just sit down, maybe we…"

Then he lifted his head again and bared his teeth like a mad dog. "But it wasn't only once. Was it, Dice? How many times before that? Huh?"

My eyes shot wide with fear as the Ace I knew disappeared and was replaced with something different.

"*How many times?*" he spat.

I closed my eyes tightly like a child hiding behind a blanket.

"A few nights later he went back…saw you again. I had to follow. I had to be sure."

My fingers gripped the door knob and began twisting it slightly. As slow as I possibly could so as not to alert him.

I've got to get out. If I can only just get the door open…

"I watched him write you a note.I watched him go to your spot."

When I opened my eyes again, his were locked on me. Fiery and wide and blood shot. My skin crawled in reaction and I could almost feel myself begin to pass out while standing up.

"I followed him to that alley. I caught him fucking red handed. He tried to explain. Tried to give me some chicken shit excuse. Told me it was all a misunderstanding."

"Ace…"

"So I…"

"Stop, Ace…"

"…I…"

"Please, let's just-"

"…Killed him…"

Then I was sure time stood still. Silence rang in my ears as I digested what was happening. My shoulders hunched as something inside of me gave up. I wanted to just crumble to the floor. It felt like I had been fighting for so long. I wanted this to be over. Finished. In my mind it was like a fog had been lifted. I wasn't crazy. I was innocent. Innocent. I could see clarity on the horizon, a way out. I knew the truth now. I could explain what had actually happened. But would I live to get the chance…

I wasn't out of the woods yet.

"It was supposed to be you," He looked up at me again, breaking the silence in the air between us. His voice was once again gentle. "You were going to take the fall for this…"

"Me? But…"

"I had it all planned out. Right down to the very last detail. All signs would point to you, and you couldn't have made it any easier to frame either, what with your bloody blackouts. You must have really hit your head pretty fuckin' hard, mate. Guess it serves you right for being such a fucking coward."

"What?"

"You heard me, you skanky son of a bitch. You RAN. You found a dead body and you fuckin' ran. Who the fuck runs when they discover their lover beaten to death in an alley?"

He was mocking me now, throwing his hands up in the air for emphasis.

"A piece of shit coward. That's who!"

He was filled with such hatred, practically spitting each word at me.

"When you fell and passed out, it was so fucking easy to get your blood all over David's body."

Jesus Christ. Of course. That's how.

I had almost completely turned the door knob. Just another inch or so and the door would be open.

"I want you to pay…Dice. I want you to be as fucking miserable as you've made me…You stole the love of my life from me and you're gonna pay for it…"

"This was all you? Everything. Wasn't it?"

He tilted his head to one side in that way.

"You…Tony? Joe…"

Oh God…Dale…

"Dead."

"How could…" My voice cracked as realisation came crashing down on me. Tony. Joe. They weren't missing…They were gone. My stomach lurched at the thought of all those near to me, gone.

"You…at Joe's house. That was you, wasn't it?"

He didn't have to respond.

"It doesn't matter now anyway. Once I notify the station, they'll find the bodies and the murder weapon with your finger prints all over it."

The way he spoke now was like it was already over.

"You'll be over, prosecuted and behind bars while I get a fucking medal for solving the case of the decade."

"You're not going to get away with this." The famous last words leaked from my mouth.

I heard a click as the knob released itself from the latch.

"Wait…" I said a little too loudly to mask the sound of the door opening. "The crash…Who was…"

"Ahhh, yes…" He pondered staring up at the ceiling again in that pensive way, "Seems like you have someone on your side. Doesn't matter who, though. I'll find them, and when I do, who's gonna believe their word over a cop's?"

I inched the door open slowly, praying he wouldn't notice, hoping he wouldn't see.

"Oh, and don't even think about it."

I didn't have time to react before he lunged himself in my direction. Like a panther with arms extended and hands like giant claws, he surged himself at me.

I raised my arms protectively to my face just in time to shield my head from his clawing hands. He connected with me, throwing his entire body weight in my direction. I slammed up against the door, slamming it shut again with my shoulder. The pain was immense as I was crushed against the wooden door.

Immediately he began punching and clawing at me, his hands getting stuck in my hair and beating down on me in any way that he could to cause the most pain. My limbs cried out in agony as he repeatedly brought his fists down upon me. I tried to shield my head and cradle myself in the fetal position. He stopped for a split second and looked around for something. I grabbed the chance and frantically crawled on my hands and knees to get distance between us. My finger nails clawed at the wooden floor boards and I kicked at midair to desperately get to my feet.

He was quick and with an animal-like howl, was immediately upon me once more. Hands grabbing at my legs. I kicked like a mad man, desperate to connect with some limb of his and get him off me. I caught a glimpse of his face. He looked almost inhuman as he savagely grabbed and scratched at me.

I was screaming now. Screaming at the top of whatever voice I still had left. Yelled for someone, anyone, to come and save me. It was the desperate cries of a victim who was grasping for a last chance at survival.

He grabbed my left leg, caught hold and pulled as hard as he could. The sheer force was enough to knock me back down on the ground. My chin smacked against the hard wood floor knocking my bottom teeth and almost dislocating my jaw. I yelped as he flipped me over with ease, his strength overpowering me, and yanked me towards him. The skin on my back scraped against the floor as he pulled me along. Instantly he was on top again. He lifted his right first up into the air and I saw what was going to happen before he even moved. His fist connected with my left cheek with the most sickening crack, like a piece of wood splitting. My vision blanked completely for what felt like minutes and I was sure I had gone deaf.

Come on, Dice.

With all the might I had left, I turned my head back towards him. He was a blurry outline above me. He lifted his hand again, raising it high into the air.

I was sure that this one would kill me. I had time to gage the look in his face once more. I had never seen such hatred and fury in someone before.

This was it. One more punch and I was sure he would knock my nose into my skull. An eerie calmness swept over me as if my head was preparing me for the end.

It was then that the front door to my flat swung open. The sudden movement caused Ace to look in its direction. A look of surprise smacked across his face as the shadow of someone else stepped into my house. I didn't see who it was before I heard the shot.

It was like an explosion inside my head. A bomb had detonated inside my ears, and my hands sprang up to protect them from the sound. I closed my eyes as I felt a hot spray plaster the skin on my face and the weight of Ace upon me suddenly lifted off. There was a thud on the ground next to me, but I dared not open my eyes yet.

Moments passed. Seconds? Minutes? I wasn't sure. Silence.

Am I deaf?

Then movement. I heard it and felt it. Then hands on me, shaking me. Gentle hands.

"*Dice?*"

Was that a familiar voice?

I remained with my eyes tightly closed, my hands still protectively sheathing my ears. I wasn't sure I should open yet.

"Dice? *Dice?* Are you alright? Talk to me!" the stranger shouted.

After another moment of silence, I opened my eyes slightly.

A shape materialised in front of me. Blurry black lines at first, which took the shape of a man. I opened them further, still afraid of whom it might be.

He gripped my shoulders slightly but not in an abrasive way. As my eyes once again adjusted to the light from above, pure and immediate relief flooded through my veins.

"Dale…" I breathed, closing my eyes again as tears flooded over, soaking my face and stinging the skin as they fell.

He wrapped his arms around me adoringly, squeezing me tightly. He buried his nose in my neck, forced me to sit up and began rocking me back and forth in his arms.

"Shhh, it's okay," he cooed into my ear as I continued to sob. "I'm here."

Those words. That reassurance. I had heard them before. All too recently. I shuddered at the not-so-distant memory.

The tears didn't stop as my brain tried to make sense and process all that had just happened. As Dale rocked me in his arms, I felt like I had been through a war. I had lived through such violence and fear, that the thought that life might ever return to normal seemed so unsure and far-off.

"Oh Dale…" I managed through sobs, "I thought you were…"

"Shhh, it's alright. You know I'm not that weak, mate. I'm made of steel, remember?"

"But…How?"

Dale looked thoughtful, like he was searching within himself for the right way to say what he was about to say. As I looked up at him, I could sense his bottom lip trembling.

Sweet Dale.

"I found him. There in the alley, just after it had happened, that son of a bitch…" His voice cracked as he gathered his thoughts.

"You were there that night?" I asked.

Dale nodded slightly, pain flashing across his beautiful features. "After we danced together that night I had to clear my head, I was so confused…I didn't know how I was feeling. So I went outside and… that's when I heard something from the alley…"

Oh Dale. This was all my fault.

"Oh Jesus…Did you see it?"

"*I was too late…I tried to help him*…He chased me and beat the shit out of me. Left me there not far from the club, thought I was dead…" Dale paused for a second and swallowed. "Someone found me. Thank Christ. They took me to the hospital."

I stopped crying long enough to straighten up and look Dale in the eye. He met my stare and wiped my cheek with his thumb.

"I was in Intensive Care for four days. That's when I came looking for you."

"Oh God, Dale."

"After that I knew I had to play it safe and find a way around him. I was never far from you. I just had to find a way to get to you safely."

It was all too much. I could feel myself begin to well up again. *My Dale.* Alive. Raw emotion was making my head ache. I lifted a hand to touch his cheek.

My Dale. My sweet Dale. Thank God.

"Was that you, then? In the car? At the Marina?"

He nodded, then cast his eyes down to the floor. "I was trying to warn you. Stop him. If anything had happened to you…I don't…"

I stopped him with a finger over his lips. He swallowed and looked me in the eye. My eyes studied his beautiful face.

My hero.

I closed my eyes once more and pulled his face down to me again, holding him in an embrace.

He let his body relax as we held each other close. Cheek to cheek, our breathing slowing as our hearts began to beat in sync with one another. I was still tense with fear, but with each passing moment, the fear transformed into relief.

Relief that this was all over.

With my eyes closed, I tried to concentrate on my breathing. I tried to block out the horrid images that insisted on playing out in front of my eyes. Pictures of Ace. Joe. Tony. The Club. Dale. They blurred and danced before my eye lids, flashed and then dissolved. They were there and then they were gone. I tried to hold them at bay, but it was hopeless. For now, I told myself, I had to just let the memories come. Memories that would hopefully someday fade away.

I held on to Dale. Held him close. The feel of his body against mine giving me warmth and security. We rocked together over and over until I lost all feeling in my legs. Silence rang in our ears until it was gradually replaced with sounds of the evening air outside the window.

A car moving up the street. Sounds of laughter from a passing couple. A dog barking out a warning. A siren in the distance. These sounds gave me comfort. Made me feel normal and safe. They came. They passed. They faded into blackness.

About the Author

Joey Jameson is Canadian born and bred, but
currently living in Brighton, UK. He can usually
be found either on the beach walking his two gorgeous
dogs, or sipping swanky cocktails in his local haunt.
He is also the author of "Candy From Strangers." Ever the
fan of all things decadent, for an insight into his daily life,
you can follow him on twitter @joeyjameson or
contact him via email at misterjoeyjameson@gmail.com.
You can also visit his facebook page
www.facebook.com/joeyjamesonauthor for
a sneak-peak of new work to come.

www.ingramcontent.com/pod-product-compliance
Lightning Source LLC
Chambersburg PA
CBHW072232170626
46813CB00003B/1186